SHADES OF GRAY

Andy Holloman

ISBN: 978-0-615-53279-0

Triple J Press

Cover Design by Matt Taft (www.SiteSkins.net) &
Laurel Holloman (www.LaurelHollomanStudio.net)
Book Interior Design, Editing & Layout by PlotLine Design
(www.Plotlinedesign.com)

Dedications and Acknowledgements

To Carolyn, Mary, and Franz: thank you for your smiles, guidance, and thoughtfulness.

To Matt Taft: the most talented graphic artist in the universe.

To the incredibly talented team at Plot-Line Designs: for your careful editing and excellent book design services.

To my mother: the kindest and most thoughtful person I have ever known.

To my father: my role model and the person that taught me to be "fundamentally sound".

To my brother and sister.

To my best friend and biggest supporter, my wife Margot. I dedicate this novel to you for giving me the gifts that no words can describe. I love you and I'm in awe of what a wonderful, caring, and giving person you are. There but for the grace of you go I.

I - March 24, 2002

He reserved his Sunday nights for the most important person in his life—his six-year-old daughter Lucy. These nights were referred to as the Sabbath and he always observed. On more than one occasion, he had mentioned his Sunday night dinners with Lucy were the source of good luck for the upcoming week. Tonight, however, would end any further mention of the delight he took in these evenings.

Lucy had always chosen the location for their dates, and the familiar ching-ching-ching-ching rattle of dollar bills being exchanged for golden tokens falling from the change dispensers rang in John's ears. The clanging of bells from the game machines and the flashing lights reminded him of Las Vegas. They were, however, quite far from Sin City as they slipped into a booth at the Chuck E. Cheese in Raleigh, North Carolina. Parents hurried past them, chasing small children. Older children stuffed chains of small white tickets into the counting machine so they could collect a prize worth ten cents after spending ten dollars to collect the tickets from games of skill like pinball, skee ball, whack-a-mole, and pop-a-shot. No doubt casino owners the world over would sell their soul for similar odds.

She reached across the table and pulled on his sleeve.

"Daddy? Are you thinking about what kind of pizza to get?"

He sighed. "I'm not thinking about anything except how perfect a little girl you are. You pick the pizza tonight."

"Well I want a pizza with double cheese and nothing else on it like that gross stuff that you like." She smiled and studied the menu. As if she would order anything else.

He removed his glasses and pushed his thinning blonde hair back from his eyes. He wiped the lens clean with his tie.

"Daddy, Nana told me that I should help you watch what you eat so you don't get any fatter."

"Hmmm, so my mom told you that?"

"Yes, but she said it was for your own good and that when I told you this, you would understand. She told me that you used to be skinnier and that wherever you went, pretty ladies would always smile at you."

"Seems like I better have a little chat with your Nana. She needs to understand that I've been working hard to be a good dad and take care of my business and that maybe it is OK to let other things slip a little."

"I will tell her Daddy. You don't have to worry. But she did say that now you look more like you are sixty instead of forty-four."

"Wow! Now I know that I need to talk to my mom."

"Daddy, you don't …"

"It's OK sweetie, your nana is just looking out for me. I know she just wants me to take care of myself so I can take care of you."

She looked up at him from the menu, dark eyes twinkling. "Daddy, when are we going on another big boat trip? You remember how you said that we could go again with Wanda and Tonya could go with us? When can we go again?"

He shook his head, leaned forward and took her small hand in his.

"Sweetie, you've been asking me the same question three times a day since Wanda and I got back from the last one a few weeks ago. I'm not sure if we are going to go again right away. I just have to wait and see if it's necessary to go again, sweetie. Wanda and I got a lot of work done on the last trip, so we probably won't go again." She pulled her hand away and sat back against the seat, turned her head to the side and crossed her arms.

"You said I could go again, Daddy! Remember, you did! It's not fair."

"What's not fair, Lucy?"

"You and Wanda didn't even take me and Tonya last time."

"Look, I know how much you like Tonya but you don't have

to be on a cruise ship to have fun playing with her. We can meet her at a park, or McDonald's or some other place to play." He watched her uncross her arms and put her hands back on the table. She didn't reach for his hand.

She spoke without looking up. "Daddy, umm, do you think that you could marry Wanda?" He closed his eyes and tilted his head to the ceiling, smiling. "If you and Wanda got married then I could have a mommy and Tonya would be my sister." She gave him a pleading smile. John was used to the question. He called it the "mommy test." It was not a difficult test to pass. Lucy's only requirements were: She had to like the potential mommy and the candidate had to be female.

"Well, honey, I've explained this to you already. Wanda and I are just friends and we just work together. We're not interested in getting married." John watched her absorb his response. She frowned and looked down at the menu.

"Is it, umm, it is because she's a, a....nigger?" she whispered.

He winced as if punched. "What, what did you just say?"

She tucked her chin against her chest, "I'm sorry Daddy."

"Lucy, sweetie, please don't ever let me hear you say that word again." He leaned forward and took her hands in his, pulling her toward him. "You know calling someone that is very bad. I don't care what color Wanda and Tonya are and you know that." John took a deep breath. Lucy pulled her hands free, "Did you hear Uncle Travis use that word again?"

"I'm sorry Daddy."

"Answer me please, Lucy."

"Umm, yes, Daddy. I heard Uncle Travis say that word when I was at his house watching movies." She didn't look up.

"Tell me what happened. You're not going to get in trouble."

"I was scared Daddy. Uncle Travis was really mad. He was yelling at somebody and he kept calling them a ... you know, the bad word." Her shoulders quivered. He wiped a tear off her cheek.

"I know, I know. I can see you were scared. But was someone else at Uncle Travis' house while you were there?"

"No."

"But you said that he was yelling at someone."

"He was yelling on the … telephone."

"So he was talking on the phone and you heard him yelling and saying the bad word, right?"

"Yes." She wiped her nose with the sleeve of her sweater. "He was on the back porch. I wasn't trying to listen, Daddy. You know how you told me that sometimes when people talk on the phone that it has to be for privacy and I'm not supposed to listen. But Uncle Travis left the window open. I wasn't trying to listen but he was yelling and it was scary."

He marveled at her intelligence. She always knew what was happening around her and there were always questions.

"I see. But you understand that just because Uncle Travis says bad words doesn't mean that you should, right?"

"I know, I know, Daddy." He reached over and dabbed her eyes with a paper napkin.

"Daddy, does Uncle Travis yell at people and fight with them all the time because he is a policeman? Just like the policeman fighting shows you like to watch?"

"No, honey. Those are just police shows. I'm sure Uncle Travis has to yell at people sometimes, but policeman have pretty boring jobs. They don't spend all their time fighting and driving their cars fast to catch the bad guys, like they do on TV."

She nodded. She wiped her eyes with the back of her hand. "So can Wanda be my Mommy?" She tugged at a pink ribbon that was barely clinging to her long black curls. He was always careful to prepare her unruly hair as best he could each morning, but most ribbons or clips rarely survived an entire day.

"Oh, Lucy, my little sweetie. I know how much you want to have a mommy. I want you to have one too, but it has to be the right person for both of us. You can't just pick out people that you like and choose them to be your mommy."

An overweight teenage waitress interrupted their conversation. John ordered a large pizza with double cheese.

"Don't forget to get me a Sprite, Daddy. You said I could have a Sprite for a treat, no milk." John smiled at the waitress and she noted the order on her pad.

"But why can't I decide who I want for my Mommy? It's just

not fair that everyone else has a Mommy but me. I want Wanda for my Mom and Tonya for my sister!" She poked her lip out in a pout.

"I understand, baby. I want you to have a mommy also, but it has to be someone that I want to marry. There is someone out there for both of us and we will find her someday. I promise you that I will keep an eye out for the perfect person for both of us." He patted her hand.

They continued to talk about other issues. None was as grave as finding a new mommy, but important issues nonetheless. She answered questions about school, told stories about playing with friends in the neighborhood, and detailed who was being nice and who was being mean. All of these things were quite wonderful items to discuss as far as John was concerned. He watched her as she spoke. She brushed her hair back so that the curls framed her perfect, round face. Her brown, almond shaped eyes were accented by her smooth white skin. He felt that warm glow in his soul that only she could deliver.

Lucy radiated a joy and innocence that John could become lost in, making the other troubled parts of his life fade away. She was his whole world and his love for her sometimes left him petrified with fear that he could lose her, especially with her recent health problems and the corrective surgery approaching. Several times a week, he would lie in bed with her while she fell asleep. Then, after she had dozed off, he would move close to her face and breathe in as she exhaled. When he was that close to her, breathing her breath, his body relaxed, and anxious thoughts faded away. Her sweet, warm breath filled the lonely spaces deep within his soul.

* * *

After dinner, a light rain fell as they walked across the parking lot. He wished now that he had not traded cars with Wanda. Her 30-year-old Mustang convertible had a leak in the roof. Wanda had expressed so much interest in his new minivan that he had offered to switch cars for a day.

When they were within a few miles of their home, the light rain became a severe thunderstorm, and John searched for the switch to adjust the wipers to a faster setting. He noticed that the car was handling strangely. The steering was out of alignment and he drifted right onto the shoulder. He jerked the car back onto the road. Lucy sang "I'm a Little Teapot," softly and he watched her in the rearview mirror as she performed the hand movements that went along with the lyrics.

"Daddy, I smell something stinky?"

"What does it smell like, sweetie?" He leaned closer to the steering wheel, wiping the window with his shirt sleeve to remove the condensation.

"It smells like the gas, like when you stop at the station to put gas in the car."

As they entered a sharp right curve he turned the steering wheel. There was no response.

"Oh God, what the hell …"

"Daddy, you said a bad w- …"

He punched the brake with both feet as the car headed onto the far shoulder. No brakes. The car kept its forty-mile-per-hour pace and slid off the road and down a steep embankment. Sounds mixed together—small trees snapping, glass breaking, metal bending, and Lucy's screams. He turned and reached back for her, but the car slammed him forward. He covered his face to cushion the blow as the car spun sideways and hit a large, old oak tree, which shuddered as it took the weight of the impact.

"OUCH! AWWWW!!!" She screamed out. "Daddy, help me! Help! I got cut by something and there's a branch scratching me. It hurts, Daddy, it's hurting me! Daddy, help me!"

* * *

Her voice came back as water dripped in his face. He had fallen forward and his head was trapped between the smashed driver's side door and the steering wheel. "Daddy, I'm hurt! Wake up! Wake up, Daddy … please … wake up!" He couldn't remember what had happened, swimming in the fog of unconsciousness.

"Daddy, Daddy, please help me. I'm bleeding. Something cut me. The blood is all over me. Daddy, it hurts. It hurts real bad,

Daddy."

His body tensed as fire-hot pain shot through his leg. He tried to speak but the words would not form. "Oh my God! Oh God!! Lucy, Lucy." He slid his right hand across his lap and felt a warm stickiness and the jagged edge of bone protruding through his torn pants leg. The pain ripped and burned through his entire body.

Her voice woke him, softer this time. Pain clouded his thinking. How much time had passed?

"Daddy, Daddy, wake up." She whimpered. "I'm hurt, wake up. Daddy, I'm bleeding. Daddy, I'm scared. Daddy, Daddy, please wake up. Please. I'm scared."

He tried to form words, but nothing came out.

Everything blurred. What had happened? Lucy? My Lucy, she's hurt.

I'm here sweetie. Daddy's coming. I'm going to get you out of here.

The haze and fog would not clear. The pain came over him in huge waves and washed him back under.

He regained consciousness. A whisper in the dark. "Daddy, Daddy, I'm cold. I'm still bleeding, Daddy. Daddy, wake up. Please wake up, Daddy."

I'm coming, my Lucy, I'm coming. Hold on, your Daddy's gonna come and save you. I promise. Tears flowed down his face. He could not turn around to see his precious Lucy. He couldn't speak. He couldn't comfort her. He could only listen to her faint cries. The rain stopped. A full moon appeared and cast a pale light through the oak tree's branches and into the car.

Hold on, sweetie. Daddy's going to get up and get you out of here. You just sit tight now, my little sweetie. Don't be scared. I'm gonna save you, my precious.

John Manning fell back into unconsciousness, and Lucy's soft cries ceased.

II – August 1975

In the sticky, humid heat of an August afternoon in Durham, North Carolina, a small girl played with a group of five friends on a barren playground. The swings were all broken, the chains having been removed years ago, destined for activities that would never be considered childlike. The only piece of equipment on the playground that had any practical use was the monkey bars. It was so badly rusted that shards of brown metal would come off on the children's hands. Occasionally, someone would get a cut or a piece of metal would lodge in one of the small hands, but this was never a deterrent. The playground was a paradise for the neighborhood children. An oasis where they could meet friends, swap stories, play tag, and avoid the hazards of their broken homes.

A mother walked across the street toward the playground.

"Hey! Hey, Wanda!" screamed the mother. "Get your ass over here now! I've called you ten times already! Are you deaf?"

All of the childlike joy of play evaporated in that instant. Smiling, happy faces turned into scared, sad faces in the milliseconds that it took for those words to travel from the speaker's mouth to the children's ears. They all looked at the ground and then at the girl who belonged to the mother. She stood and gave a timid, frightened wave to the others. She walked toward the mother.

"Are you gonna answer me? I can't wait to get you back to the house and tear your ass up for not coming when I call you. This has got to stop, you hear?" said the Mother.

The timid girl whispered "OK, Mama, I'm sorry."

"Shut up and don't say anything. I'm too pissed off to listen to your bullshit right now," she growled.

The girl and the mother walked away from the playground, across the street, and around the corner to their home. Often the girl wished the playground was further from the house, maybe closer to her other refuge: the elementary school. The mother took the two cinder block steps up to the porch that was just large enough to hold two rusted card table chairs and a dirt-stained love seat. The sofa's stuffing material remained in some places. It still served its purpose whenever someone found a board to cover the rusted springs. The small girl followed, but at a greater distance than when the two had left the playground. Dread and fear covered her body like the worn out blanket on which she slept. She slithered up the steps as her mother was going through the door.

Inside the front door, the living room held a tan couch with a green blanket strewn across it in an unsuccessful attempt to cover the many stains on the cushions. There was a nineteen-inch black-and-white TV opposite the couch. To the left was a small kitchen with dirty dishes piled in the sink, as well as remnants of past meals still lying on the counter top. A white Formica table and two metal chairs stood against the wall opposite the sink. A short hallway, which began by the couch in the living room, led to the only bedroom. Mother and daughter shared this room, most of the time, and it had a small bathroom attached to it, with a mildewed shower, commode, and sink. There was a hole large enough to fit a basketball near the wall across from the sink.

"Get in here now. Don't be dragging your ass behind me. I got to go to work and you got to eat. Go sit at the table. I've got some chicken and rice for you."

The girl sighed and slipped into her chair. She was hungry and because of this she let her guard down and reached for the bowl of food on the table instead of keeping her eyes on her mother. As she picked up the spoon in the bowl, the back of her mother's hand flew toward the small girl's head and connected with tremendous force, just below her left ear. The girl fell to the floor screaming, holding her ear and trembling.

"This is the last time you're ever going to go to that playground! Are you listening to me? I know you could hear me and I'm not going to put up with your shit no more! Do you understand?" The mother loomed over the girl, eyes bulging with anger. "Answer me right now or you're going to get smacked on the other side of your head!"

The girl's face was wrenched in pain. Her lower lip quivered, her checks soaked with tears. "Y-y-yes, Mama. I'm sorry," she whispered. Past experience taught her to show how sorry she was to minimize the possibility of further punishment. "I won't do it again. I promise." These words came out with a clarity that surprised her. It worked. The mother opened the oven and pulled out a pan of biscuits, dropping them with a bang onto the stovetop.

"You better do exactly as you are saying right now, because if you don't, I'll give you something to cry about. Now get back up in your chair and shush up." The girl wiped tears and snot from her face, watching the mother from the corner of her eye. She slipped onto the chair and sat on the corner with one leg still on the ground, in case of another attack.

The mother placed two biscuits on a plate and shoved them onto the table. "Here, eat your dinner. Lock the door behind me 'cause I'm leaving for work now. Get in bed by nine o'clock and don't sleep on the couch, sleep in your bed."

"Yes, Mama. I will. I will." It was better when Mama went to work. Wanda was glad to have these few hours to be alone and unafraid. While her other friends' parents worked in restaurants, fixed cars, or simply stayed around the house, Wanda had no idea what her mother's job was. She just knew that her mother worked at night and sometimes brought home a friend. Twice during the summer, Wanda had witnessed her mother's return from work just before sunrise. Her mother didn't work every night, just the nights when Wanda didn't have to go to school the next day. Sometimes when she came home from work, she had trouble walking and she stumbled over the porch steps. Wanda preferred to sleep on the couch, which was further away from the bedroom and any guests.

After her mother left, Wanda finished eating and locked the front door. She opened the only window in the room and walked back to the bedroom, returning with a square fan the same size as the TV, which she placed by the window. Next, she went to the kitchen and picked up one of the metal chairs, which she brought back and placed underneath the window. She plugged the fan in and set it up on the chair, adjusting it to point the stream of humid air toward the sofa. She turned on the television, ate two Oreo cookies that she had hidden between the cushions, and fell asleep as the Captain's blue hat gave Gilligan his fourth swat of that evening's episode.

* * *

At the end of the school year, Travis' third grade class had been studying weather. He learned hurricanes were powerful storms and that North Carolina's Outer Banks were a frequent target. Though it was still early in the hurricane season, 1975 was shaping up to be a mild year for the big storms. Only Hurricane Amy, in late June, had threatened the North Carolina coast.

Travis felt that being with his brother and his father was like watching an approaching hurricane. Each day they were together, the storm grew in intensity. He knew hurricanes had an eye in the middle, where it was calm and peaceful, and he hoped the eye would arrive soon. He loved the fishing trip that he, his brother and father took every August, and hoped it wouldn't end badly, as some other trips had. It was early in the morning and they were thirty minutes from the marina. Cape Hatteras is the closest point on the East Coast to the Gulf Stream, which brings up warm water from the Gulf of Mexico and also abundant game fish, like marlin.

Yesterday, John and Travis' father had gotten into their loudest argument of the summer. John would be starting college in two weeks and Travis did not want to think about him leaving. He understood that John was his stepbrother, because they had different fathers, but John made Travis promise him last summer that they would never use any other word but brother to refer to each other. They were heading out to the Gulf Stream to catch marlins. Travis loved it when they went way out and tried for the big ones. The three of them had been deep sea fishing together at Hatteras since Travis was four. John and Travis' father, Hank Hanson, had gone fishing together once before Travis was old enough join them, but it had not gone well. John and Hank argued most of the trip. Hank had purchased a fifty-foot Sea Ray the previous summer and all of them enjoyed the greater number of fishing trips. As much as John disliked his stepfather, he loved the boat. Travis also loved the boat, especially the soft bed in the lower cabin. He was tired and it was easy to catch a quick nap while they were heading out. The loud engine drowned out all the sounds around him and he fell asleep quickly.

John always drove and, after another hour-and-a-half, he slowed the boat when they were close enough to their destination to begin setting out their lines. Travis awoke from his nap and watched his father climb the ladder to the upper deck where John was. Travis walked up the three steps, out of the cabin area, and stood under the deck, listening to them.

Hank sat down on a small bench, opposite of the console where John was holding the ship's wheel. "You know John, if I had talked to my father the same way you've been talking to me on this trip, he'd have kicked the shit out of me."

John continued to look out over the bow and the gently rolling swells. "Hank, if you weren't such a stupid, bigoted fool, then maybe I wouldn't have to talk to you like this. But if you're saying that you think you should kick the shit out of me, then go ahead and give it your best shot."

Hank waved his hand in the air. "Now don't go saying stuff like that. I ain't going to do nothing of the sort. Why don't you just let it rest for the day, John? You ain't going to change me and I ain't going to change you."

"I'm not worried about you or me, Hank. It's that wonderful little nine-year-old boy sleeping down there that I worry about. Your attitudes, the way you talk about blacks, he doesn't understand how wrong your old ways are. I can't stand to see him picking up your habits."

"I just tell it like I see it, John. I know what I know. Like I said, you ain't going to change me." Hank took a sip from the beer he was holding. "There's no need to bring up what happened with that little darkie boy at the marina if that's where you're heading with this."

"You're goddamn right I am. That was the most insulting thing I've ever seen you do. You told that little boy that you didn't want your son using the bathroom after a little 'nigger' and you pushed Travis up ahead of him."

Hank leaned forward on the bench. "You don't need to be worrying about Travis. I'm a good father and I know how to raise my boy. He knows what he sees in the world. Some people just ain't the same as others and I didn't make it that way. God did." He paused and took a long sip of his beer. "I guess since you're heading off to college, you think you're a lot better than me. Maybe you think you know how to raise a kid. You don't."

John turned and pointed his finger at Hank. "I know one thing Hank: Travis is a wonderful boy who loves his father, even if you are a prejudiced ass. You can bet I'm going to do everything in my power to make sure he knows your ways are wrong. I'm not going to let him grow up with your attitudes." Hank looked down at this beer and shook his head. John pulled the throttle back and the boat shifted into neutral. "I'm done with this. I'm going to starting rigging up the lines." Travis scurried back into the cabin as John came down the short ladder from the top deck.

* * *

John wasn't going to let Hank ruin this trip. It was a glorious August morning, with calm seas and a bright sun. Hank was right about one thing: John was never going to change him, no matter how much he argued with him. John would never understand why his mother chose to marry someone like Hank. She claimed to love him, that he provided well for all of them, and that down deep, he did have a good heart. John never saw it. He suspected his mother rarely did either. His mother once said loneliness and poverty force you to make compromises. John's father had abandoned him and his mother when John was only a year old. Hank owned five auto repair shops in the Raleigh area. They had married when John was eight, and his mother no longer struggled to make ends meet. Travis arrived a year later and both John and his mother were elated to have a new family member.

The three of them had fished hard for two days. John knew his conflicts with Hank would diminish if they concentrated more on the task at hand. This was the way it was, yelling and fighting at first, then getting down to business. On every trip, the amount of fish caught was inversely proportional to how much he fought with Hank. Their catch so far had been poor, but today was to be exceptional. They hauled in a dozen large fish and John reeled in the largest blue marlin any of them had ever caught. After the four-hour ordeal of landing the fish, he could not contain his delight. Even Hank was jumping up and down and whooping with excitement. The fish was twice as long as Travis, and Hank estimated it weighed three hundred pounds. After they had finished securing the fish to the side of the boat, Travis ran back to the cabin and grabbed a small camera. He took pictures while Hank held up John's arm and pointed to his bicep. In the last picture he took, Hank had even thrown his arm over John's shoulders. They were both covered with fish blood, seawater, and broad smiles.

The drive home to Raleigh was filled with pride and laughter as the three of them revisited the success of their outing. John was already talking about coming home from college in a few weeks so they could take the boat out again. They left Hatteras around seven o'clock, and after the sun had gone down an hour later, John fell asleep in the back seat.

"Son, you make sure that you get those pictures developed right away, and get some extra copies for us to give out. John really bagged us a good one."

"Are you going to show the pictures to the guys in the garage?"

"Damn right! My guys are going to shit their drawers when they see the size of this marlin."

Travis looked out the window and then down at his hands.

"Umm, Dad, uh, can I ask you something?"

"Sure son, what's on your mind?"

Travis brushed a fish scale off the back of his hand. "Why do you and John fight about black people so much?"

Hank smiled and glanced in the rear view mirror to see that John was still asleep. "Well Travis, it's like this. See your brother is still young. He ain't seen much of the world or the people in it. You understand?"

"Yes sir."

"He just doesn't know yet that people are different. See, I know them darkies ain't the same as you and me. They just ain't the same."

"But John said everyone is the same and it doesn't matter what color their skin is."

"A lot of people say things like that, but they just don't know. It's just the way it is in this world. John would see the same things the same way too if he had grown up around them like I did. I started helping my Dad fix cars up when I was just about your age." He flashed a smile at Travis. "He told me about how they ain't the same as us. I worked with them when I got my first real job as a mechanic, when I was only fifteen. I saw that what my Dad said was right. Even hired a few when I opened my own shop, but don't anymore. You just get a feeling for types of people and what they're like after you've been around them some. You just need to listen to your Dad about these things. You'll see too as you get older." Hank turned and smiled at Travis.

Travis was silent for a minute. "Remember you said I could start working in one of your shops next summer, right?"

Hank reached over and patted him on the leg. "Now that's my boy. You bet you can start next summer. Already been thinking about some good things you can do to learn your way around. I bet … oh shit." Travis looked up and saw the flashing lights reflected in the windshield. "Goddamn cop is pulling me over." Travis turned around in the seat and rose up on his knees to see the patrol car following them. Hank slowed the car down and pulled onto the shoulder of the road. "Son, reach over in the glove box there and get out the car registration. Goddamit, I sure don't need another speeding ticket."

Travis handed his father the slip of paper from the glove box, and watched him as he opened his wallet and pulled out three $20 bills. He smiled at his son as he folded them into the car registration form.

"Here's you first lesson son in how the world really works. This little trick has bailed me out of a couple of problems in the past."

The highway patrolman walked to Hank's window. All

Travis could see was his enormous belly as it hung over his belt. He hiked his pants up and Hank rolled down the window.

"Howdy, officer. What's wrong?" Hank's voice was friendly, surprised.

The patrolman shone his flashlight into Hank's face and then moved the light to the back seat, pausing on John for a few seconds. "Let me see your driver's license and registration please, sir."

"You bet, officer." Hank took his wallet from the dashboard and removed his license.

"Sir, I was following you for five miles and for that entire time, you've been traveling at least fifteen miles per hour over the speed limit."

Hank's eyes opened wide, "Oh my God! Was I really going that fast? Damn, officer, I've just been chatting with my boy here and I guess I wasn't paying close enough attention." He handed the officer his license and the car registration.

The policeman studied the license with his flashlight. "Well, Mr. Hanson, I'm sorry, but I'm going to have to write you up for speeding," Travis saw the patrolman's plump hands unfold the car registration, revealing the cash. He lifted his arm and wiped the sweat off his forehead with his shirtsleeve. The patrolman looked at Hank. Hank smiled, reassuringly.

"Hold on for just a second, Mr. Hanson. I'm going to have to call this one in on the radio." The patrolman turned and walked back to his car. Travis turned to look back.

"Just keep looking ahead son. He's just going to take a look at the paper work I gave him. Then he'll come back and tell us to be on our way."

Three minutes later, the patrolman returned to Hank's window.

"Mr. Hanson, I've decided to let you go with just a warning. But if I catch you speeding or doing anything else wrong around here again, you won't be so lucky." He handed the license and registration back to Hank, who in turn handed everything back to Travis. Travis returned the empty registration to the glove compartment.

"That's mighty nice of you sir. I was just telling my boy here how cops don't get the respect they deserve. You guys do a great job for us law abiding citizens. I just wish you didn't have to spend any time with us good folk so that you can spend more time chasing down the bad guys."

"That's mighty nice of you, Mr. Hanson. We can take care of the bad guys if all you good guys would just slow down a little. Looks like you got some precious cargo in that car with you. You wouldn't want to have anything happen to that boy of yours because you're driving too fast now, would you?"

"Good point, officer. I'll pay closer attention, you can bet that."

"Well good night, Mr. Hanson. Drive safe now, you hear?"

"Yes sir, officer. You have a good night now."

Hank pulled out from the side of the road. He was smiling. He drove on as the police car caught up with and then passed them. A few minutes later, the tail lights had disappeared.

"Now son, you got to understand what just happened here. I mean really understand. You're old enough now to start learning about how things work."

"But Dad, I didn't know that you could pay for your speeding ticket like that. You told me about one that you had to mail in some money to pay."

"I paid for the ticket, son. I just put the money into the hands of someone who needs the money a lot more. Cops don't get paid for shit. I just did that cop a big favor. Why, he'll be able to buy his kids some new shoes or maybe something nice for his wife."

"You mean that when you pay for a speeding ticket, the cop always gets the money?

"No, that's not how it works."

"Is that what you did when you mailed in that money before? You just mailed it to the cop instead of handing it to him like tonight?"

"Nah, son. That ain't what you're seeing here. Now, officially, that cop was supposed to give me a ticket for driving too fast. Then he turns that ticket in to a judge who sends me a letter saying that I've got to pay the money to the courthouse or I can come and see the judge and tell him why I think I shouldn't have to pay. Only the judge don't listen very well, so if you go to court, you just end up paying the money anyway. Plus, I gotta take off a day from work, sit in this big courtroom until they call my name and then I've wasted almost a whole day. See, this way, instead of giving the money to the judge, I just give it to the cop. The cop decides to take the money and then he lets me go. The cop can go on and spend more time catching bank robbers, muggers, and niggers who are breaking into people's houses. I mean bad guys, criminals. Then the poor, tired cop goes home with the cash and helps his family and I don't give my money to the judge and my insurance don't go up. Everybody comes out a winner."

Travis sat up on his knees and turned to look in the back seat. John was still asleep. "But Dad, it's against the law, isn't it? John told me about one time when you did this and he was in the car. He said you could go to jail for doing this since you were breaking the law."

Hank snorted and waved his hand toward the back seat. "Oh, that John! Listen, my boy. He sees things the wrong way because he just don't understand the world. He and you are just kids. To John, everything is either right or wrong. But that ain't how things work out there in the world. You're better off listening to your ole dad than listening to John. You gotta trust me on this, son. I know it's hard to understand, but in time you will. Right now, you just gotta trust me. You trust your old dad now, don't you, Travis?"

Travis turned to the window and stared out at the sky. It was a clear night and Travis noticed the number of stars he could see was greater than he could ever remember. He could see John's reflection in his window. What would his brother add to this conversation? What would he say about his father's opinions? It was best that John was sleeping. They would have just ended up shouting at each other again. Yeah, it was better that John was asleep.

"Yeah, Dad, I trust you."

Hank reached over and tousled Travis' hair. "Now that's my boy."

"Can we stop and get something to eat? I'm starving."

"Yes sir, my boy. I'll stop and get you anything you want."

III - July 2001

A woman, a man, and a young girl waited to check-in for their flight to San Francisco. The woman, who appeared to be near the end of her pregnancy, was in a wheelchair. The man handed their tickets to the airline ticket counter agent. The agent smiled and opened the tickets. After typing in the names on the tickets, he retrieved their reservation.

"OK. I've got the three of you traveling first class from RDU to San Fran. Does that sound right?"

The man nodded. "Yes."

"And the name is Brandon, right?"

The man nodded again, smiling.

The agent continued typing as he spoke. "Looks like you got a new arrival coming soon. Is it a boy or a girl?"

"It's a boy and we still have about a month to go. Going to make that last trip to see some family. Won't be doing much traveling after our boy comes."

"You're right about that. Got two teenagers myself and after they were born, we never made it out of the neighborhood. Got any luggage to check today?"

"No. Just taking these carry-ons. We travel light."

The agent nodded and bent down pulling the boarding passes from the printer. He assembled them with the tickets and handed everything back to the man. "Here you go Brandon family. The flight leaves from Gate 12." The agent leaned over the counter and pointed to his right. "If you push your wife around that corner, you'll find the elevators. Take it to the third floor and you'll see directions to the gate. Good luck with your new baby."

"Thank you." The man pushed the woman toward the elevator while the young girl lagged behind.

"Tonya, please catch up. Don't you want to push the elevator button?"

"OK, Mama. I'm coming." The girl skipped up beside her mother's wheelchair. "Which button do I need to push, Mr. Jamel?"

The man pushed the wheelchair faster. His face tightened into a frown. "Hit number three and don't be falling behind. We're late so we gotta hurry." He leaned down as he walked and whispered to the woman in the wheelchair. "Is everything safe in there?"

The woman patted her stomach. "Yes. Yes. Yes. Why do we go through this every time? Don't you think I know what I'm doing by now?"

"Look Wanda. It don't matter how many times we done this, I still got to know that everything's cool."

"Mama, this game is so much fun. Did you see that man ask when the baby was coming? Why can't we pretend that it is a girl? I want to have a sister!"

"We will, Tonya. We will next time."

They arrived at the gate in ten minutes. Wanda felt most nervous at this point. They had made six other trips, just like this one, but she could never relax. Jamel said they looked like the all-American family and no one would ever question them about what she might be carrying. The prosthesis that made her look pregnant held $40,000 in hundred-dollar bills. On their return flight, it would carry two kilos of cocaine. It had been Jamel's idea to make their pickups with this disguise. Her supposed condition also let them board the flight earlier. As they settled into their First Class seats, Jamel smiled at Wanda.

"Relax baby. We're on our way. You look like you're going to puke."

"I'll never get used to it. Get me a rum and coke."

"Don't be stupid. You can't be drinking rum when you're supposed to be pregnant. I'll get you some juice." He reached up and touched the attendant call button. "You want a 'lude to help you slow down?"

"No." Wanda glanced at Tonya. She was holding a Barbie doll up to the window and whispering about the planes coming and going on the runway.

She leaned closer to Jamel and whispered, "This is it for me, Jamel. I can't be putting my little girl at risk no more. I'm done."

Jamel closed his eyes and shook his head. "Don't be starting this shit again. There ain't no way that I'm going to make these pickups without you and Tonya. The five-oh would be all over me. Besides, it ain't like you're doing it for free."

"I don't care about that. She's asking questions. I can't be your mule anymore."

Jamel's face darkened. He slipped his hand over Wanda's forearm, gripped it and leaned closer to her. "Listen, bitch. You owe me." Wanda tried to pull her arm away, but he held tighter and jerked his chin toward Tonya. "I know what she means to you, so hear this. You blow this thing that's working so well for us right now and that little girl is going to get hurt. Hurt bad. Don't fuck this up, Wanda."

Her eyes narrowed. She yanked her arm out of his grip, smacking her fist into the opposite arm rest. She turned in her seat to face him. "Now you listen to me you sorry ass motherf-"

Tonya noticed the rise in her mother's voice and turned around. "Mama, can we go again to the 'quarium when we get off the plane?"

Wanda paused and turned to her daughter, her gaze fixed on Jamel until the last possible moment. "OK, honey. We'll go again. Remember to say Aquarium not 'quarium." She stood up and took Tonya by the hand. "Come with me, honey. We're going to sit somewhere else. Mr. Jamel wants to be by himself for a little while."

They moved back one row and sat down. Tonya continued playing with her doll in her new window seat. Wanda closed her eyes and the pilot announced they were next for takeoff.

* * *

The next day, Jamel headed out at 9:30 a.m. with a rental car to scout the area where the exchange was to take place. This was part of his ritual. He would be considered a very talented businessman by any normal measure. But his industry did not lend itself to normal measurements. Unlike other businesses that gauged their success as members of "fast growth" lists or as a Fortune 1000 company, Jamel's success wasn't publicized to the rest of the world. He gained no advantage by receiving business awards or garnering a fluff piece on his management style in the business press. As is the case with other industries, some of his suppliers, competitors, regulators, and employees suspected he had achieved great success, but no one knew the real story. Unlike others in his industry, he drove an old car and lived in a simple home in an average neighborhood. He worked hard to keep his financial success private.

Jamel would describe his enterprise using the same terms and phrases that any business operator would use. His product line consisted of cocaine and crack cocaine. He had several suppliers from whom he could buy his product. All of these suppliers differed in the quality of their product, pricing, and delivery schedules. One even offered favorable credit terms, an extraordinary feature in a cash-only industry. Six commissioned sales representatives sold his products. (He had moved out of direct selling himself two years ago, which had relieved him of quite a bit of stress and worry.) He had a solid base of customers and some growth in new customers, most of which came through referrals. Since he was inhibited in his ability to advertise and market his products, he depended on word-of-mouth advertising and the hard work of his sales force to meet the demands of his customers while maintaining a reasonable profit margin. He had competition. As a result, he made pricing decisions with the objective of maintaining his current customers as well as attracting more. He had systems in place to monitor product quality. Employees were fired if he suspected they were diluting the product without authorization. If he thought it necessary to send a stronger message to the rest of the staff, he used other techniques to punish employees in addition to firing them. He was quite adept at the use of technology. In fact, the Internet had brought his operation tremendous advances in communications with suppliers, employees, and customers. He used his PC daily. He enjoyed his ability to manage his substantial bank accounts in the Bahamas and Aruba via online banking. Even though he always made his bank deposits in person on various business trips to Nassau, he could move funds from his Bahamian account to other accounts in Aruba. Because his banking was done offshore, he could avoid the scrutiny that one might face if they chose to work with a U.S. bank. He also faced issues regarding regulation of his product and, just as other companies do, he had developed tried and true methods of avoiding regulation (or, perhaps, better described as detection). Falling afoul of the regulators would mean he would have to close his operation and spend many years revisiting his error. Recognizing the huge risks, he had taken great care to cultivate connections within the police force in his hometown of Durham, North Carolina. They provided "advice and consultation" in regards to the oversight of his industry by the regulators. Anyone examining a Profit and Loss statement for his enterprise (and he did construct one of these every month, though it was written out and destroyed in the same day) could not help but note his second largest expense was labeled "Professional Fees." Keeping the regulators off his back was his most significant cost. Financial advisors would identify this expense as one that was variable and was moving upwards in direct proportion to his company's growth. This would be an accurate assessment.

Whenever they flew to San Francisco to pick up product, Wanda did not attend Jamel's meetings with his suppliers. They stayed at a Holiday Inn near the airport. Five hundred yards from the hotel, there was a small car rental company whose rates were outrageous, but they accepted cash payments and did not require a credit card deposit. Wanda rented a Ford Taurus and she and Tonya started their drive to the Monterey Aquarium, two hours away. On their last trip, Tonya had stared at the sea creatures for hours. Wanda enjoyed the sea lions that lounged on the rocks around the facility.

"Mama?"

"Yes, honey?"

"What were you and Mr. Jamel fighting about on the airplane?"

"Nothing important. You know, just grownup stuff."

Tonya looked down at her seat belt. Normally, she would ride in a car seat in the back, but this was a special occasion. "Were you fighting about going on the airplane again?"

"Something like that honey." Wanda took a sip from a Coke

can. "Why don't we talk about fish? Do you want to see those sharks again? Remember those sharks with the funny looking heads called hammerheads?"

"Yeah, I do remember them, but I want to look at the big tuna fishes." Tonya paused and put her finger up to her chin. "Are you sure those fish get squeezed into them cans of tuna?"

Wanda chuckled. "Well, honey, remember I told you how it works. They don't put the whole fish in the can; they just put little pieces of him in. If the can was big enough to hold the whole fish, we wouldn't be able to fit it in our car to bring home from the store." Tonya brought her hands to up to her mouth and covered her laugh and Wanda laughed loudly.

"Mama, can we eat some tuna fish for lunch today?"

"You bet. We'll get whatever you want." They smiled at each other.

"Mama, can I ask you another question?"

"Sure honey. What is it?"

Tonya twisted a braid around her finger. "Why aren't you wearing your pretend baby costume today?"

Wanda leaned forward, checking traffic in the rear view mirror, before moving into a faster lane. "Well honey, the costume is for when we ride on the airplane. Mr. Jamel and I just like to have it on for fun when we're flying on the plane. You remember us talking about this, don't you?"

"No."

"You know what a joke is, honey. That's what we're doing when we wear the baby costume. Just like when you dress up for Halloween." Tonya stopped twisting her braid and looked up and her mother.

"But I don't want to pretend anymore. I want to have a real baby." She furrowed her brow pushed out her lower lip. "I want a sister."

Wanda slid her hand across the seat and patted her leg. "Oh, honey, I know how much you want to have a sister. Maybe someday we can get you one. Right now, let's just talk about how much fun we are going to have at the aquarium." She let her hand rest on Tonya's knee.

Tonya paused, her face still tight. She took her mother's hand. After a moment she smiled and looked up. "OK. Can I get a beanie baby seal?"

"You bet."

They drove for ten more miles without speaking.

"Tonya, honey?"

"Yes, Mama?"

"Would you like to live near the aquarium someday?"

"Could we come every day?"

Wanda laughed. "No, but we could come here a lot more if we lived here nearby."

"Could we get a new house and new Barbies to go in it?"

"Do you mean a new Barbie playhouse and new Barbies?"

"No, I mean a new house for you and me to live in and some new Barbies for me to play with."

"Maybe, sweetie, maybe."

"If we live near the 'quarium, can I have a sister too?"

Wanda laughed again and pulled one of Tonya's braids.

She thought about it daily. It was time to get out. They'd been lucky so far, but the risks scared her more now. They could move here. It wouldn't be that hard. Wanda had a recurring dream about it. On other trips, they had visited Carmel and Big Sur and these were the places that would appear in her dream. She laughed sometimes thinking of herself and Tonya, a pair of backwards folk from North Carolina, living here, among the giant redwoods. Big Sur was her favorite. She loved the open spaces, the friendly people, the farms, and the huge trees. She pictured a tiny house, way up in the hills, overlooking the ocean. They would have a home and a life that was safe, and she and Tonya would be together, always.

IV - August 2001

John always drove her to school. The previous year, he had spent one morning a week reading to her class. Lucy adored school and John was proud to be there to watch her thrive. Her new teacher was Cindy Alston-Capps and John felt as if Lucy and he had hit the lottery. She was patient, funny, and a big hit with the children. They called her Mrs. A-C and she asked John to call her Cindy. He always found it disappointing to meet attractive women and then have them introduce themselves with a hyphenated last name.

"Daddy, will you read that Arthur book again?" Lucy called out from her car seat. "You know the one where he plays April Fools on his friend. Can you read that book when we get to school, Daddy?"

"I think it would better to try some new books this week Lucy. I know it's one of your favorites, but we can read it at home. I want you to try to read it again."

"I can't read those big words, Daddy."

"I bet you can if you try. Remember how you read that Clifford book to me a few days ago?

"But you had to help me a lot."

He smiled as he watched her in the rearview mirror. "That's OK, honey. That's how you learn. You've got to keep trying."

He glanced back again and saw her twisting a rogue black curl with her finger. It was a common action in advance of a well thought out question.

"Daddy, can I ask you something?"

"Of course."

"Do you promise that you won't get mad?"

John sighed and closed his eyes for a moment. "I won't get

mad Lucy. You know that you can ask me anything."

She looked at John and then down. "Did, umm, did my Mommy put a divorce on you?"

John winced. She asked questions about her mother regularly, but not this one. "Now that is a very interesting question. How do you know about divorce?"

She twisted the curl tighter. "Well, I kind of, you know, heard Mrs. A-C talking to one of the ladies that works in the cafeteria, and she said she was getting 'super-rated' and that she was putting a divorce on her husband." She paused and looked back down. "Did my Mommy do that to you?"

John eased the car over to the curb and turned off the engine to discuss the matter. He turned around in his seat. "Well, in way, yes. But we don't say 'put a divorce'; we say that people 'get divorced.' And most of the time before people who are married decide to get divorced, they get separated. I think you called it 'super-rated.'" He rolled his head around to relieve the tension in his neck. These questions about Ellen always gave him a headache.

She looked up at him and smiled. "So you and my Mommy got a divorce, right?"

"Yes, sugar. We decided that it would be better for both of us if we weren't married any longer."

Lucy turned to look out the window. A man and a boy Lucy's age walked past them holding hands. The man carried a Spiderman book bag that looked much too large for the boy. Lucy looked back at John.

"I understand, Daddy. I'm just glad that you didn't get a divorce on me like Mommy did to you."

"Thanks sweetie. You know that I love you more than anything else in the world and I will never leave you. You're my sunshine, right?" John turned back to the steering wheel.

Lucy smiled and covered her face with her hands. "Yes, Daddy, I know. I'm your sunshine."

"And, sweetie, parents don't divorce their children." He watched her in the rear view mirror. "Your Mommy loves you and wants you to be happy. She decided that she wanted to move away and do some other things for her work. She was very good at her work."

"I know, Daddy, I know. You told me that before."

I need a new topic, he thought. He pulled away from the curb and continued to their destination.

"Now I have a question for you. Tell me again what you heard Mrs. A-C say about getting divorced."

"Well, I just heard her say that she was putting, I mean getting a divorce on her husband. Did I say it right?"

"Yes. And there's something else to remember about this, Lucy."

"Yes Daddy?"

"Grown-ups would call this thing that you heard Mrs. A-C say 'private' and you shouldn't tell anyone about it. You remember what 'private' means, right?"

"Yes, Daddy. I won't tell anyone else."

"Good, sweetie." John pulled his car into one of the visitor parking spaces.

"Here we are. Ready for a great day at school?"

"Yes. I love school and I love Mrs. A-C."

"That's good, sweetie. Mrs. A-C is a very nice lady."

John parked the car and they both got out. Lucy carried her Barbie backpack and matching lunchbox. John had made her favorite, a peanut butter and jelly sandwich without the crust. He always felt proud to walk in with her, like a knight delivering the princess to her throne. The school's principal, Jennifer Lang, waved at John as they walked past her office.

John waited in back of Lucy's class while the students watched the morning announcements over the school's closed-circuit TV system. After announcements, the students recited "The Pledge of Allegiance." Then, Mrs. A-C gathered the students together on the floor in front of a large rocking chair. She reminded the students that every Tuesday Lucy's father, Mr. Manning, read to them. John nodded to the class and sat down in the rocking chair. He had already selected a Dr. Seuss book for today's reading. As usual, the twenty students in the class listened attentively. As soon as John finished, several small hands shot into the air. Lucy smiled as he answered their questions and listened to several personal stories. These stories began with some connection to what he had read, but quickly went off on a tangent. John reveled in how much Lucy enjoyed having him in the class. The simple act of reading to a group of small children filled him with immeasurable joy.

After finishing his reading duties, John walked over and returned the book to Cindy as the assistant teacher moved the children back to their desks for another assignment.

"That was terrific, John. They enjoy your stories." She stood up behind her desk and took the book from him. She turned her back and bent down to place it on a low shelf. John noticed her thin, long legs and the waistband of her panties as it peeked out above her skirt. She turned back around and John's face flushed as he looked down. She sat back down at her desk and pointed to the adult desk a few feet from hers.

"Why don't you grab Jan's chair and have a seat? I've got a minute or two while she gets them going on their writing workbooks." He smiled and moved to the chair, placing it close to her desk as he sat down.

"You know, Cindy, you're magical with these kids. How long have you been teaching?"

"Thanks, you're very sweet. I started teaching right after college, so this year will be sixteen years. Wow, that seems like a long time, doesn't it?"

"So I'm guessing that you must have been a child prodigy and graduated from college when you were twelve?" Her smile grew larger and she blushed. John liked her angular features and the smattering of brown freckles that ran below her eyes and met at her nose.

"That's a really nice thing to say. I'm afraid I wasn't a prodigy, not by any means."

"Well, maybe it's just that time flies when you're having fun."

"That's a good way to describe it. Although it does get tiring some days."

"No doubt. I'm worn out just keeping up with one kid." He glanced back over his shoulder to see that Lucy was busy at her desk. Cindy brushed her hair back and smiled.

"You should be proud of Lucy. There's no doubt that she's

inherited your intelligence." John returned the smile.

"I'm afraid she inherited her intelligence from her mother. I didn't make much of a contribution in that area."

Her face tightened again. "I would argue with you about that. Listening to you read and the few times that we've spoke, I would bet you're very intelligent." Cindy glanced down at her desk and picked up a pencil. She placed it in a chipped white coffee cup that held a collection of pens, pencils, and assorted markers.

"I've wanted to ask you about Lucy's mother but if it is too personal, please just tell me so."

"No, it's fine."

"I've never heard Lucy say anything about her mother. Is she not in Lucy's life right now?"

John sighed and glanced over his shoulder again. "One of those long stories I'm afraid. But you're right; she's not in Lucy's life. We divorced about a year after Lucy was born and she took a job in Europe. It was a big promotion for her."

Cindy's face tightened. "And she left you all alone to raise Lucy?"

"Well … I guess, yeah, but like I said, it's a long story. She's a good person. Really, she is." John shifted in his chair. Cindy leaned forward and patted John's hand.

"Well, I'm very sorry. It must be difficult raising Lucy alone."

John smiled at her touch. "It was in the beginning, but things turned out fine. My brother and my mother are both a big help and Lucy adores both of them."

"Oh, I know about Uncle Travis the policeman! Lucy mentions him frequently." Cindy nodded. John turned back to check what the children were doing. Cindy smiled at him when he looked back at her.

"Umm, Cindy, there's something I've been meaning to ask you, but it's a little awkward since you're Lucy's teacher. You asked me to tell you if a question about Lucy's mother was too private, so please let me know if I'm out of line with this question."

"Sure, John."

"I was just wondering if maybe you might like to, umm, maybe have dinner sometime."

Cindy sat up straighter and tapped John's hand playfully.

"Why John, that's a very nice offer and it shouldn't make you feel awkward. Lots of parents invite me over for dinner to talk about school and to help me learn more about their child's needs. Tell you the truth; the kids get the biggest kick out of it. I mean having their teacher sit down to dinner with their family is a big deal to them."

John scratched his chin and smiled. "Uh, well, actually I was thinking that it would be just you and I having dinner. I guess you'd call it a date."

Cindy's face flushed and she looked over John's shoulder at the students. "Oh … umm, well, I see. Uh, I'm flattered that you asked, but, I can't really do that John. I'm married."

John bowed his head and touched his forehead. "Oh, no. Oh, my gosh, I am so sorry. I never would have brought this up, but I had heard that you were getting a divorce.

Cindy fidgeted in her seat and looked down at a stack of papers in front of her coffee cup pencil holder. "Hmm, now where did you hear such a thing?"

"I think, I just, umm, heard someone mention it at the volunteer meeting that I went to last week. Another person asked why you didn't have on your wedding band."

Cindy smiled and looked down at her finger. "Oh that. I've, umm, I'm getting it resized right now. I lost a little weight over the summer."

John nodded and pushed his glasses up further on his nose.

"Good for you. I could stand to do the same myself."

"If you like, I can give you some information on the program I used this summer. It's a great system. If you stay with it like I did, you'll lose weight. I mean, not that you need to or anything, but just if you felt like it."

John smiled and looked down at the floor. "Well, Cindy, that's a nice offer. Maybe when I come back next week, I'll pick up the information from you."

"Excellent." She stood up and John followed. "I've got to get back to the kids. I'll, uh, see you next week then." She turned and walked to the front of the class.

"You bet. Thanks, Cindy." John cursed under his breath and

closed his eyes. He stood up and began walking toward the door, blowing Lucy a kiss as he walked out the door. As he passed the principal's office, Mrs. Lang was outside her office posting a list of names on her door.

"Hi, Jennifer. How are you?"

"Well hello there Mr. John Manning. I'm doing just great. I hear that Lucy of yours is one smart cookie."

"Thanks. Thanks a lot. She loves school. Thank you for having such a good staff." John pointed to the piece of paper she had taped to the door. "What's that you're posting on the door?"

"Oh, just some boring old duties that a few of my teachers have to do next week."

John rubbed his chin. "Hmm, interesting. So this is the crew for lunchroom duty next week. Sounds like a very tough assignment to me." He smiled at Jennifer. "Are these staff members up for this hard job?"

Jennifer chuckled and touched John's elbow. "Very funny, John. Yes I hand-picked this crew for this very difficult assignment."

John pointed to the list again. "Hey, you've got a typo there. You forgot to write out 'Cindy Alston-Capps'. You've just got 'Cindy Alston.'"

Jennifer leaned forward and looked at the name that John had pointed to. "My goodness John, you are very observant." She leaned forward and glanced behind John and down the hall. "Actually, Cindy started the process of getting divorced this summer. She asked us to drop the 'Capps' from her name right away." Jennifer's dropped her voice to a whisper. "Between you and me, I heard that things have been pretty rough between them."

John nodded. "Hmm, that's too bad. I feel sorry for Cindy."

Jennifer returned the nod.

John stared at her for a moment, looked down while he scratched the floor with the toe of his shoe, and then looked back at Jennifer. "Well, it was good talking to you. Thanks again for running such a great school. I'm very happy to be part of it."

"And we're very happy to have you, John. See you later."

John walked back to his car. His day ahead at work was going to be busier than usual. Maybe he could explain to Lucy that he was now just a little too busy at work to continue reading to her class. She wouldn't be happy, but he wouldn't be comfortable in the classroom anymore. She'd be OK. Kids adapt and there would always be next year and a different teacher. Things would work out so that he could be around more next year.

V – August 2001

Two Durham police detectives sat in an unmarked, black sedan watching an empty parking lot from across the street. Travis Hanson sat on the passenger side, finishing off a large, black coffee. His lean, six-foot four-inch frame made it difficult to find a comfortable position. He shifted his legs for the fifteenth time since they had begun their midnight vigil. It was 2:00 a.m. and cooler than usual for an August evening in North Carolina. Jim Keefer was behind the wheel, his eyes closed, seat tilted back, and his head lolling on the headrest. He was fifty-five, twenty years older than Travis, and a foot shorter. He was tired and not happy to have been drafted to go along on this stakeout.

Travis slapped Jim on the arm, "You're starting to snore again, man. Cut that shit out."

Jim's head lolled forward, making a slow circle, while he rubbed the back of his neck. "Look, Travis, don't be hassling me about my snoring, I didn't ask to come on this ride tonight. Boss said you needed some company, so if I need to get some rest, you gotta let me close my eyes for a while."

Travis shifted in his seat and looked out the window. "I'm so fucking tired of needing babysitters. They told me that when my probation period was up, they'd cut this shit out."

Jim looked over at Travis, shaking his head. "I wouldn't sweat it, my friend. You're almost out of the dog house." He looked out toward the parking lot. "You tired?"

"Nah. I'm juiced up on coffee and looking forward to kicking a little ass tonight."

"How did you find out about this thing?"

"One of my regular snitches. The most reliable one." He

shifted in his seat again. "He didn't know much. Just the date and time of the meeting. This snitch has always given me good information."

"You think this buy has anything to do with that Jamel guy you've got such a hard-on for?"

He stared at the parking lot. "Doubt it."

"I've been wanting to ask you about this Jamel guy. If he is such a player, why haven't I heard of him?"

"'Cause the guy's smart as shit. Doesn't operate the way most dealers do."

"What do you mean?"

"Nothing sticks on him. We've got nothing from his home phone tap. Nobody we bring in that we think is connected to him will roll over. Nothing."

He scratched the stubble on his chin. "Damn. That's all we need, a smart dealer."

"Like I said, he's smart. Most of these dealers are mouthing off about their business on the phone all the time so you can pick up clues or at least match the calls to other phone numbers and put the pieces together. Not with this dude. Another thing, this guy don't even drive a new SUV like all the others. In this city, you can pull over five new Nissan Pathfinders in one day and two of them are being driven by players. This guy drives an old Audi. He flies under the radar."

"They all got a weakness, man. Some dip into the dope, some like the ladies too much, some like to flash the cash. You'll find his."

"Don't know about that, my friend. Only weakness we can connect this guy to is that he likes to fly First Class. Someone watched him get on a plane with a pregnant lady and a little girl. They flew to the San Fran area, probably doing a pick up. We never did find out when he was flying back. The guy only buys one-way tickets. If we'd known when he was coming back, we could've asked the guys at the airport to give him a little extra attention. Smooth operator. Just like the song."

"So you need to find out about this guy's flying habits, huh?"

"Yeah."

"What about asking your brother? He owns that travel agency over on Hinton Road, right?"

"Yeah."

"You ought to talk to him. My sister worked at an agency in Raleigh, and those folks know all the ins and outs of dealing with the airlines, making reservations, shit like that. He might know some way you could track this guy better when he's on the move."

"Good idea."

Jim rubbed his eyes and yawned. "Didn't I read about him in the newspaper winning some kind of business award a while back?"

"Yup, that's my brother. Half-brother really. And yeah, he's won some business awards."

"So the guy's a good businessman?"

"Oh yeah. He grew that little agency from nothing. He's a good guy, good brother. Always ready to help. Bailed me out of a big jam one time." Travis looked down. He turned back to Jim, smiling. "Have I told you about his daughter Lucy, my sweet little niece?"

Jim leaned back on the headrest and laced his fingers across his large stomach. "You've got a niece, huh? Uncle Travis. Has a nice ring to it."

"You should hear the way my Lucy says it. She can melt your heart and she's a real beauty."

"How often do you see her?"

"Usually once or twice a month."

"How about your brother?"

"I talk with my brother a little more and we swap email messages once a week or so. We're going to Hatteras in October to do some fishing."

"So you leave the niece with the Mom and the boys do some fishing. Sounds good."

Travis grimaced. "No mom. Lucy stays with my mom, but John's bitch of a wife left him and Lucy about a year after she was born and moved to Europe for another job. She's a nut job, so don't get me started." He raised his coffee cup and took a long drink.

"How in the hell can a woman just leave her family like that?

Goddamn bitch."

Jim shook his head and stared out the window. "Your brother's older, right?"

"Yeah. Nine years older. His dad divorced our mom a couple of years after John was born. The guy moved somewhere out West. She raised John all on her own. She married my Dad and I was born when John was nine. Ever since I was a kid, John watched out for me." Travis leaned back in his seat and ran his fingers through his hair. "Good thing too, 'cause my dad died when I was twenty. The bastard stuck my mom with a lot of bills from his auto repair business that was going under. He ran all over town borrowing money from people trying to keep his company running. Lied about everything he was doing. He even forged my mom's name on some bank loans."

Jim frowned and shook his head. "Damn, man. That's some bad shit. I'm sorry."

"Yeah, I know. But John worked it all out. He helped her get out of just about all of it. My mom and I call John 'Mr. Fix-It.'"

"Sounds like a good guy."

"Yeah, he's a good one." Travis scanned the parking lot again. "What time is it?"

"Two-thirty."

Just then, a late model Chevrolet Camaro appeared at the intersection to their left. When the light turned green, it drove through the intersection and turned into the parking lot, heading toward the far corner. The car's headlights switched off and they watched it turn around and back into a parking space. Jim patted Travis on the leg and nodded toward the car.

"OK, here we go," whispered Travis. "There's two of them. I'll take the driver."

Jim started the car. They spun away from the curb. In ten seconds they were in front of the Camaro. Jim turned the headlights to bright. Travis was out of the car quickly.

"Police! Police!" He shouted. Both hands clasped his .38 revolver handle. "Get the fuck out of the car, right now! Keep those hands up where I can see them! I'll blow your motherfucking head off if you so much as flinch!" Jim was a few seconds behind Travis.

His first step after he rounded his door was on a pile of gravel. His foot slid forward and he flailed backwards, arms swinging wildly, falling hard on his right hip, and grunting loudly. Travis turned to the sound of the fall.

"Jim? What the fuck man, get up!" Travis shouted, his head turning back and forth between the Camaro and where Jim lay on the ground. The Camaro's passenger side door flew open and a small man began running away from the scene. He had covered a hundred yards before Jim managed to get back on his feet.

"Shit that hurt." Jim leaned on the hood and looked over at Travis.

Travis pointed in the direction of the fleeing man. "Jim, look … Get him, man!"

Jim grunted. "I got him. I'm alright." He switched his gun to his left hand and grabbed his hip with his right. The man had a three-hundred-yard head start.

"Jim, get your ass moving man!"

Jim gained speed as he trotted to the end of the parking lot and turned right down an alleyway, following the runner.

Travis turned back to the driver. "Now, you want to go with your friend, asshole?" No response. "Go ahead, 'cause I'll shoot you in your white ass and you'll limp for the rest of your shitty life. Now get your hands back on that steering wheel." The driver's hands trembled as he moved them back to the steering wheel. "This is the deal you sorry ass punk. You're going to keep your hands right on that steering wheel and I'm going to open your door. You quiver the wrong way and I'll blow you away. Got it?" The driver nodded, his eyes wide with fear. Travis reached down and opened the car door.

"Now put your hands up on your head and lace those fingers together nice and tight, then get out real slow." The driver stood up and walked around the open car door. Travis pointed to the front of the car. "You know the position." The driver turned to face the hood of the Camaro and in one swift motion, Travis lifted his left foot and drove into the lower back of the driver. His body slammed onto the hood.

"What the f— !" said the driver, barely preventing his head from snapping down onto the hood. "Cut that shit out, dude, I'm not going anywhere." He raised himself up from the hood. He appeared to be twenty years old. He was six feet tall, about one-hundred-seventy-five pounds, with stringy brown hair."

"What's your name, punk?"

"Why the fuck does that matter, dude? You don't have no right to be kicking me in the fucking back." Travis put his left hand on the driver's shoulder.

"You want to try that again?"

The driver snorted and jerked his shoulder away. "Eddie, man. Name's Eddie."

"OK, Eddie. Here's a little news for you. I'm in a real bad mood tonight. When I was leaving the station tonight to come out and catch your ass, I stepped in a big load of dog shit. Really pissed me off, too. If you think that what I just did hurt, then try something stupid right now. 'Cause if you do, I'm going to turn you into my own personal doormat by shoving my foot so far up your ass, I'll be able to use your tongue to wipe the dog shit off my shoe."

Eddie turned his head to locate Travis. "C'mon, man. I've told you already I ain't going to do nothing stupid. What the hell are you hassling me for, anyway?"

"Keep your ugly eyes on that hood, Eddie. We got a tip from some of your cokehead friends in West Palm that you were going to be in this parking lot trying to sell a big bag of blow."

Eddie looked back over his shoulder again, "What're you talking about man? I don't do that shit. I'm just on a trip up here and I wanted to catch a little sleep, that's all."

Travis shook his head slowly. "I'm real glad to hear that, Eddie. Then I guess you won't mind if I take a look inside your car, right?"

Eddie rose up from the hood. "You can't go looking around in my car, man."

"Get your goddamn hands back down on that car, Eddie." Travis kept his gun pointed at Eddie, while looking in the direction that Jim had gone. All was quiet.

"Let's cut the shit, Eddie. Here's the deal. I know you're here in Durham to sell someone a nice load of blow."

Eddie shook his head. "That's bullshit, man. Nothing but

bullshit."

"I doubt it, my man." Travis wiped the sweat from his forehead with the back of his left hand. "Now, you've got a choice to make and it's a real simple one. You can put the dope in my hand in the next sixty seconds and then you get to drive out of here." Travis scanned the parking lot again. "You don't give it to me right now, then I'll bust your ass and put you away for possession with intent. Got any idea how much time you'll get for that, Eddie?"

"Fuck that, dude. I don't know what you're talking about."

Travis grabbed his head and forced it down onto the car hood, jamming his gun into Eddie's ear. "I don't think I heard you, Eddie," he hissed. "You want to do some serious time, or do you want to drive away from here like nothing happened?"

Eddie squirmed under Travis' weight. "Get the fuck off me, man!" Travis held him down for five more seconds then pushed down hard and stood back up. Eddie raised himself slowly. He brushed his chest twice, indignantly. "So what if I do what you're saying. You'll just take my shit and bust me anyway."

Travis chuckled. "Now, Eddie, I don't give a rat's ass about busting a little fuckwad like you. I'm just here to help clean up my fair city of Durham. I want your dope and then I want you to take your ugly ass back down to Florida and never show up here again."

It was Eddie's turn to scan the parking lot. He turned back to Travis. "If I'd known that I was going to be dealing with the same types of cops that I deal with in Fort Lauderdale, I would've never made this fucking trip," he snarled.

Travis smiled. "You're getting smarter by the minute, asshole." Travis raised his eyebrows and held out his left hand. Eddie shook his head and jammed his finger toward the driver's side front tire. Travis nodded and took a step backward. He tightened his grip on the gun and pointed it at Eddie.

"Take it slow, my man. Real slow." Eddie knelt down and reached up behind the fender. His faced grimaced in concentration as he pulled out a small piece of the tire well. Placing it on the ground, he reached back up and removed a plastic bag about the size of four large candy bars, the middle of which was bound with duct tape.

"Good job. Now stand up nice and slow and hold both of your hands away from your body." Before he had stood up all the way, Travis snatched the bag from his hand.

"Now don't say another fucking word. Get your ugly ass in the car and go." Eddie's mouth opened and Travis brought the gun to within a foot of his face. "Don't talk. Go."

Eddie stared at Travis and then down at the package before getting back into the Camaro. He drove out of the parking lot, accelerating quickly and squealing his tires, as he turned onto the street.

Travis glanced around the lot, stuffed the package into the crotch of his pants, walked back to the driver's side of the car and sat down. His sweat-soaked shirt hung on him like a wet towel. He leaned his head back against the headrest and closed his eyes. Five minutes later he put the car in gear, drove back onto the street and headed out to find Jim. One block later, he saw Jim limping toward him. Travis pulled over and rolled down the passenger side window. Jim walked over and stood beside the car. He put his hands on the roof above the door.

"Get in the car, Jim. You look like a perp leaning on the car like that."

"I just … got to … try … catch … my breath," sputtered Jim. He laid his head on his hands, his shoulders heaving as sweat dripped onto the car seat.

"Where's your guy?" asked Travis. Jim shook his head.

"Never even got close to him. I must've run in five different directions. Hip is killing me." He rubbed his hand across his face. "What about you?"

Travis smiled. "Sorry to tell you man, but the guys were just couple of lowlifes who wanted to park and smoke weed." Jim grimaced and shook his head.

"What the hell, Travis? You mean I broke my hip for a couple of potheads?"

"Sorry, man. All I found on him was a half a joint. I jacked the guy around a little and then shoved him off."

"Damn, man." Jim slammed his fist on the roof and groaned, grabbing his hip.

"Then let's get out of here." He opened the car door and lowered himself into the seat. He reached out to pull the door shut but stopped short, wincing with the pain. He looked over at Travis. "Hey, man, you mind walking around and closing my door?"

"Sure, man." Travis stepped out of the car and walked around to Jim's door. The phone attached to his hip started to vibrate

"Damn, man. Who's calling you at 3 a.m.?" Travis slipped the phone out of his belt and brought the small screen up to his face.

His face tightened, then he smiled. "Umm, oh damn. It's this chick that works at Topper's."

"You mean that strip club over at I-85 and Roosevelt?"

"Yeah. She gets off late. I gotta take this. Be right back." He looked down at the phone again and walked away from the car.

"No shit you're gonna take that call. If I had a stripper call me at this time of night, I'd be jumping for joy."

Travis turned back to him and held up his finger. "This'll just take a second man. We'll stop at that 7-11 over on Nelson Road and get you some ice for that hip, OK?" He didn't wait for Jim's response and continued away from the car.

He pushed a button on his phone and raised it to his ear. "What? Didn't I tell you I was gonna call?" He turned back to look at the car.

"How many times do I need to tell you don't fucking call me, I call you," he whispered, then paused to listen to the caller.

"I don't give a fuck. I'm hanging up. I'll call you back from a land line." He closed his eyes as he listened.

"OK whatever. I took care of everything, just like I always do. Hey, I called you on this one, remember?" He turned again to look back at the car. "You got real lucky, too, man. My partner got pulled away so I got the stuff off the guy and sent him back home." He paused, listening to the caller. "No problem. It's done. I took care of it, just like before." Travis rubbed his head and looked up at the sky. He continued walking away from the car.

"Yes. Yes. I told you it's done, now fuck off. They won't be back, you can bet your ass on that." He shook his head. "Has anyone ever come back after I've had a little chat with them?" Travis nodded. "That's right. That's fucking right. Now just drop my cash off in a couple of hours. I'll be swinging by there before seven. Don't come back to get your stuff until after nine or ten this morning." He listened again. He took two steps toward the faded brick wall of a deserted T-shirt shop and turned to lean his back against it. "You don't have to remind me about that. Go jump back in bed with your boyfriend of the week and just make sure my cash gets there." He frowned and moved the phone down to his waist, tapping his foot. "Stop your damn shouting. Just stop. Yeah well we all got secrets, huh? And I bet you wouldn't want yours to get around to all your business associates. How do you think all your soul brothers would feel about doing business with you if they knew you spent so much time at your special 'men's' club? I told you a hundred times that I could care less who's in your bed, just stop your yelling and I'll shut up about that." He held the phone away from his ear and looked at Jim. He pointed at the phone, shook his head, and mocked the caller by mouthing 'blah, blah, blah.' Jim nodded back. "Yeah, yeah. Got it. I'm hanging up now. Stay the fuck away from me. I'm just about done with you." He pushed the end button on his phone, shook his head, sighed, and wiped his forehead with the back of his hand before walking back to the car.

"So I guess you'll be getting some action tonight, eh?"

"Yes, I will. And it will be some mighty fine action my friend."

"Does she look as good as the gal that tracked you down the night we were all drinking at O'Hara's Pub?"

His brow furrowed in concentration. He smiled and shook his head. "Oh yeah, you mean Terri. She doesn't look quite as good as Terri but her body is to die for. Perfect little heart-shaped ass and beautiful tits. All natural, too." He looked down at Travis' shirt. "Man you're sweating almost as much as me. Did this chick get you a little worked up on the phone?"

"Nah. I just got a little hot and bothered dealing with that punk."

He snorted and shook his head. "Now this is one fucked up situation if you ask me. I break my hip chasing some pothead jerk off, now I can hardly walk, and you get to go off and bang some beautiful stripper." He looked over at Travis and tapped himself on the chest. "Don't you think the guy who took the fall tonight should be the one laying some pipe?"

"Hey, man, all you got to do is wake up that wife of yours and then you can get all the action you need."

"Now that's a fucking hoot! I'm sure she'll be fired up and ready to go when I limp in at sunrise. I'll be lucky if I get a cup of coffee."

Travis patted his hand. "Sorry about the hip, man. That was a nasty fall."

"Screw it. When you've been beaten up, shot at, and had your finger almost chewed off by some kid jacked up on dust, a busted hip is a treat." Jim waved his hand at the windshield. "Let's get out of here. Skip the ice. Just get me home."

VI - August 2001

Attorney Paul Gittano was taking steps to improve his financial situation. He was broke. Not the kind of broke that made it difficult to pay the mortgage— he was near financial ruin. All of his credit cards were maxed out, as was his bank line of credit. He hadn't had a big case in the last twelve months. As a criminal defense attorney, he needed one of those every year to make a decent living, but there just wasn't enough work available outside of those types of big cases to sustain him. Strung out and desperate, he had hit up everyone he could think of for clients. But what he really needed was the type of client that Travis could deliver. That's why he had arranged to meet Travis at his health club. Travis had referred clients before, and he was ready to squeeze Travis too, if that was what it took. Travis owed him one, and it was time to collect.

* * *

Travis first walked into Paul's office in June1996, after being indicted on grand larceny charges for pocketing $25,000 in cash during a drug raid. He needed help badly. Paul already knew about Travis' situation. His connections on the police force kept him up to speed on current events. This was going to be the kind of case that could bring in big bucks. Police corruption always brought out the media and the media always brought in more clients. Paul's connections on the police force had suggested Travis talk with him. Paul might be Travis' best chance at beating the charge.

Travis knew the drill. What to say about what had happened two months earlier and what to leave out. You can share most things with your attorney, but not everything.

Travis laid out his story: They had received a call about a domestic disturbance in the middle of the day. Both Travis and his partner knew the address well because the guy was a known dealer. Travis was driving a black and white then. He and his partner pulled up just in time to see a woman chasing the dealer out of the apartment with a knife. It was comical, at first.

She said, 'I'm going to kill that sorry ass, kill 'em dead, I'm telling you that. Kill 'em dead. He been beating me for two years now. I done snapped when he started in on me this time. I'm a kill 'em. I mean it and nobody's gonna do nothing to me when I do. 'cause it'll be self-defense, just like on TV, you know.'"

Travis then went into her kitchen and returned with some ice to put on her swollen, bloody nose, and handed her a glass of water.

He asked if anyone else was in the house. She replied, 'No. My boy's at school and he won't be home until four.'

Travis then proceeded to look around the apartment while she sat on the sofa. In the front bedroom, he had spotted a rumpled, brown grocery bag that had been jammed between the bed and the wall. It contained cash, mostly hundred dollar bills. Travis sat on the bed looking at it. He told Paul that he thought about taking it but threw it back between the bed and the wall and left the room. His partner brought the dealer back into the apartment after Travis took the woman out the back door. Poor guy had been running around in his underwear. He needed to get dressed before they took him back to the station.

When they brought the dealer back to the station, no one paid much attention when he started screaming about how the cops had taken his money. His lawyer was going to raise hell over this. Travis and his partner smiled at each other. Dealers were always going on about cops stealing from them or planting drugs or guns on them to make a bust stick. Everyone in the station laughed.

Five days later, a local minister showed up with his lawyer. The Durham police knew them well. The minister claimed he had concrete evidence that a Durham patrolman had stolen cash from a law abiding citizen. As he had in the past, the minister and his lawyer held a news conference the next day to announce more details.

The Durham police chief agreed to speak with them.

The next day, Travis was asked to speak with two officers from internal affairs. He was glad to do so. They asked him ten routine questions and told him they were just going through the motions so that the minister would go away. Travis understood and they all chuckled at how the minister had become the media spokesperson for every criminal claiming to have been wronged by the Durham police. It was disgusting how these claims of police corruption, beatings, and misbehavior were so blown out of proportion. It was a tough job, and every cop knew that sometimes a few eggs got broken.

One week later, Travis was notified that a warrant had been issued for his arrest.

Everyone said it was unavoidable. The minister had evidence, which had convinced a few more people that bringing charges against Travis was necessary. They told Travis to just come in the next day with his attorney and they would book him. 'Come early in the morning,' they said. 'That way no one would be around. You'll be done with everything in about two hours and then you can go back home. You'll be placed on temporary suspension with pay. Hell, Travis,' they said, 'You're getting a long paid vacation thanks to this preacher.'

The case was so juicy, that after Travis met with Paul and told him what had happened, Paul spent ten minutes jumping up and down and punching the air with delight after Travis left. This case was going to be big. His biggest yet. He'd have to get on the phone to some of his press contacts. As instructed, Travis returned three hours later and gave Paul a check for $10,000 as a retainer.

Early the next morning, two TV station trucks were at police headquarters when Paul and Travis pulled into the parking lot. Paul instructed Travis to smile and stand tall. He had no idea how the press had found out about this, but this could help their case as long as Travis appeared calm and let Paul do all the talking. When they finished the booking process and left the station, the reporters were still there. Paul stopped for a moment and started in on his well-rehearsed speech.

"Ladies and Gentlemen. The charges that have been brought

against my client, Travis Hanson, are completely without merit." Paul thrust his finger up into the air, his voice rising.

"My client has done nothing wrong and is looking forward to clearing his name. He is a well-respected member of the Durham police force and well known for his courage and integrity." Paul turned slowly, pausing to smile into each of the TV cameras.

"Within the next week, I will be filing a civil suit against the police department and the City of Durham for wrongful prosecution. My client will be exonerated and this horrific black mark against his exemplary record will be erased."

Standing together in the parking lot, Travis and Paul were quite a contrast. Travis stood behind Paul, a full foot taller. Paul's body was stocky and he was bald. Travis had thick blonde hair and a thin, athletic build. Paul knew that Travis' good looks would be an asset. As they drove away, Paul smiled at Travis. "What did you think?"

"You did good, Paul. Real good."

"Do you think I was emphatic enough?"

"What's that mean?"

"You know, aggressive, loud."

"Definitely."

Paul turned and looked at the window. "Oh yeah, don't let me forget something when we get to jury selection."

"What's that?" asked Travis.

"We need a lot of women on that jury. You've gotta dress up and look good every day. You got the good looks for that. I'll do the talking; you just look good."

"No problem, Paul, no problem."

* * *

Two months later, the biggest case of Paul's life was set to begin. The judge had not considered Travis a flight risk and set his bail at the minimum amount. The minister's use of the media had increased pressure on the Durham police department, and Paul's attempts to negotiate a lesser charge were rebuffed. The key to the prosecution's case was the eyewitness—that much was clear. Paul had to find a way to cast doubt on his credibility. Travis had an excellent record as a police officer, so Paul advised him to smile at the jury and look confident. He believed his looks and demeanor could help sway the jurors, eight of which were women. The case had taken on so much significance in the area that one local TV station was broadcasting live coverage of the proceedings, and using its lead reporter, Laura Lapsley, a former runner-up Ms. North Carolina. She had been a fascination for Paul since her TV career had begun two years earlier. He planned to get to know her better.

On the fifth day of the trial, Paul and Travis were eating lunch together at a popular diner near the courthouse.

Travis glanced around the diner. They sat in a booth near the back. The diner was packed with courthouse employees. The waitress set down plates of food and smiled at Travis. Travis leaned across his plate. "We're sucking wind here, Paul. What's up?"

"Just feels like that because the prosecution goes first. Wait until we get your partner and your boss up on the stand. They're going to shine when they talk about what a good cop you are."

"But those damn drug dealers, man. You didn't get nothing decent from them."

Paul didn't look up from his food. "They were smarter than I thought, Travis, that's all. I didn't think that the bitch was going to drop assault charges against the guy. They kissed and made up. I can't know how everything is going to go. Plus, I had no idea that the judge was going to block me from bringing up their criminal record. That hurt us, but it's not fatal." Paul jammed french fries into his mouth, smearing ketchup across his chin. His cell phone chirped and he pulled it out of jacket pocket.

"Hello, Paul Gittano."

"Hey Paul, it's Laura."

"Oh, hey there. Hold on just a second will ya'? I'm at lunch. Just let me step outside for a second." Paul stood up and signaled to Travis that he needed to take the call. Travis waved him off and took a bite of his cheeseburger.

"Well, hey there! Haven't heard from you in a while," crooned Paul.

"I know, I've been busy with this trial. You left me a message that you had something for me. Got some more insider info for me?" asked Laura.

Paul moved further away from three people who were waiting outside the diner for a seat. "Now, Laura. I'm not giving you insider info. Remember, we're just a couple of folks having a little chat. So how about if you meet me tonight, say eight o'clock at Barry's Pub. We can chat a little more, how about it?"

"Can't do it, Paul. I'm too busy, spending all day at the trial and then sitting in the editing room for five hours cutting all the footage down for the next day's news."

"I know, I know. And by the way, you sure have been focusing a lot on what the prosecution's been doing. Don't you think you're reporting has been a little one-sided?"

"Now Paul, you know that I pride myself on balanced journalism. I'm just reporting the facts as they come out."

"Well, just wait to we get our turn, my dear. Then you're going to really see me shine."

"OK, Paul. Can't wait. So look, if you haven't got anything for me, I really gotta go, OK?"

"Laura, look, let's just get together and chat. Why don't you meet me tonight? Just for a drink," pleaded Paul.

"Sorry Paul, really I just can't. But hey, look, call me if you have anything else you want to share, OK?"

"Sure, see you later."

"Bye," said Laura.

Paul put the phone back in his pocket. He went back inside and sat down in his chair, shaking his head, and then started in on his cheeseburger.

"What happened? You pissed about something?" asked Travis.

"Hell no. Leave me alone for a minute. I'm hungry and I gotta eat."

They both finished their meals in silence.

* * *

Paul estimated they were two days away from the prosecution calling their final witness and resting their case. He and Travis were in Paul's office. Travis paced across the floor in front of Paul, who was sitting on a couch, his head tilted back and his eyes closed.

"We're going to lose, man, we're going to lose."

"Relax, Travis, just relax. We're going to put on a good defense. Just wait."

"If that last witness comes through, Paul, we're screwed. He told the cops that he saw everything, everything. The guy's a saint too. Been working at the same job for 25 years, coaches basketball at the Y, active at his church. The guy has put two kids through college on a goddamn janitor's salary," said Travis as he sat down on the edge of Paul's desk.

"Doesn't matter, Travis. I've taken on other supposed eyewitnesses. It's easy to trick them. I know how to make them say contradictory things. It's not that hard."

Travis closed his eyes and rubbed his fingers across his forehead, then reached in his pocket and pulled out the last billing statement Paul had given him.

"I've got a better idea, Paul. A sure thing. Take your bill and add another fifteen grand to it." Travis unfolded the paper and threw it at Paul. Paul jerked upright.

"What? I can't just go and jack up my fees like that, Travis. That would be unethical."

"Screw unethical. I'm your client, and I'm telling you what to do. Add fifteen grand to the bill and you'll win this case."

"Not that I'm even entertaining the thought, but tell me how doing what you're asking is going to insure I'll win the case?"

"Don't ask any questions, Paul. Just do what I say. My ass is on the line and you need to win this case. So far, you've been doing a shitty job, so we're going to try my plan."

"No."

"Listen to me, Paul. You and I don't have a choice. That extra money is going to win the case for both of us. Just do what I'm asking. It won't involve you. I'm going to set this thing right," said Travis. He stood up from the desk and started pacing across the small room again. Paul leaned his head back on the couch and stared at the ceiling. Neither spoke for several minutes.

"Can't do it, Travis, sorry."

"Sorry? That's all you got? Sorry? The whole reason we're even talking about this is because of your shitty work. Think for a minute Paul. What's going to happen to your reputation if you lose this case? What's going to happen to my ability to send you more clients if I'm locked up? I can drop those good paying clients on your doorstep. You know, the kind who like to pay cash and have plenty of it." Travis was shouting and waving his arms around wildly.

"Calm down, man. Calm down," said Paul. Travis continued to pace. Paul leaned back on the couch and looked up at the ceiling. Neither spoke for three minutes.

"Well I guess I could go back and readjust my fees to better reflect my normal billing rate. I've been cutting you a little discount, but the trial has taken up a lot more time than I expected."

"Whatever, man. Just do it."

"As long as you understand, Travis, that I'm not doing anything but going back and adjusting my fees. That's it." Travis nodded as Paul walked over and sat behind his desk. He tapped on his computer keyboard for one minute and pulled a new billing statement off of his printer. Travis leaned across the desk and jerked the statement from Paul's hand.

"I'll be back in one hour with a check for you. Then you're going to give me the fifteen thousand back in cash." Paul started to protest, but Travis cut him off.

"Don't give me any bullshit about not having it. Open up your little safe there and just take out some cash. Or go to the bank and get it. I don't care where it comes from, just have the cash when I get back."

"But Travis, wait, ummm, I've got to ..."

"Shut up, Paul. Just get the cash. I'll take care of everything else." Travis turned and walked out the door.

* * *

The morning the witness was to appear, the prosecution team was late. Paul and Travis sat at the defense table, with Paul tapping his foot loudly. His anxiety was bordering on unbearable. Travis had been right about the case. It wasn't going well. If he couldn't discredit this witness's story, he would lose the case.

The prosecutors arrived 30 minutes late. The flustered lawyers obeyed the scowling judge's command to step up to the bench.

"I don't like to be kept waiting. This is the second time you've been late. Do it again and I'll hold you in contempt." Paul had scurried up to the bench in time to hear the judge's admonishment.

"I'm sorry, Your Honor, but we have a slight problem," said the District Attorney.

"I hate problems, Mr. Thompson. What is it?" said the judge.

"Our witness is missing, Your Honor. We haven't been able to find him."

"What? Now how in the world could you lose this so-called key witness right before he's supposed to testify, Mr. Thompson?"

"We're sorry, Your Honor. We can't find him and no one seems to know where he is," said the District Attorney. He glanced at Paul and leaned in closer to the judge.

"We'd like you to call a two day recess, Your Honor. This witness is very important to our case and we'd like to have two days to find him."

The judge stared at the District Attorney. Paul was stunned. He could not believe his luck. The most important piece of the puzzle for the prosecution was gone.

"Well, Mr. Gittano? Did you hear my question?" asked the judge.

"I'm sorry, Your Honor, I didn't hear you."

"Do you have anything that you'd like to say in regards to the prosecution's request for a recess?"

Paul regained his focus. "Yes, sir, Your Honor, I most certainly do. I must insist that you deny this request. My client has endured a lengthy trial already. His good reputation has been forever marred by these proceedings. If this witness cannot be delivered by the prosecution, then you must declare a mistrial. We must assume this witness has changed his mind about testifying against my client and is now reluctant to come forward. You must end these proceedings now, Your Honor. It is the only fair thing to do," said Paul, his voice rising with his conviction.

"Mr. Gittano, please lower your voice."

Paul nodded. The judge leaned back in his chair and waved the attorneys back to their seats. As the lawyers followed the judge's instructions, the judge wrote on a legal pad. A buzz of whispers began to take over the courtroom.

The judge turned to the jury. "Ladies and gentlemen of the jury. The prosecution has just informed me that their key witness is not available to testify. Our legal system is set up to protect the rights of defendants at all times. One of the key components of our system is the right to a fair and speedy trial. I cannot, in accordance with the law, delay these proceedings any further while the prosecution locates this key witness. Therefore, I'm declaring a mistrial. Mr. Hanson, you are free to go." The judge slammed down his gavel.

Travis leaned back in his chair and crossed his hands over his head as Paul thrust his fist into the air with a loud "Yes!" They both stood up and shook hands and Travis gave a quick wave to the jury.

Out on the steps of the courthouse, Paul beamed as the cameras and reporters encircled them. The courthouse steps allowed him to add some height and he stood shoulder to shoulder with Travis, putting his arm around him. Paul held his hands up to silence the crowd and reiterated the injustices Travis sustained personally and as a member of the police force because of this trial. Paul continued his winner's speech as Travis slipped out of his grasp and through the crowd to where Laura Lapsley was standing. He held out his hand and she took it.

"Congratulations, Mr. Hanson. Looks like things worked out well for you," said Laura, smiling and touching her hair.

"Thank you, Laura. I came over here because I wanted to say thanks for your coverage of the trial. I watched some of it. You did a terrific job," said Travis.

"Why thank you, Mr. Hanson."

"Please, Laura, call me Travis, OK?"

"OK, Travis."

"Look, I've been thinking that now this is all over, you and I should get together so you can get my side of the story. You know, the real story about what happened."

"I'd like that very much, Travis."

"Good. Then I'm going to give you a call later today and we'll set something up. Maybe we could have dinner tomorrow and just chat some. How about that?"

"Sounds great. And maybe, in addition to your story, you can tell me how a handsome man like you could still be single," said Laura. She tilted her head and touched her hair again. Travis returned the smile.

* * *

As he pushed open the door to the health club, Paul reflected on the number of good clients Travis sent his way after his trial. There were three damn good cases, and all clients paid in cash. But that was four years ago.

He needed more clients and fast.

Travis was sitting in the snack bar. His light gray t-shirt had turned dark gray from the sweat of his work out. He stood up and held out his hand for Paul.

"Hey, my man! Damn good to see you, Travis!"

"Yeah, Paul. Good to see you." Travis sat back down. Paul pulled a chair over from the next table. He spun it around and sat in it backwards, his arms resting on the back of the chair. Travis looked around the snack bar. It was empty. He leaned in closer to Paul.

"What's on your mind, Paul. I've got to get going on my workout."

"You bet, my friend. First, tell me how you've been doing. Haven't talked to you in about a year."

"Not too bad. You know, life goes on. Like I told you, since the trial, the brass treated me differently, but I've been winning them back over. Can't keep a good cop down."

"Damn right. You bounced back. I knew you would."

"Couldn't have done it without your help, Paul." Travis lifted a half liter bottle of water to his lips and drank loudly. "You know it's not so good for me to be seen chatting with a defense lawyer. You're on the wrong team. Tell me what's on your mind."

Paul shifted in his seat. "Hey, man. I'm not just any defense lawyer, I'm your lawyer. You don't have anything to worry about with me. We're just a couple of friends chatting about the past and strategizing about the future, that's all."

"I'm not sure that we've got a future together, Paul. I'm laying low now. Just doing my job well, paying my bills, and being Mr. Joe Normal Citizen. Don't think I'll be needing your services."

"No one hopes that is the case more so than me, Travis," said Paul. A woman walked past their table toward a small cooler against the wall. She reached into it and removed a bottle of water, shaking off the ice as she lifted it up. Both Travis and Paul turned as she walked back past them. She smiled at Travis and he nodded. They watched her as she got on a stationary bicycle and started pedaling.

"Damn, man. That is smoking hot," said Paul.

"Yep. Nice, huh?" said Travis, still smiling at her. She lifted her water bottle in a mock toast and smiled back at Travis. He turned back to Paul.

"So what's up?"

"I need some help, my friend. Haven't had a decent case in over a year. Gotta get something going, you know, like one of those you sent me after your trial, remember?"

"Yeah, I remember. I sure as hell don't remember getting my finder's fee for any of those people I sent you either."

Paul smiled and rubbed his hand across his forehead. "Now, Travis, you know I can't be giving money to cops! Hey, how would that look to everyone in my profession?"

"Based on what I've learned about your profession, Paul, I'd say that it would just be standard procedure."

"Travis, Travis, now that's a terrible thing to say. Especially to the guy that worked so hard to help you beat your bad rap."

Travis looked at Paul and took a long drink from his bottle of water. "We both know, Paul, that your hard work was going to put me in the can."

"Not a chance, my friend. Even if that witness hadn't disappeared, I had some great contingency plans. I had your ass covered, my friend."

"Sure, Paul, whatever man," said Travis. He looked back over at the woman on the bicycle. Paul glanced at the woman and then leaned in closer to Travis.

"Hey look, I never asked you anything about that special bill we created. You wanna tell me a little more about it now?"

Travis turned back to Paul. His smile faded. "What special bill, Paul?"

"Come on man, you know what I'm talking about. You asked me to boost my fees an extra $15,000 to help us win the case."

"Fuck off."

"Now, Travis, don't be hostile. We were a good team. Come clean with me man. What was up?"

"I told you not to ask questions. Why in the hell are you here asking me about this shit now?"

"Just curious. Maybe I could use some of your special techniques to help with my clients in the future. Maybe there is something I can do for you."

"Look, Paul, you can't do shit for me. Go to hell." Travis stood up.

Paul was desperate. This conversation was not going the way he had hoped.

"Travis, you better sit down and tell me a little more. I know that you wouldn't want any details of that event to be leaked out to anyone."

"Why you little sack of shit." Travis grabbed Paul by his lapels and lifted him up off the seat. Paul stood up and jerked his coat out of Travis' hands. He brushed the lapels and looked around the gym. He smiled at Travis.

"Just kiddin', man. I wouldn't do something like that. Like I told you, I'm just visiting with an old friend who might be able to refer some more clients to me, that's all." Travis sat back down in his chair. Paul followed his lead.

"Goddamn you, Paul. You come back around like the fucking little rat that you are and think I'm going to throw you a piece of stinking cheese. Like I said, fuck off."

"Look Travis, I'm sorry, man. You know me pretty well. I'm never going to say anything. Calm down a second and talk to me. I'm practically beggin' you for help."

Travis stared at Paul. Paul was right about a few things. Defense attorneys could help cops. It was a mutually beneficial relationship. Besides, Paul's little threat to tell the story to others about the boosted bill was just that. It would be more detrimental to his reputation then to Travis'. Besides, in a strange way he was fortunate that Paul had been his attorney during the trial. Most attorneys wouldn't have gone along with inflating their bill and then giving him some cash back. Travis tossed his empty water bottle into a trash can next to their table and turned back to Paul.

"Can't you cut me a little slack? I also helped you connect with that lovely TV reporter. What was her name? Lisa something, right?"

"It was Laura."

"After the trial you were banging her pretty regularly for a few months, right? Man, I was pissed about that. I was working on getting her in the sack myself. Whatever happened to her anyway?"

"No idea. I think she took a job somewhere in California."

"Wasn't she like a beauty queen or something?"

"Yeah. She was runner-up Ms. North Carolina a few years before the trial. Killer body, but not too much happening upstairs. We had some good times for a while." Travis leaned back in his seat and crossed his arms. "Do you really think you stood any chance of getting in her pants?"

"Oh hell, I don't know. I felt like we had a little connection during the trial. She would flirt with me every now and then. Wouldn't have happened for me. At least I connected you with her."

"Yeah. Just another way you've been so helpful." Travis stared at Paul and shook his head.

"Travis, tell me what was up with the bill. Why did you ask me to do it?"

Travis looked at Paul and then glanced around the snack bar. He leaned forward and put his arms on the table.

"Let's just say that I needed to buy a little insurance."

"But your brother was paying for my services, right? I mean the checks came from his business."

"Yeah, he was paying. I didn't have a pot to piss in then."

"But why didn't you just borrow it from him? He seemed OK with helping out."

"Couldn't do that with John. He's a straight arrow. He wouldn't have gone along with my need to buy a little insurance. He doesn't understand the way the streets work. You and I, we know that sometimes you got to break a few eggs to make an omelet, right?"

"Sure, Travis, sure. But speaking of straight arrows, I would have never thought that the witness could be bought. I mean, he was such a clean-cut guy. Remember how we checked his background and everything. How did you get him to take the money?"

Travis turned to look over his shoulder and then back at Paul. His mouth tightened. "Who said that I gave the money to him? He didn't get anything. I sent him on a little vacation."

"Damn. I knew that was what happened. Smart move, Travis."

"Damn right it was smart. Goddamn drug dealers. I mean, how in the world can people raise so much hell about some drug dealer losing his cash. Doesn't anyone get it? These guys deserve to have someone steal their cash. Especially when it's put to better use and ..." Travis stopped suddenly.

"So you took the dealer's cash and did something better with it, right?"

"Yeah. I had to help someone out."

"You helped your mom, right?"

"How the hell did you know that?" Travis leaned back in his chair.

"I saw some court filings against her. It looked like a private individual was suing her to get back some money she borrowed."

"She didn't borrow anything," said Travis, touching his finger on the table. "It was my scumbag father. He had borrowed money from people and from a few banks. Even forged her name on some documents. He died and left her stuck with some big bills. My brother had negotiated most of the things down to where he could cover costs. My mom didn't have shit to pay anyone. Neither one of them even asked me to help because they knew I didn't have any money. I had to help in some way, I mean, it's my mother, and she needed me. There was one person that my Dad owed money to that just wouldn't go away. He filed a lawsuit. My brother couldn't get him to drop the claim. He found out that my brother was covering most of the debts, and figured that if he put the squeeze on my mom, then maybe my brother would come up with the cash. John was having tons of other problems anyway because his messed up wife left him and his newborn daughter. Damn bitch just decided she didn't want a husband or a child." Travis wiped his brow with the back of his hand. "So I went to the guy and gave him enough cash to make up the difference between what he wanted and what my brother offered him. It worked out good for everyone."

"Hey man, I understand. Kinda like Robin Hood if you ask me. You were just taking cash from a criminal and putting it to good use."

"Yeah. That's me, fuckin' Robin Hood." Travis smiled. "Damn I'm glad that's all over. All I've got to do now is pay my brother back for covering my legal fees and a few other things. Almost got enough now. He won't take the money, but I'll figure something out. I owe him. He's a good brother."

"Sounds like you're a pretty good brother too, my man."

"Sure, Paul." Travis shook his head. "Damn. I have no idea why I spilled all this out to you. I hope you know how bad things could get for both of us if what I just said got around."

"Travis, man, I didn't hear you say a thing. Besides, I could lose my license for helping you the way I did. Look man, the way that everything played out, everyone came out OK. You and I, we did the right thing here. Maybe it wasn't pretty, but it worked."

"Yeah it did work out. We got lucky, mainly. Now, you're saying that you need a big case, right?"

"Sure do. Is anything in the works right now that might create a good client for me? You know, the kind of client who has money and is looking at a lengthy trial?"

"I think so. Could be a few more weeks before anything happens. I'll whisper your name in the right places. Can't guarantee anything, though."

"So tell me more. What's going to happen?"

"Shit, Paul. Haven't I told you enough already? Look, you'll know what happens when it happens. Hell, from what I know about you, you'll know about this before I do!"

"Maybe. I do have some good sources. But they haven't been as good as they've been in the past. Get me a good case and I'll figure out some way to reward you, Travis. I promise."

"OK. Now I've got to get on with my workout. You've got me running late."

Travis looked back over his shoulder. The woman they had both noticed earlier was stepping off the stationary bicycle.

"Besides, I've got to go have a chat with that little lady."

"You go ahead and have a good 'work out.' I've got to get on home anyway. Thanks for helping, Travis. I mean it. Get me something and I'll make it worth your while."

"I'll try, Paul. Take it easy and remember to forget everything we talked about."

"You bet. See ya' later, Travis." Paul walked out of the club and stepped out into a heavy rain. Cursing under his breath, he jumped over a puddle and pulled his suit coat over his head. As he glanced back into the club, Paul saw the woman that was on the bicycle touch Travis' bicep and smile.

VII - September 4, 2001

"Hey, pal, you doin' OK? Need another beer?" asked the bartender.

"No thanks, I'm good," replied John. He was sitting at the bar in Raleigh's hot spot of the moment, Leon's. Thirty-somethings in their dark suits filled the place—men with unbuttoned collars and loosened ties; women with loosened blouses and dark high heels.

Loneliness had been creeping up on John for the past year. He felt it like the fog that rolled in off the ocean some mornings at Cape Hatteras. Most mornings you woke up and the fog was simply there. Other times, you watched it move in slowly from the ocean and cover everything. The feeling grew since Lucy started school and increased in proportion to Lucy's growing level of independence. School was a delight for Lucy and John loved to hear her stories. He enjoyed supporting her by visiting her class during story hour and reading a book to everyone while Lucy sat in his lap. School was, most often, about children and their parents. During the annual carnival, John watched sets of parents walking the halls with their sons and daughters. The couples laughed, complimented their children, and shared looks that married couples shared. The kind of look that said, "Isn't he a beautiful boy and aren't we lucky to have this child and each other?" Often the child had a brother or sister. Lucy deserved one of those. He needed someone.

"Hi … I'm supposed to be meeting a John Manning here. Are you John?" John had arranged a blind date via a dating service he had been trying for the past three months. John smiled at her. Her name was Allyssa. They had first connected by email and then chatted a short while on the phone. She said she was 41, but she looked younger. He noticed her pale blue eyes and blonde hair. He was surprised since they had not exchanged photos.

"Hi … I said, 'Are you John?'"

"Yeah, I'm sorry. I'm John. Good to meet you Allyssa." John stood up and they shook hands. "I forgot to tell you last time we talked on the phone how much I like your name."

"Well, thank you, John." John pulled out the barstool he had been saving for her and she sat down.

"It's a little crowded tonight. Can I get you something to drink?"

"A glass of merlot would be fantastic. Bad day at work. I've had a little headache most of the afternoon. A glass of wine should help." John nodded and smiled at her. He signaled the bartender, who arrived and took the order.

"You work in customer service, right? Like some kind of software support?"

"Sort of like that. It is a little different than most types of software support. We sell a software product to realtors and I provide training and support by phone. I've only been doing it for a few weeks. I had a lot of hassles today." She sighed and brushed a strand of blonde hair from her eyes. The bartender placed a wine glass in front of her and she took a small sip. "You'd think realtors would be nicer than they really are, but they get mean when they're having problems. Aren't realtors supposed to be friendly? Especially with all the money they make, you'd think they could lighten up."

"Sorry about the hassles." John stopped a running drop of sweat on his beer glass. "Actually, realtors don't make that much money on average. A lot of them just work part-time. I saw some article about how bad their pay was. Something like $25,000 a year. Maybe that's why they're grumpy."

"I didn't know that." Alyssa took another sip of wine. "That's what I make working full-time. Guess I need to switch professions."

John shifted in his seat. "Twenty-five thousand was a good year for me until recently. My business didn't really pay me much until about five or six years ago."

"You own a travel agency in Durham, right?" Allyssa glanced over John's shoulder.

"Executive Travel. Have you ever heard of it?"

"No. I don't do much traveling. All my family lives near Charlotte, so I mostly travel by car."

"Family in Charlotte. Great. Tell me about them."

"Not much to tell. I've got a brother and a sister, both married. My brother has two boys and my sister has two girls and a boy. My mom and dad are both remarried and living in the area. My sister and I never have gotten on too well. But my brother is a great guy and I love his little boys. You said you have a daughter, right?

"Sure do. My sweet little Lucy. She's the center of my universe. She'll be six in a few months. She is a real treasure. Just wish she'd quit hassling me so much about finding a mother for her," said John. Alyssa turned away to look at the other end of the bar. John blushed and reached for his beer.

"What happened to her mother, if you don't mind me asking?" said Alyssa. "You know what, just forget I asked that question. It's too personal."

"No, I don't mind you asking. How about we get some dinner here and I'll give you a few more details. I'd like to hear more about those nephews you were talking about." Alyssa hesitated and looked over John's shoulder again.

"Do you know someone over there? You keep looking behind me." John turned and looked in the direction of her glance.

"No, I just thought that I saw someone from work, but I'm not sure now."

"Do you wanna go say hello?"

"Ah . .. no. That's OK. Look, I don't really want to eat here. Too crowded. I've got another place we can go. Do you know the Steer House over on Strickland? Great steaks there. Is that OK with you?"

"I know the place. Haven't been there in a while, but sounds good to me. Do you want to ride with me or just drive over separately? It's close by."

"I'll just meet you there. How about if you go ahead and then I can run to the bathroom? Meet you in the bar over there, OK?"

"Wonderful. I could use a nice filet mignon. See you in a

few minutes."

Alyssa turned and headed to the bathroom. John picked up his jacket as the bartender put his bill in front of him. He paid it and pushed through the crowd to the door.

He waited in the bar at the Steer House for more than an hour. Why didn't she show? He knew his physical appearance had gone downhill lately, so he wrote it off to that. Hell, they had only met for fifteen minutes. Why couldn't she have given him a little more time? Maybe the dating game was never going to be his thing. He walked back out to the parking lot. As he opened the car, he set off the alarm. It wasn't the first time. He put the key in the ignition and silenced the noise. Then he looked around the parking lot, which was empty except for five cars. Placing his hands on the steering wheel, he tapped his forehead lightly on his hands and proceeded to weep for fifteen minutes before driving home.

VIII – October 2001

The only decent thing that Travis' father and John's stepfather had left them was a love of fishing. He took the boys fishing on the Outer Banks almost every fall until a few years before his death. It was a fond memory for both men, and a tradition they continued after his death. On some trips, they chartered a boat and trolled for blue marlin in the Gulf Stream. John and Travis were adept at boating and navigating the waters around Cape Hatteras. Some years they fished from the beach. Travis liked to surf fish but John preferred to be on the boat twenty miles off shore, trying for the bigger fish. Their trip this year couldn't have come at a better time for John. His anxiety about his business was at an all-time high.

After the five-hour drive from Raleigh, they checked into the Hatteras Harbor, a classic, old motel that had always been their home base in Hatteras. Travis wanted to head out to the beach and start fishing immediately. They drove down toward the ferry station and out onto the beach. Pick-up trucks and SUVs stretched up and down the beach for miles. They found an open spot and backed their truck into place. Nearby fisherman waved hello and gave an enthusiastic thumbs up when Travis asked how they were biting. They unloaded a few things from the truck.

"Ready for a cold one?" asked Travis

"Sure. Hand me a couple of pieces of bait from the cooler, too."

Travis returned from the back of the truck with a beer and four large pieces of squid, their preferred bait. "Did I tell you that the weather for the next few days is going to be perfect? Cool temperatures, light winds from the southeast."

"Yeah, you told me that twice during the drive down."

"Sorry. I'm just excited to be here again. Not getting that same feeling from you, though.

"Just have a little more than usual on my mind right now. Like I said in the car, the business has been chopped in half since 9/11. I don't know what to do to get it back on track." A vertical rack of foot-long PVC pipe attached to the front of the car held four long surf casting rods. John pulled one out and released the hooks from their secured position. He worked the cut squid onto his hooks.

"Look, I understand how bad it is. But let's try this: Neither one of us can bring up the subject again. Nothing we do for the next few days will make any difference anyway. Agreed?" asked Travis.

John pulled the tab on his beer and took a long pull. He wiped the foam from his mouth with his shirt sleeve. "Sounds good to me. If I start going on about it, just tell me to shut up."

"You keep forgetting how much you've grown that business and the success you've been having up until recently." Travis looked at John and smiled. "Oh shit, I forgot to change the subject." John nodded and returned the smile.

John got up from his chair and walked twenty yards through the sand to the water's edge. The sea was calm; John took a deep breath. The ocean was good medicine. Releasing the bailer on his reel, he tilted the tip away from the water and then jerked the rod toward the ocean. Just as the tip snapped forward, his finger released the line and his first cast sailed out into the blue-green Atlantic. Ten seconds after his tackle hit the water, he put his finger back on the line to let it out as he walked back to the seats that Travis had put down. He snapped the bailer back in place and turned the reel several times to tighten the line. Then he sat down and placed the rod into a three-foot length of PVC pipe that Travis had already driven into the sand beside John's chair.

"Good first cast. Remember what Dad use to say about the first cast?"

"Yeah." John chuckled. "Didn't he tell you that if you didn't get your first cast out beyond the breakers, you'd turn into a girl?"

"That's right. And he'd say that a girl didn't need a dick so he was going to cut mine off and then he could use it for bait on his next cast. Travis walked to the water and waded in to his knees. His cast was not as long as John's but it did clear the small group of waves that were forty yards out from the shore. He trotted back to his chair and sat down beside John.

"I guess I won't be losing my dick today!"

"And there are hundreds of women across the state of North Carolina who are very happy about that," said John. Travis laughed and held up his beer. They bumped the cans together in rough toast. Half of John's beer spilled down his arm. He flicked his hand toward Travis, raining droplets of cheap beer on him. They both drank down the remainder of their beer and tossed the cans back over their heads and into the bed of the truck. Travis pulled out two more from the cooler. He opened them both and handed one to John.

"Tell me what's up with Lucy. I really miss her. Has she been asking about me?"

"Every day. Whenever there's a hint that she might need a sitter, she says you have to come over. What in the world do you do with her that has her so attached to you?" asked John.

"Nothing. I just can't help myself. When I'm with her, it feels like a drug and I've got to drink in every drop. You know how it is. I just ask her what she wants to do and we do it. We do all kinds of stupid stuff. She's my doll baby."

"And you're her big play toy. You know how to make her happy, Travis." John took a sip of his beer and looked up at the tip of his surf rod. It moved with the gentle rhythm of the small waves.

"I need to check with you about something in regards to Lucy."

"Sure. Anything." said Travis

"We talked about this last year but I just want to check with you again before I have the papers drawn up. You will be her legal guardian if anything happens to me. OK?"

"Of course. But why don't you just be safe and then we won't have to worry about anything like that." Travis took a long sip of beer and pointed to the waves. "Hey, if I threw you out in the ocean and you never made it back, would I get to have her right away?"

John frowned and looked down at the sand. He kicked a

small piece of driftwood away. “This is serious, Travis. I’m not planning on having it come to that, but I need to know that you will devote yourself to her and be a good guardian.”

“I promise, John. Nothing matters more to me than Lucy. If I ever become her guardian, I swear that I will do my best to be as good a parent as you are.”

“OK, it’s a done deal.” John took another sip of his beer and he saw Travis’ surf rod bend forward and snap back. “Hey look, you got one!” Travis grabbed the rod and pulled back quickly. He stood and turned the reel a few times and then pulled back on the rod again. The line went slack.

“Damn. That felt like a good one. I didn’t set the hook fast enough.” He sat down again. “Since we’re talking about this serious business of me taking Lucy if something happens to you, I want you to know that I can provide for her. I’ve been making better money lately. Been saving up.”

“I don’t care about that. Just take good care of her.”

“Look, I owe you big time for how you helped me with the trial and everything. Since you’re in this bad spot with your company, why don’t you let me pay you back some now.”

“No, I don’t need the money. I’ve got a rainy day fund that will see the business through this bad spot. It will last until things get better. Keep your money for yourself. Why don’t you get a new car and get rid of this piece of crap truck you have?”

“Hah! Get rid of Ole Willie? You have got to be kidding. Do you know the memories this truck has for me? Do you know how many girls I banged in the back of this thing? I’m going to keep Ole Willie until he dies. Besides, I’ve spent so much time fixin’ up Ole Willie to keep him going, I’m going to make sure he never dies.”

“Well, brother, Ole Willie is a shining example of your two biggest talents: auto repair and seducing beautiful women. Hey, that reminds me to ask you about Jackie, or was it Jasmine? What happened to her?”

“You mean Jacqueline? The red head? I haven’t been out with her in about six months. We had some good times but I’m not in the settle down mode, but man, she sure was. What about you? Have you been seeing anyone?”

John looked down at the sand again. He gulped down the remaining half of his beer and tossed the can back into the truck bed.

"Another bad subject. Nothing to talk about. I've been trying a little, but no luck. Now that Lucy is getting a little older, it feels like I could do more to meet someone. God knows she wants it to happen. I can't even bump into a woman without Lucy getting all starry eyed and asking about having a mom."

"Still nothing from Ellen, huh?" Travis looked up at the tip of his surf rod. His faced darkened. "You know I hated that bitch from the beginning, but, man, leaving you and the kid too? If you ask me, things turned out well for Lucy not having Ellen around." Travis rubbed his hand across the side of his beer can.

"Honestly, I haven't thought about her much lately, which is a welcome change." John leaned back in his chair and looked up at the sky. "She never wanted a child. Didn't want me, either. Everything just happened too fast for both of us. You're right, things did work out for the best." Travis glanced over at John and then back at his surf rod. He leaned forward in his chair, elbows on his knees.

"You know, that is the most I've heard you say about the situation with her. How come you never talk about what happened?"

"It's just too painful. Like I said, only recently have I been able to start putting it behind me. I'm not as good with women as you are, and I just thought I had won the lottery when we started going out. She was such a beauty. It hurt even more that she didn't want Lucy. Her work always came first. I know you're right that it was best for everyone that she left, but I wish she had been more willing to try to work things out. Some couples make it because they're invested enough that when things get difficult, they want to see things through, to make it work. Some people don't make it because they hit a rough spot and one of them realizes they don't even want to try. Ellen and I, unfortunately, fell into the second category."

Travis turned and saw John reach up and wipe his eye with the back of his hand. John leaned forward in his chair and stared out at the water. He looked down at the sand and shook his head.

"Looks like we now have two topics that are off limits for this weekend. I'll get you another beer," said Travis. He turned to reach into the cooler. John watched the tip of his surf rod bend and then jerk twice. He jumped up and pulled it out of the rod holder, walking toward the surf as he reeled. When Travis looked up, John was already knee-deep in the water. Travis jumped out of his chair and grabbed a small net from underneath his chair. He ran down to the water and then walked another fifteen yards until he was standing beside John. Both men stood waist deep in the water, as John reeled the fish into shore gently, but quickly. As it neared them and came to the surface, Travis whooped at the size of it. He jabbed the net into the surf and brought up the fish quickly.

"Hell yeah! Look at that bluefish! Hey bro, this has got to be the biggest one yet. Better get out the scales and the tape measure. This one's going into the record books!"

John laughed. It was about an hour before sunset. They fished for a couple more hours after it got dark.

IX - November 2001

September 11 drove the airline and travel industries almost to a complete stop. For three days after the event, not a single commercial flight left the ground. For weeks afterward, business travel limped along and vacation bookings were non-existent. No one wanted to get on a plane. Anyone who had booked a vacation was calling and demanding their money back. The airports were deserted, cruise ships were empty, hotels and resorts were barren. Travelers got in their cars and drove to the beach, the mountains, or somewhere else. Before 9/11, John's phones were always ringing. Afterward, the silence was deafening. John cut back staff hours and reduced expenses where he could. In the past, he could count on steady cash flow that covered everything he needed to pay. He sat in his office looking at the stack of bills that were due. With his revenues cut in half, he'd have to cut expenses faster and deeper. The cash was running out. He stood up and began pacing in front of his desk. After two minutes, he hurried out the door and onto the sales floor.

"Mary, will you come back to my office? I need to discuss something with you."

"Sure, John."

Mary Thomas had been with John since 1995. She was a superb salesperson, manager, and confidante. John valued her opinion on every topic. She made it possible for him to cut his work week back to only 25 hours so he could be with Lucy as much as possible. He was the brains of the operation, but she was the heart and soul.

When they entered John's office, he shut the door and she sat down across from his desk. He picked up a piece of paper and waved it in the air. "What the hell is this account doing past due for 60 days? They owe us $26,000. Who's been doing the ticketing for T-3 Enterprises?"

"Well, John, if you'd take a moment you'd remember we talked about this back in the summer. I told you about this woman, something Branden or Brenner, or at least that's what she claims her name is. She comes in two-to-three times a month and always buys First Class tickets to the West Coast. She buys tickets for herself, her supposed husband, and a six-year-old girl. She started out paying cash, maybe like a year ago. Remember those nice commissions you saw back in the spring and summer? I know you can recall us discussing it."

John looked back down at the piece of paper. Mary had a perfect memory. "Sounds familiar. But what jackass approved her to go on a billing basis? We stopped offering billing accounts last year," growled John.

Mary rolled her eyes and crossed her arms. "Well, John, you would be that jackass. Let me repeat: Back in the summer we discussed the situation, what she had been buying, the commissions, how she had been paying, how long she had been a customer ..."

"OK, OK. I think I remember now." interrupted John. He dropped the piece of paper back on his desk, walked around to his chair and sat down hard, his mind racing. He needed to get that money. "When was the last time she bought something?"

"I haven't heard from her since 9/11. I guess she's not interested in traveling with all the extra security."

"Why would she care about the security changes?"

"Because she's a drug dealer. Last minute travel, First Class, always paying with cash. When she first started buying from us, she got irate over the fact that someone issued her ticket so that it read "Cash Payment" instead of "Check Payment." She claimed she never wanted her ticket purchases recorded as cash and had mentioned this in the beginning. That was such a crock. I've never seen anyone care about the form of payment recorded on their ticket. She made up some story about having problems in the past getting refunds or making changes. None of us believed it. She's just trying to avoid any scrutiny because she's involved in something illegal, like drugs.

She knows the airlines sometimes flag reservations like hers because they fit a certain profile." Mary stopped and looked down at the floor. "I'm guessing that we need to collect that money."

John was staring out his office window onto the sales floor. "Have you or anyone else called her about this bill?"

"I haven't heard from her in months. I wasn't aware she was so far past due. I just don't have the time to monitor everything now that you laid off the two part-time agents. I'm overloaded just taking care of the customers that are left." She stared across the desk at John. He softened. Mary was always right.

"Look, no one knows how hard it has been more than me. Just get me her phone number so I can talk to her," said John.

"She never gives us a voice number. Just a pager number. That is the only way we have to get in touch with her. She always comes by the next day to pick up the tickets she's purchased. "

"So get me whatever number you have for her." He stood up and came around the desk. He sat down on the corner and folded his hands across his lap.

"Hey, I'm sorry that I'm being short with you. This is not your fault. I'm just worried about the company. We're getting a little low on cash, and I just want to get this receivable collected. There are a few other small ones to collect, too. We always run a little thin on cash near the end of the year, you know that," said John.

"I know. But please don't try to tell me that this is like last year, or the year before. I'm here to help; you know that, so just keep me up-to-date. You know, you could stand to be here a little more and show everyone that you're rolling up your sleeves and working hard to turn everything around."

"It's too hard to do that right now, Mary. You're right, I should be here more. I just can't juggle taking care of Lucy, the company, and all this. I know the company has suffered because I've been here less, but it just had to be that way. Lucy always comes first."

"John, no one is ever going to fault you for that. I'm just letting you know what the staff is saying and how I feel, that's all."

"Your feelings are noted. Please get me this woman's phone num-, I mean pager number, so I can get in touch with her."

* * *

John paged the woman several times a day for a week to no avail. He checked his accounting records to see if they had her address, another phone number, anything. There was nothing. After the first week, he started inputting different phone numbers for her to call back—his cell phone, a pay phone near the office—but nothing worked. He made several attempts on Saturday and Sunday. It was pointless. Why would she call a travel agency that she owed money? She wouldn't call anyone back unless she recognized the number. That was the whole purpose of using a pager—anonymity. He had to get that money. The company needed it.

Ten days after he and Mary had discussed outstanding debts, he received a call from her.

"John, it's me. Look I'm at the McDonald's on MLK Parkway picking up lunch and I just saw the woman that owes us the money. Remember the drug lady? She just walked in with a little girl."

"Are you sure it's her?"

"No doubt. I remembered she has this awesome old convertible mustang. Beautiful car. Anyway, it's her. What're you going to do?"

"Damn. I have no idea."

"You need to just stay away from her. If she's selling narcotics, and I think she is, you're asking for trouble. Let it go."

"Can't do it. Thanks for calling. I'm going out the door. What does she look like?"

"Black. Nice Hair. Looks a little like Angela Bassett."

"Who's Angela Bassett?" asked John.

"An actress. You don't …"

"What was that, Mary? Hey, you still there?"

"Sorry, they just walked past me. She has a beautiful little girl with her, wearing a pink dress and her car is a candy apple red convertible mustang, real old."

"Got it. Bye."

The McDonald's was nearby. John knew it well because Lucy loved cheeseburgers and the kids play area. He noticed the car that Mary described in the parking lot and made a mental note of the license number. He walked in the door and saw the woman and her child eating at one of the tables near the play area. He bought a Coke and a Big Mac and sat down at a table nearby. The mother and daughter were discussing kindergarten. The little girl's name was Tonya. The mother noticed him watching and shot John a concerned look.

John picked up on the look and smiled. "I always bring my daughter to this place. I'm just taking a lunch break and I just sat by the play area without even thinking about it. Funny, huh?"

The woman frowned. "Yeah. It's pretty weird to see some guy sitting in here without a child."

"How old is your daughter? Mine's six."

"Five. Look, we'd like to have a little mother-daughter chat in private. So give us some space."

"No problem. I'm just going to finish my lunch and I'll be outta here."

Tonya looked up from her French fries. "Mister, why didn't you bring your little girl to play today?"

"Tonya, sweetie, that's none of our business. Let the man eat his lunch. Have you finished your chicken nuggets?"

"No mama. I need some more ketchup. Will you get me some more?"

The woman moved several pieces of paper around on the plastic tray, searching for ketchup packets. "I'll get you some more, sweetie. Why don't you come with me?"

"No. I want to stay here."

The woman looked at John and then back at her daughter. "I'll be right back," she said.

As soon as she walked away, John smiled at Tonya.

"My little girl is in school right now. That's why I didn't bring her."

"I'm in kindergarten and I go to Jennings Road Elementary. My Mommy said I didn't have to go today. Does your little girl go to my school?"

"No. We live in Raleigh. She goes to a different school."

"Does she ride the bus?"

"No, I always take her to school in my car."

"My mommy always takes me to school, too."

The mother returned. John continued eating. Tonya smiled at him. John nodded at them and left his seat. He dropped his half eaten sandwich into the trash can and walked to his car. He sat low in the driver's seat trying to figure out what to do. Should he confront her? What would he say? Did he have any leverage to force her to pay? Why wasn't she traveling anymore? He smacked the steering wheel in frustration. He watched the woman and Tonya walk out the door and get into the mustang. He'd never get any money out of her if he didn't find a way to get in touch with her.

The next morning, he arrived at Jennings Road Elementary fifteen minutes before the school was scheduled to begin receiving students, parked in the back of the large parking lot in front of the school and opened his newspaper. He had finished reading most of it when a trickle of cars began arriving and circling through the drop-off area. They stopped and children popped out, waving as they walked to the front door, struggling to get oversized book bags mounted on their small shoulders. He removed an envelope from his shirt pocket that had "Ms. Brendan" typed on the outside. Inside the envelope, he had included a statement of the money she owed. He had also included a handwritten message that he hoped would increase her desire to resolve the matter quickly. She had traveled with Tyrone Brendan and Tonya Brendan six times to San Francisco over the last three months. There were four trips prior to these but they had been paid in full at the time of purchase. Ms. Brendan owed John $25,432. He was going to collect it.

He dipped down lower in his seat as he saw her car turn into the front of the parking lot. The car swung into a parking space near the drop off circle and mother and daughter walked toward the front door, holding hands. John waited until they had been inside for two minutes and walked to the convertible, and slipped the envelope under windshield wiper. He jogged back to his car and drove to the office. The staff wouldn't begin arriving for another thirty minutes.

Ms. Brendan arrived within ten minutes. She knocked on the door and John walked from his office to the front door. They both could see each other through the glass door. When he unlocked the front door, she stepped back, scowling at him. “You’re the dude who was talking to us at McDonald’s yesterday, aren’t you?” John looked from side to side. No one else was nearby. He looked back at her.

“I’m so very happy that you decided to come by, Ms. Brendan.”

“So … so you want to talk with me?” she snarled. “You just made a big fucking mistake leaving this note on my car.” She flapped the note in the air and crumpled it into a ball. She let it fall from her hand. John watched it hit the ground, looked up at her and smiled.

“Actually, you are the one who has made a mistake, Ms. Brendan, or whatever you name is. I don’t have patience for people who buy tickets from me and don’t pay their bills. Please give me my money and I won’t call the police.” Her face darkened further. He wished they weren’t alone.

“Screw the police and forget about your money. You don’t have nothing to talk to the cops about. I’m just an ordinary business person who bought some tickets from you and now my business has dropped off and I don’t have the money to give you. You want me to pay you twenty-five thousand? Shit, it might as well be $25 million.”

John stared at her for a minute and she glared back. Neither broke the gaze. “That’s really too bad, Ms. Brendan. See, I need that money right away. My business is suffering also, what with 9/11 and all this terrorism stuff. People just aren’t in the traveling mood right now.”

“Sorry, can’t pay the bill. No money. You got it?” she challenged.

“I’m so terribly sorry. Why don’t you step inside for a few minutes?” John stepped backward and held the door open, motioning with his hand for her to come in. She looked past him into the office, and then scanned the parking lot behind her before stepping into the office. John locked the door behind her.

“Sit down in this chair and I’ll make a call right now to see if the Durham police would be interested in knowing more about your travel patterns.” John moved toward the closest desk and slid the phone near him.

The woman moved closer to him. John took a half step backward.

"Look dude, don't try to mess with me on this." She pointed her finger at him and glanced back at the front door. "Do something stupid like call the police and you'll get yourself hurt. Or maybe your little girl will get hurt. You hearing me?"

He crossed his arms and stood straighter. "Well Ms. Brandon, it appears that the cops make you nervous. How did you want to pay your bill, cash or cash?" John's gamble led her back to his office, but he knew it was unlikely he would collect any money, but he had to try. He had to.

John noticed movement at the door. Mary looked through the glass and saw John. She pointed at herself and then into the office. John nodded with too much enthusiasm. He walked to the door and opened it.

"Hi, Mary. You remember Ms. Brendan?" Mary nodded and smiled, but did not receive a response. "She just came by to talk with us about her bill. Wasn't it nice of her to do that? Looks to me like she is an honorable person who intends to make good on the money she owes."

Mary's eyes moved between John and the woman. "Oh, OK, that's good, John. Hi, Ms. Brendan, how are you?"

Again there was no response. "Let's talk in your office," said the woman.

"Let me show you the way, Ms. Brendan." John pointed to the back of the store. She walked ahead of him.

The office's longest wall had a glass window that allowed for viewing of the sales floor. John walked toward it and pulled the small string to lift the closed shades so his staff could see in. He sat down at his desk while the woman paced back and forth, hands trembling, and noticed another employee come in. Mary was talking with her and they both looked back at John.

"Why don't you sit down, Ms. Brendan, so we can resolve this amicably."

"I don't know what that word means, but there's nothing to solve. I ain't got the money. Doesn't matter what you do, I can't pay."

"Here's a thought: Why don't you sell that nice car of yours? I'm betting that it's worth about half of what you owe me. That would be a good down payment on your debt and would prevent me from calling the police."

She stopped pacing. Small beads of sweat were visible on her forehead. "I can't sell the car. Your business is down, so is mine. There is no way I can pay."

"Now I don't recall you telling me about your line of work. What do you do?" asked John.

"Does it really matter?"

"Maybe not. I'm just wondering why things are so bad."

"They're just bad. So I don't have any cash to give you."

John continued to probe. "I'm guessing that your business has been hurt by 9/11, just like mine."

"Yeah, that's part of it."

"So what else has hurt your business?"

"Look, forget this shit. It doesn't matter what kind of work I'm doing, I'm telling you there's no money. Go talk to the cops, it don't matter to me." She sat down in a chair in front of John's desk.

John removed his glasses and methodically started cleaning them with a Kleenex before putting them back on. "I'm thinking you're business is illegal drugs and that you bought tickets to pick them up in the San Francisco area. That's why you got so pissed when someone issued one of your tickets as a cash sale rather than a check sale. You know the authorities look for people who buy tickets with cash and travel on short notice. I'm betting that ..."

She jumped up and slammed her fists on John's desk. He lurched backward, just out of her reach as she lunged across his desk, trying to grab him. She nearly fell onto the desktop, but regained her balance and shoved everything on the desk onto the floor. Two picture frames shattered and a coffee cup filled with pens and pencils sprayed its contents against the wall.

"Listen to me right now." She was leaning over his desk, her face dark. Her spit sprayed John's face as she spoke. "I ain't listening to your shit anymore. You're going to get hurt if you don't shut up. You keep pushing me and you'll find out that you're messing with the wrong girl."

John rebalanced himself, brushed his hands across his chest and took off his glasses. "You better sit down." He wiped his glasses on the front of his shirt to remove her saliva. "You're about to do something stupid. Something that is going to cause you a lot more harm than trying to work with me." He put his glasses back on. He spoke in a low voice, without emotion. "I've written a letter detailing your history with my company and included copies of your flight records. It's ready for the cops. You want to mess with me, well then you're messing with the wrong guy. I'm betting that you don't want to spend time in jail and lose that pretty little daughter of yours. So listen up. There's a simple solution. You want to hear it, sit down. You don't want to hear it, walk out the door." She stood, wiping spit from the corner of her mouth as she glared at John and looked over her shoulder at the others in the office. The entire staff was busy at their desks.

"My name is Wanda. Don't be calling me Ms. Brendan anymore." She sat in the chair behind her. "Start talking."

John sat up and slid his chair closer to the desk. "OK, that's better. I've got to have that money. You owe it. So here is the plan, and it's good for me and you. You give me a down payment of $2,500 today and then another $2,500 in two more days. I'll give you a thousand off your bill. You'll come back in one week and give me another $5,000 in one lump sum. I'll give you another thousand off your bill. Keep doing that every week and you'll be paid up in one month and you'll be saving five grand because I'm only going to charge you $20,000 if you pay everything on this schedule. This is it. Give me the cash now and let's get on with it." Wanda looked down at the floor and rubbed the back of her neck. Neither spoke for one minute.

"I've got a thousand on me right now. I'll try to get you some more." She rolled her head around and looked at him. "Can't promise anything for sure. I ain't got nowhere near the kind of money you're asking for."

"Well. Why don't we see how it goes for a few weeks? Can't say that I'd take any less than what I offered."

She stood up and opened her purse. "I need you to hand me an envelope." John obliged. She put the envelope inside her purse and placed ten $100 bills in it before tossing the envelope onto John's desk. She took a few steps toward the door and paused. "Hey, look, umm … I'm sorry about the papers on the floor and everything. Sometimes my temper gets the best of me." She glanced out again at John's staff. "You promise that you aren't going to the cops about this, right?"

"As long as you pay, you'll be OK. See you next week." She smiled and walked out the door. John reached into a drawer and removed two paper towels. He leaned back in his chair and ran the paper towels across the top of his head, soaking up the sweat. There was no way she'd be back with more money. No way.

X - November 2001

She came back. Two weeks in a row. Each time with the amount that she had indicated she could afford. They even exchanged a few jokes on one visit and discussed how bad 9/11 had been to their respective businesses. John always asked about Tonya. Wanda enjoyed talking about her. Especially her reading skills. When she returned for a fourth time, John tried to get her to talk about her work.

"So, things still really bad in your business?"

"Yeah. Like I said, we can't get any product to sell. Can't fly around doing what we need to do."

"Why not?"

"Security is too tight. They're checking everyone."

"So you can't carry your products around?"

Her brow furrowed as she leaned forward in her chair, which was in front of John's desk. "Maybe." She looked at his face and then scanned his waistline. "I need you to take off your shirt."

"What?"

"You're asking a lot of questions. Take off your shirt so I can see you ain't wearing a wire."

He patted his chest and stomach. "I'm not wearing a wire. I told you I was only going to talk with the cops if you didn't pay. You've been paying. I'm just interested in what you do, that's all."

"We're done talking and I ain't bringing you another dime until you stand up and take off your shirt." She leaned back, crossing her arms. "I'm good at seeing when folks are lying to me."

John looked out through his office window. Only two staff members were in the office. He needed her to keep delivering the money.

"Alright. Walk over to that window and close the blind." She followed his instructions. He stood up and unbuttoned his dress shirt. He pulled it open.

"OK, see. No hidden surprises."

"That's cool. Now drop your arms so that the shirt comes off your back and turn around so that I can see back there." He snorted in meek protest. He lowered the shirt and turned his back to her, stopping for a few seconds so that she could see his back clearly.

"Alright, you ain't wearing no wire." She smiled. "You need to cut back on those Big Macs."

"Yeah, thanks for noticing. Now can I sit down or do you want to give me a few more diet tips?"

"Sit down. I knew you weren't wearing no wire anyway. I can tell these things."

He buttoned his shirt and sat down.

"So, what do you want to know?" she asked.

"What kinds of products do you sell?"

"Can't tell you. Just call it product."

"So you fly to the West Coast and pick up your product. But now you can't do that because of the extra security since 9/11. So your product is illegal. Why do you do it?"

Wanda shifted in her seat. "Good money. Been doing it a long time and I don't got any other skills."

"How good is the money? What are your margins?"

"Margins? What the hell is that?"

"The difference between what you pay for your product and what you sell it for. Let's say you go to San Francisco and buy a pound, no a kilo, of your product. How much does it cost you?"

"About twenty grand."

"Then when you get it here, what can you sell it for?"

"Depends. Prices vary."

"Just give me a guess. Do you get double for it, say forty grand?"

She smiled. "More like sixty."

He returned the smile and shook his head. "Damn, that's a big margin."

"I guess so. Don't know what else to compare it to. Funny

thing is now we could get even more for the product. Everyone is short because of this shit with airport security. Customers are paying more because there ain't no supply."

"How long does it take to sell a kilo of the product?"

"Hard to say. Depends how much people want. Sometimes you sell it in large bags, but you make less. You know, volume buying, just like Wal-Mart." She chuckled. "Are you looking to get into my business?"

"Nah. Like I said, I'm just curious. I've seen the movies and TV shows and wondered if it's true, how much money you can make."

"You got other things you got to pay for, too. You don't just buy the stuff for twenty, sell it for fifty, and keep thirty. You gotta slip some people some cash. Make sure that you can move the product without anyone getting suspicious. Besides, I just sell the stuff. I get a cut on what I sell. I work for someone else who does all the other stuff. Course he gets to keep a lot more of the … what did you call it … margin?"

"Like who? Who do you have to pay?" asked John.

"Just people. People who can help. People that can keep you informed. Don't matter who it is, you just have to get it in the right hands."

"Fascinating."

"Yeah, whatever. Don't matter much now. Nothing to sell anyway." She stood up. "I've gotta get out of here. I might see you next week."

"Good. I'm looking forward to it."

She didn't wait a week to return. The next day she arrived at 10:30 a.m., with twice the usual amount of money.

"Hmm. So you're going to pay $2,000 today?"

"Yeah, but this is our last visit. I'm tapped. No more cash."

John opened the envelope and thumbed through the hundred dollar bills. "That's bad, real bad. You're nowhere close to paying what we agreed on. Remember, I was even offering to knock off a few thousand from what you owed me if you paid up quickly.

"Don't matter what we talked about. I've already told you that I ain't got the money. You better be happy that you got as much as you did."

"And you'd better be careful because I'm still thinking the police are going to be very interested in your past travels."

She shifted her weight to one leg and crossed her arms. "Look, John, don't be saying that shit again about the cops. We both know you were never going to go the cops. You ain't got shit to talk with them about and anyway, if you did somehow get me busted, then how in the hell were you ever goin' to get any money from me?"

He stared at her and ran his hand across the top of his head. "I've meant every word I've said. Every word." He walked over to the window and looked out at his staff. "So now you're telling me that this is it? You've got to be able to come up with more. You owe me twenty-five grand!"

"Hey, man, you can complain all you want. I done told you that I just can't make a living like I use to." She stepped closer to him, her hands palms up. "You seem like a smart guy so you got to know that I ain't making any money. You figure out some way for me to move my product and then I'll be able to work and pay you back."

"That's not my problem," he said, turning back to face her. "Look, here's a deal for you. Just get me five grand more and we'll be done with it. You can do that."

She shook her head. "Might as well be $5 million. I just ain't got it."

"Look, Wanda. I need that money. My business is sinking. I've got lots of people depending on me. The people who work here need to make a living; I've got to make a living. You gotta agree that I've been very fair about all this."

"Maybe you have. I ain't bullshitting you. There ain't no money." He shook his head and walked around to the chair behind his desk, sat down, removed a tissue from his desk drawer, and began cleaning his glasses.

"Look, you said I should come up with a safer way for you to move your product. You said that if there was a way, then you'd be back in business, right?"

"Yeah, I did. But what do you think you're going to come up

with? You got some inside connections that can get us past all the airport security?" She pushed away a strand of hair that had fallen into her face. "Maybe since you're in the travel business you've got a few tricks."

John leaned back in his chair and looked up at the ceiling. "I do have an idea. Something that I know will work for you and it does come from me being in the travel business. But it doesn't have anything to do with airplanes."

She rubbed her chin. "So? What is it?"

"Before I tell you, you've got to do something for me, OK?"

She shook her head slowly. "C'mon now, John, don't be asking again for me to give you money I ain't got."

"Wanda, I know you can get more money. You come back tomorrow and bring me another $2500, and I'll tell you my idea. If you don't think it will work, then you can have the money back."

"You giving me some kind of money back guarantee?" She smiled. "You must think your idea is some hot stuff."

"It's good. Hey, look, I'm a businessman. A good one. My whole business life has been about solving problems. One day I've got cash flow problems. Another day I've got problems with a customer. The next day two of my employees quit on me. This is what I do, solve problems. You've got a transportation problem. I have a solution to your problem."

"So I guess I've got nothing to lose, huh?" She walked to the door and opened it slightly. "I don't know where the hell I'm going to get any more money."

"Don't come unless you bring the cash. No cash, no solution," he said. She paused a moment at the door and then left.

He sat down across from his desk, one hand drumming fingers on the arm of the chair. He didn't know why he was going down this path. Was he really going to give this woman, a criminal, ideas about how to get more drugs into Durham? Was he so desperate to save his business that he was going to do something like this? Something illegal? He stood up and walked around to his phone. No. This was stupid. There were other ways. He'd find the money somewhere else.

* * *

The next morning, she tapped on his office door. He didn't look up from the report he was reading. "Come in, close the door. I don't have a lot of time to mess around with you today."

"OK, OK. Man, what's up with you this morning? You need some more coffee or something?"

He turned a page over and looked up at her. "No. I changed my mind. I don't have any ideas to share with you."

Her face darkened. "You and your big ass ideas. Now I came here with the money, just like you said and now you ain't gonna come clean with me?" She pointed a finger at him. "You ain't keeping up your end of the bargain here, John."

"Hold on a second. Don't be twisting this thing all around here." He stood up and pointed back at her. "You're the one who owes ME money. I don't owe you shit."

She smiled. "That's right. But how you gonna get any more money from me unless you solve the problem like you said you could?"

His face reddened "Are you mocking me? You … a … a … goddamn criminal, making fun of me?" He pointed to the door. "Get the hell out of my office."

"Whoa, man. You are in a bad mood."

"Damn right. It's about the money. I need the money. Things are bad." She paused for a few seconds and then reached into her pursed and pulled out an envelope.

"So here's a little. Two grand. Tell me your idea. If I like it, then you get the two grand." She put the envelope back into her purse. "And if this idea of yours works, then I'm back in business and I can pay you back in full."

He sat down and put his face in his hands. A minute later he looked up, took off his glasses, and wiped his hand over his face.

"Alright. Here it is." He paused and looked out at his staff. "You can move your product by taking a cruise."

She frowned. "What? That's your idea?" She sat down across from his desk. "Sorry but a couple of dudes I know got busted trying to smuggle stuff back on a cruise ship. That ain't gonna happen."

"Being in the travel business, I've been on a lot of cruises. I've got connections and I get special access at ports of call. I can move around without a lot of folks noticing. I deliver a lot of business to a couple of cruise lines and they treat me well."

"Hmm, well that would help a lot. So you're saying that I can just get on some cruise and then when it stops at … umm … what ports are you talking about?

"Just about any place you can think of in the Caribbean. You get off the ship and have a full day enjoying some port and then you get back on the ship at the end of the day. Overnight, the ship sails to a different port and you wake up and do the same thing again."

"OK. How 'bout Mexico?"

"Yes. They stop at a couple of Mexican ports. Would that be a good place for you to pick up product?" asked John.

"Hell, yeah!" She smiled and shifted forward in her chair. "And, we could get a better deal on the stuff if we pick it up in Mexico rather than in California. The further south you go, the cheaper the product is."

"So that's it. That's the idea. And you even got a bonus because I didn't know that you would be getting a better deal if you picked up the stuff in Mexico."

He folded his arms across his chest and leaned back. "I'll take my money now."

"So you're saying that you take one of these cruises and stop for the day in Mexico, and hop back on the boat without any hassles?"

"Yes."

"And there's no security at all? No baggage checks? No x-ray machines? No sniffing dogs?"

"Well not when you get off in a port. I mean, well there is but like I said, I can get around that."

"So is there security when you come back to the U.S.?

"Yeah, it's pretty tight then. I bet the guys you're talking about got caught at that point."

"Yeah, they did. In Miami."

"So anyone taking on this venture would need a way to get around that choke point."

"OK, so since you know so much about cruise ships, then you've got a solution to this problem too, right?

John ran his fingers through his hair. "Don't know, maybe. Well, yeah, I got a way to work around that. But it doesn't matter because I'm not getting involved with something like this. I must be crazy. Anyway, I'll take my cash now." He came around to the front of his desk and held his hand out in front of her.

She stood up and looked at his open hand. "Hold on a second. You've gotta tell me some more about how this would work. I ain't never been on a cruise ship. You've gotta give me more on this man."

"No. I told you the idea." He thrust his hand further out. "You're on your own." She removed the envelope from her purse and put it in his hand.

"OK, but look, you've been thinking about this thing. I know you've got some more ideas about how this could work."

John stood up and jammed the envelope into his pants pocket. "No. Thanks for the money. Like I said, I'll be in touch in a few weeks." He walked to the door and opened it for her. She gave him a long stare, and then walked out. John closed the door behind her. He sat back down at his desk, shaking his head and staring at the floor. He looked up at the old shoebox on his desk where he stored his bills for the month. It was overflowing.

XI – December 2001

John fidgeted, struggling to get comfortable in the waiting room of Lucy's pediatrician. Lucy had been having mild back pain for the past two weeks. He should have brought her in sooner, but he preferred to avoid doctors when possible. After being unable to determine the cause of Lucy's back pain, they had given her a battery of tests to see if they could discover the cause. Dr. Jessie Cayton, Lucy's doctor, had called John herself and asked him to come in right away to discuss the test results. Panicked at first, his preoccupation with the business erased the worries and he almost missed the appointment. The receptionist was surly as she reminded John that he was forty five minutes late.

"Hi Jessie. Thanks for seeing me so fast," he said, standing at the door to her office. "Sorry about being late. Work problems."

"No problem, John. Come on in and have a seat." She stood up behind her desk, waving him in and pointing to a chair across from her desk. "I'm glad that you could come in today."

He sat down and crossed his hands in his lap. "So, what's up? Did you figure out what is wrong with my Lucy?"

"We did, John, and I'm afraid that it is not very good news." She opened a file on her desk and put on her reading glasses. She lifted a page and scanned it quickly. "We're going to have to run a few more tests, but based on what I see from the results of the tests we just did, it looks very likely that Lucy has a condition called Juvenile Polycystic Kidney Disease. PKD for short."

He closed his eyes, his body tensing. "What? Kidney disease? How, uh, I mean, I can't, what, uh, what does that mean? Can you break that down for me? What is wrong?"

"Sure, John, but stay with me on this and don't let your

mind rush ahead to something horrible, OK?"

"PKD is a rare condition that causes cysts to grow on the kidneys." She continued, placing her glasses back down on the desk. "It causes gradual deterioration in kidney function. I'm not an expert in this field by any means, but I have seen one other case and I did consult with a colleague about that case and I will for Lucy."

"So how bad is it?"

"It's very serious. Right now there are some medications we can try to help her with the back pain and maybe slow down the progress of the disease, but these are only temporary solutions. Ultimately, Lucy will need to have a full kidney transplant—the sooner the better."

His eyes closed and his chin fell down on his chest. He removed his glasses and rubbed his eyes, bringing his fingers together at the bridge of his nose.

"My God. Are you sure about this? I mean, a kidney transplant is a very complex procedure, right?"

"Yes, it is."

We're not just talking about a few days in the hospital are we?"

"No, it is a complex operation and there are great risks involved. But at this time, it is the only solution for Lucy. Unfortunately, if left untreated, most children with this condition rarely live for more than a few years."

He stared at his hands, shaking his head slowly. "Goddamn. I … I can't … can't believe this."

"I know, John, but we're very lucky with Lucy. She is a healthy girl and it appears we detected this condition early." She stood up, walked around her desk, sat in the chair beside John, and leaned toward him. "This news is really hard, I'm sorry."

He looked up at her. A tear leaked from the corner of his eye and ran down his cheek. "No, it's OK. Keep going."

"Like I said, we'll do more testing, plus I'm going to recommend that you visit a doctor in Boston who is much more familiar with this condition. I want him to examine Lucy and the test results and give his opinion on what is best. We're all going to do everything within our power to help Lucy, and you. I promise."

His body slumped and he covered his face with both hands. She reached across the chairs and patted his arm. "Right now, we all just have to acknowledge that she has this condition and work to get her the best treatments available. I've already made arrangements for her to be put on a waiting list for a transplant. It's difficult to predict when a donor would become available, but I'm positive that we have enough time. I did some checking and it takes about five months for donor organs to become available."

He looked up. "Donor? I'll be the donor."

"Well it has to be a child. I know you'd be the first one to do whatever it takes to help her." He looked out the window behind her desk. A young mother walked down the sidewalk, holding the hand of a small child that stopped to jump over every crack in the sidewalk.

"John? Did you hear me?"

He shook his head and looked at her. "Sorry."

"I understand. This is overwhelming." She straightened her skirt. "I find that it helps parents to roll up their sleeves and get involved in the process. Sometimes we all get relief by getting on with the things that need to be done. Lucy can make it through this and have a long, healthy life."

He gave her a weak smile and sat up in his chair. "You're right. I know you're right. That's how I've been about other things in my life. I find that if I dive in and start trying to solve the problem, things work out."

She smiled. "Good. Good." She stood up and walked back around her desk. She picked up a folder and held it out to him. "I've taken the liberty of printing out some things from my internet sources that will help you understand more about what we are dealing with. I think ..."

"Umm, Jessie, excuse me just a second. This might seem like a strange question right now, but how much does something like this cost?"

"That's not a strange question at all, John. This type of procedure will cost several hundred thousand dollars. It depends on several factors: how the operation goes, what happens during the rehabilitation process, etc. You've got good insurance coverage, so you'll just have to spend a few thousand dollars and your insurance company will pick up the tab for the rest. I'm sure that we'll need to alert your insurance company and file the appropriate paperwork before the operation but we'll help you with all that."

"OK, good. That's a relief. Wouldn't matter anyway. I'd come up with the money somehow even if it wasn't covered by insurance. I want to make sure that Lucy gets the very best medical care during all this. Let's not spare any expense that you think is necessary to get this done properly. She's my life, my whole life."

* * *

December was always the slowest month for John's company. He took this time to catch up on year-end issues and plan for the upcoming year. One morning he sifted through a large stack of unopened mail and pulled out a certified letter from his health insurance company. The shortage of money had caused him to return to an old bill paying habit whereby he paid things in order of importance or in preference to those vendors that were the most demanding. The certified letter advised him that his company's group health policy had been cancelled effective November 30, due to non-payment. Panicked, he called the insurance agent who sold him the policy and received the news that the company would reinstate the policy if John rushed payment to them as quickly as possible.

The insurance company notified John within a week that his policy had indeed been reinstated. They also advised him that due to his cancellation and reinstatement, the terms of the policy dictated a change in the major medical coverage for his employees and their dependents. The insurance company would disallow any claims for major medical issues that arose any time prior to the policy cancellation date and going back six months. Another call to his insurance agent confirmed this was true. She reminded John that when they set up the policy, she had made it clear that if there was a cancellation due to lack of payment, there could be severe consequences for any member of the policy that was facing a new, expensive medical issue. No insurance company can afford to let customers cancel only to have them rush back and reinstate the policy because of a medical need. It was standard procedure for all of them.

His next call was to Jessie Cayton's office manager. She informed John they had filed the pre-admission request for Lucy with his insurance company two days after he had met with Dr. Cayton. The pre-admission request detailed Lucy's medical condition and the procedures necessary to treat the ailment. She told him they had indeed received an electronic confirmation from the insurance company for the request and she expected to get an approval from them any day. After John hung up the phone, she called back and left him a message that there was no need to worry. She was certain the medical help that Lucy needed would be fully covered. Another call and description of the issue to his insurance agent confirmed John's fears. There would not be coverage for the procedures necessary for Lucy's new medical condition.

* * *

Two days later, John made himself a Seagrams and Seven-Up and sat down in front of a blank TV screen. He had put Lucy in bed earlier than usual. Glancing at the phone beside him, he swallowed the drink in one long gulp. It was a phone call that he hoped would never happen. From the small number of details he had accumulated about Ellen's parents they seemed to be good people. Ellen had rarely spoken of them and John had only met them twice. She seemed embarrassed by them, but John was never sure why. When he had pressed her for more details, she became defensive. Maybe she was embarrassed by their simple lifestyle. They had been teachers, quite good ones according to Ellen. After Ellen had moved out, her parents sent birthday and Christmas presents for Lucy for a few years. Beyond that, he had not heard from them or Ellen for three years. No matter how painful it might be to track down Ellen, he had to try. He needed money for Lucy's procedure, and she might have it. He had to try for Lucy's sake. Ellen's parents lived in a small town outside Cincinnati. John found their phone number on the Internet. He poured another drink, this time without the Seven-up, and sat back down. His body felt heavy and tired, as if he were wearing a rusted suit of armor. He took a deep breath and dialed the number.

"Hello," a faint voice answered.

"Hi, is this Barbara?"

"Yes, who's calling please?"

"Barbara, it's John Manning calling. Ellen's ex-husband." There was a pause.

"Oh my God, John, is that really you? Wow, this is quite a surprise! I can't believe you called. I was just thinking about Lucy today. How are you? How is Lucy doing? How old is she now?"

"She's a delightful six year old, Barbara. She's quite a beauty and so intelligent that it's sometimes tricky to keep up with her."

"Oh, John, that is so wonderful to hear. I think about you and her all the time. How are you?"

"I'm fine, Barabara, just fine. We're both doing fine."

"Wonderful! That's just terrific, really terrific. You don't know how many times I've wanted to pick up the phone and just check in on you two. Dick and I never knew what to do, you know, with the situation being just so awkward. But I so wanted to know how you and Lucy were doing. It really is great that you called. I only wish that Dick was here to talk with you too."

John heard Barbara sob and then there was a loud crash on her end of the line.

"Barbara? Are you there, Barbara?" He heard the muffled sounds of her sobs and the banging of the phone against the wall as Barbara pulled the receiver back to herself by the cord.

"John? John, you there still?"

"Yes, Barbara. I'm here."

"Dropped the phone on the floor. I'm sorry." She continued crying. He waited. "My hands can shake so badly now when I get upset. It happens so much lately."

"I'm sorry, Barbara." He waited another minute. "So you said Dick wasn't there. Is he out somewhere?" He wished he could take back the question.

"He's … he's not here … anymore," Barbara sobs grew louder. "He … he passed away."

"Oh God, Barbara, I'm so sorry." He waited again. Her sobs soften.

"It's OK. I'm … I mean, it's … it's just recently been enough time that I can talk about it. He died eighteen months ago."

"I really am sorry, Barbara. Very sorry."

"That's OK. I mean thank you. But I'm thinking that you didn't call to listen to a blubbering old lady go on and on about her life."

"Well, actually, I'm looking for Ellen. I need to get in touch with her about something important."

"Oh John, I'm … uh, I, I … uh … I'm afraid I don't know where she is."

"You don't have any idea?"

"Nothing. I've been so worried about her too, every day. I just hope that she hasn't had another episode, like, you know, with her problem."

"Yes, me too. I mean, you're talking about her bipolar disorder, right?"

"Yes. I mean it caused some real problems for her. Maybe it was even a part of why she left you and Lucy. I don't know."

"That was a part of the reason. But I thought she was fine as long as she took her medicine."

"Sure, she was very conscientious about the medicine. Except when she got into her excitable periods. She always thought the medicine dulled her down, made her mind cloudy. Sometimes, when she got, you know, excitable, she wouldn't take the pills."

"I know. She told me the same thing. So you don't have any information about how I might find her?"

"Well I did get some information about her two years ago. When Dick started to get really sick, I remembered the name of the company that she was working for in Paris and I tried twice to contact her. I thought that maybe they just didn't understand me because I couldn't speak French."

"Was the company called Aster-Evans?"

"No, no. That was the first company she worked for. She went to work for another one. Can't remember the name now, but I've got it written down somewhere. Some French sounding name."

"Can you find the name of the company for me? Maybe I can get through to someone there that can help."

"It won't matter anyway John, because I found out that she left Paris."

"What?"

"Yes. Like I said, the second time I called, I just kept insisting that it was an emergency. Finally, they connected me to this British woman, I'm pretty sure her name was Elizabeth."

"So did this British woman give you any information?"

"Yes, she did. She was very sweet. They must have been close friends because of the things she said about Ellen. She even seemed to know about Ellen's problem because when I asked her about how Ellen had been feeling, she told me that Ellen had was doing well and had been taking her medicine. Anyway, she said that Ellen had been working really hard at her job and that she had gotten several promotions. She said Ellen was very talented. She said Ellen had met some man from Russia and that they were ... I mean that they were seeing each other and that Ellen had changed. She said Ellen talked all the time about the man and how he was a very important businessman back in Russia. After they had been seeing each other for about three months, Ellen told her they were going to move back to Moscow and start a company together. The woman said Ellen even tried to convince her to help them get the business started. She said that Ellen was working on this new project all the time. Ellen was even taking some of her vacation time and traveling with the Russian man to do business things. Then, after one long vacation, I mean, you know that the Germans take very long vacations, I mean, after that, she just vanished."

"Hold on, Barbara, you just said that the Germans take a lot of vacations. Was she working in Germany or Paris?"

"Oh gosh, did I say something about Germany? See how I forget things so easily."

"So where was she?"

"It was Germany, definitely Germany. The British woman told me that both she and Ellen were put on a special project and were living in Munich together because that's where Ellen met this Russian man."

"So Ellen was living in Germany?"

"Yes, definitely. Now the British woman said that after project was finished, she moved back to Paris, but Ellen asked the company if she could stay longer in Munich. The British woman said that when she couldn't get in touch with Ellen, she went back to the apartment that they had lived in and it was empty. All her things had been removed. She was just gone. The woman said that she never got a phone call or an email or anything from Ellen. She was just … just gone … no word or anything."

"So this woman didn't have any idea where Ellen might be?"

"Nothing, nothing at all," she sobbed. "Oh God, why John, why? Why would she do this to me? How will I know if she's OK? What am I going to do?"

He listened as her sobs grew louder. She blew her nose and the phone dropped on the floor again. He waited for her to pick it back up.

"I'm sorry, my hands just aren't so good anymore. Seems like I drop things all the time now. Did I tell you about how my hands shake now?"

"Yes, you told me. But please tell me if you can remember anything else that this woman told you."

"That's all, really. I didn't even tell Dick all this. I just told him that I couldn't get in touch with her. Ellen had broken his heart so many times. You know how much a father loves his daughter. You've got a daughter now. He was just too sick. I didn't want him to be burdened with anything else. Don't you think that was a good idea?"

He sighed and he looked at his watch. "Yes, it was. You did the right thing. But I need to ask you some more questions about this. See I've really got to get in touch with her, so I need you to try to remember.

"I can't remember John. I really can't. I even called back again after Dick's death and tried to get someone at the company to put the nice British woman back on the phone. Someone that spoke better English said she had moved back to London to care for a sick relative. Now isn't that what children are supposed to do? Shouldn't Ellen have been here helping her father when he was sick? Helping me now? Why did she do this to me John? Why?"

"I'm sorry, Barbara. I just don't know. Maybe she was really sick again. Maybe something else was happening. So, this British woman, do you remember anything else about her?"

"I don't remember very well, John. I just know that she was nice and that she and Ellen were friends and that I couldn't talk with her again because she had moved back to London. That's all I know."

"OK, Barbara. Thanks for trying to help me anyway. I guess I'll try a few other ways to see if I can get in touch with her. I'm sorry that I had to bother you with this. I've got to get going now. I'll be sure and call you if I find out anything."

"John, you've got to promise me that you'll tell her about our conversation if you get in touch with her. Tell her everything I said. I miss her so much sometimes. Just tell her to call me. Can you tell her that?"

"Of course I will, Barbara."

"And Lucy too. Will you tell Lucy I think about her every day?"

"Of course, Barbara. I'm sorry that things didn't work out better for all of us, especially for you."

"Oh, John, I've got to hang up now. I just think I'm gonna lay down for a little while. You promise you'll call me if you reach her, right?"

"Yes, Barbara, I will. Good night."

He hung up and laid down on the sofa and stared at the ceiling. Even though the pain of her departure had lessened over the years, he couldn't shake the fantasy that someday she would arrive back in his life. They would reunite, Lucy would have her mother, and all would be right with the world. There was some comfort that she had not only abandoned him, but she had also abandoned her parents. Not that he wished Ellen's parents any ill will, he just felt reassured that Ellen's actions might have been because of her illness more than anything else.

* * *

A week before Christmas, John agreed to meet Wanda. For the past three weeks, she'd tried to get his advice several times. He refused her requests, but she persisted. Each time she called him, her enthusiasm for the idea had grown and so had her determination to get him involved. She had framed the whole concept in such a way that he was almost touched. She spoke about the importance of making the trip for herself and Tonya. She reminded John that she could pay him back if they made a run. She also relayed to him just how much money could be made. They met in John's office after everyone had left for the day.

"No, I'm not kidding. I told you a few months ago how much money there is in this business. Wouldn't a couple hundred grand help your business over this rough patch?"

"Yes it would, but you don't really expect me to think that it's possible to make that much in a couple of days do you?"

"You better believe it. All we've got to do is come up with about thirty grand and then we can buy five or six kilos of pure stuff. We get it back here and I could sell it in about week, maybe two. Everybody's looking for product right now."

He leaned back in his chair and took off his glasses. He rubbed his eyes and put the glasses back on. "What would each kilo go for?"

Wanda smiled. "Right now, big bucks. Someone might pay $35,000 around here for a kilo. Like I told you, everything is jammed up because the five-oh is all over the airport. I'm sure I could get $50,000 for each, maybe more." She smiled. "Easy money."

"So, based on what you're telling me, we buy five kilos of the stuff for five grand apiece and sell each one for fifty. And you've got the connections to sell all the stuff. That means we'd net about $220,000, after taking out the $30,000 we used to buy the stuff." He leaned back in his chair, locking his fingers together behind his head.

"That sounds about right. Now, we're going to pay a few people. Some of the people I deal with are going to want a little cash for connecting me with their friends. Kind of like a finder's fee, you know. And they'll be some other expenses, something that we didn't count on, but yeah, the way I figure it, we both will come out of this real big."

"You do make an appealing case."

"See, man, you and me, we make a good team. You know about cruise ships and how we can use them to move the stuff. You can come up with the cash. Then when we get back, I'll take care of the really hard part. I'll be the one taking most of the chances trying to sell the stuff."

He closed his eyes and sighed. "Look, I have to admit that some of what you're proposing sounds interesting. But I'm not getting into something like this. I can't risk my whole life. If things went bad, I'd lose Lucy. I can't even begin to tell you how much the thought of losing her scares me."

"I know, I know, I really do. I use to worry about losing my girl too. But I learned how to be smart and what to look out for. I've been doing this for a long time and ain't been busted yet. I learned that if you got enough cash, you can make it safe. Hell, those guys moving stuff all the way from Columbia, through Mexico, to LA have to pay a lot of cash to people along the way. One dude told me that you've got to grease about a dozen different people to move a nice sized load all the way to the U.S. If you pay, you get to play, that's it."

"But we're not in Mexico," he sighed. "It's just too dangerous."

"You're looking tired."

"Haven't been sleeping well. Only got about four hours of sleep in the last three days. Got a lot on my mind."

"Understand. Well, you're right, this ain't Mexico. But what you came up with cuts out so many problems. Hey, it's simple, like you said. You ride on the big boat, stop and buy the coke. Then you get us back on the boat, past any security checks, and we bring it home. Goddamn it's good. I mean everyone on the boat is partying right, having a big vacation, right?" He nodded. "It ain't going to be like they have cops on board or something. I mean, I've been checking out a few things about it myself. It's just a big party boat and we'll ride back all safe. Hell, we don't even have to worry about some dudes jacking our stuff. Everyone else that moves coke not only has to worry about the cops, but they also have to worry about some bad asses pointing a gun in their face and running off with the goods because somebody tipped off someone else who wants to make a big score. Hell, talk about a good deal, imagine letting someone else take the risk of moving the stuff and then you just steal it somewhere along the line. And this type of stealing don't get reported to the cops either." She smiled at him. He frowned and shook his head.

"Let's cut the shit right now. No more talking. I can't become a drug runner in order to save my business. I'm not going to do something like that. I'm just not that desperate. I'll figure something else out."

"I'm telling you, John, this ain't that risky. You've got to trust me on this. We can both come out big on this, real big. Don't just blow this off. I can help you save this business." She leaned forward in her chair. "Look, how long you been doing this anyway?"

"Twelve years."

"And don't you know a lot about how to run this business after all that time? I mean, didn't you make some mistakes in the beginning?"

"Of course. Everybody gets smarter over time."

"Me too. I've been pretty much doing my gig for about ten years and I've gotten a lot smarter over time too. I'm smart enough to know that you and I could partner up on this thing and make some good bucks." She leaned forward further and crossed her arms on the desk, placing her chin on top of her right hand. She gave John a wink and her best smile. This time, she received a slight smile in return.

"Why don't you just get some of your work buddies to do the deal with you? You don't need me. You're a smart woman. You can handle this without me."

"Can't do it. Too many problems come up that way. Number one, I need a way to get the stuff off the boat when we land in the U.S. and you know how to do that, right?"

"Maybe. I've got an idea that might work."

"Ok. Number two, some people won't like that I'm doing this." Her smile faded.

"I guess you're talking about your boss, huh? Is this the guy that you travel with?"

"Yeah. That's the guy. We've been working together for a long time and I know that he does everything he can to get rid of people trying to move in on his turf. He's done me pretty right though. I just ain't been able to make enough and save enough. That's why I don't have any money. He knows what we all make so he's careful to make sure that we don't make too much. If we all get some extra cash, then he knows that one of us might want to make more by getting the product ourselves or from someone else." She sat up and leaned back in her chair.

"What do you mean 'he knows what we all make'? What other people are you talking about?"

"He's got other people who sell the stuff for him. We keep a piece of what we sell, like a commission. Anyway, there's five of us and we all make enough to get by on, but nothing more than that."

"You mean this boss of yours has an actual sales force that works on commission and you're part of this team?"

"Yeah, I guess you could call it that. Like I told you, it's a business just like yours and my boss is damn good at it. Knows how to make it work and how to keep me and the others working for him." She fidgeted and brushed a loose piece of thread from her leg.

"Seems like the guy makes you uncomfortable."

"Maybe he does, but I'll deal with that."

"I guess you get free product from being a part of this team, huh?"

"Nah. I don't mess with drugs. Did a little when I was younger. That shit can really mess people up. I've seen it wreck people. That ain't for me. Anyway, we're getting off the subject. You asked me why I don't get some of my people to do this with me and I told you. So what would it take for you to be in?"

"Just stop it. I'll never be in. I'm sure you think I might change my mind since we keep on talking about this, but it's not going to happen. No way. Not a chance." He looked at his watch. "I have to get Lucy."

"I forgot to ask you about the security when the ship returns. You called this the choke point, right?"

"Yeah. Basically, anytime you're arriving into the U.S. from a foreign county you must go through a customs check. Even if you're coming in on a cruise ship. The custom guys know what to look for."

"OK, I got it. This is where folks get busted, just like those guys in Miami. So maybe you have a way around this with all your cruise connections?"

"Don't really know. One time they even had one of those drug sniffing dogs running around checking out everyone's luggage." He glanced at his watch again.

She sat up straight in her chair and leaned forward, smiling. "I'll get us past that. Let me take care of that part." She paused. "I'll carry the shit through. You won't have any chance of getting caught. If it goes down wrong, I'll take the fall."

He sighed and shook his head. "Nice gesture, but my answer is still no. Maybe everything would be fine. We pick up the stuff in Mexico, sail back up here, drop it off the ship, and then go pick it up. Then you go out and you sell the stuff. But a dozen things have to go right for us and they only have to get lucky once. Then we're screwed. I can't lose my Lucy." He took off his glasses and rubbed the bridge of his nose.

She frowned. "Wait a second. You just said, 'We drop it off the ship and then go pick it up.' What the hell does that mean?"

He squirmed and looked out the window into his empty store. "Umm, that was, I mean, I just meant to say we bring it through customs. I don't know what I was thinking about."

Wanda's brow relaxed. A smile formed slowly. "You've got some special idea about this security thing."

He rubbed the back of his neck with his hand and rolled his head around slowly. "I don't have any ideas Wanda. This whole discussion is giving me a headache."

"C'mon. What'cha got in that smart head of yours?"

He stood up quickly. "Cut this shit out! Look, I'm tired and I'm not going to talk about this anymore. We're done. Goodbye."

He walked around his desk and to the door, holding it open for her. She stood up and walked past him like a scolded child. He followed her out the front door, locked it behind him, and watched her drive away. He got into his car and leaned forward, tapping his forehead on the steering wheel.

XII - January 2002

Golden Cruise Line's smallest ship, the Blue Heron, sailed around the Florida Keys on her way to the Western Caribbean. The ship had been refurbished in 1997, so she hid her actual age of twenty-five very well. The five hundred passengers had finished dining and were heading off to enjoy the evening's entertainment. John and Wanda had sent the girls back with John's mother to go to bed. They'd been fortunate to have had a calm season and warm temperatures. Lucy and Tonya spent most of their time in the children's play area, which was staffed with three crew members who excelled at entertaining the fifteen children aboard the ship. They had become fast friends within one hour of meeting for the first time while boarding the ship in Norfolk, Virginia. John's mother, as always, was delighted to be with Lucy and happy to take care of the girls. She would take care of them on the ship while he and Wanda inspected hotels in the ports of call and met with excursion operators. Over the years, he had described to her the growing success of his group cruise business, but she wasn't aware that he had hired someone to assist him with this part of the business. She had only met one of John's employees, Mary. So meeting another one, and one so charming and attractive, only added to her enjoyment of the trip.

John and Wanda walked into the casino and sat down to play blackjack. The night they left Norfolk, she won $700. But things were not going as well tonight. After playing for an hour, John picked up his few remaining chips and signaled to her that he was going to sit down in the bar area near the back of the casino. He found a booth and ordered a vodka tonic. After thirty more minutes of playing, it was obvious that she was still losing.

He watched her frown at the dealer and the cards, and then slam her fist down on the table. She stood up, cursed, and kicked her seat backward into the hostess who was bringing her another rum and coke. She leaned forward over the table, glaring at the dealer as the three other players leaned back, covering their chips with their hands. She stomped over to him and threw herself into the opposite side of the booth.

"Goddamn dealer wasn't throwin' me jack tonight. How could I rake in so much last night and then lose it all so fast." He shook his head.

"You better quit getting into arguments. You can't be making scenes like you just did. Do you remember what I said when we first got on the ship? Were you listening, because what I just saw looked pretty goddamn stupid."

She raised her hand to hit the table but dropped it without a sound. "I heard what you said." The bartender approached their table and she ordered another rum and coke. "I'm laying low. Just like you said. So I'm a little drunk, so what? I'm just happy about being on a cruise ship. You never told me how damn cool it was going to be."

He looked at her and then at the blackjack tables.

"Hey, I'm sorry. You're right. I was out of line. I just forgot for a few minutes. I'll be cool." The bartender delivered her drink and she drank half of it.

He turned back to her. "Thank you for saying that. Now just make sure you remember from now on." He leaned forward, lowering his voice, "We're just like everyone else on this ship, OK? Having a vacation, relaxing, and enjoying the ride. We don't want to stand out."

She frowned. "You need to do some relaxing yourself, man. Everything is going to be fine. I got my end under control. It's going to be smooth sailing. Ha! That was a good one. Get it, smooth sailing?"

He still had not been sleeping well and was not much in the mood for chatting. He glanced at the clock above the bar. "OK, OK, whatever. Look, it's almost ten o'clock. I'm going to pack it in early. You should, too." He started to slide out of the booth and she reached out and touched his arm.

"Wait, umm, I gotta ask you something about all this." He turned back to her and she finished the rest of her drink. "It seems to me that there's something more going on here besides you needing money for your business. The last few weeks that we've been chatting, you just look worn out. I mean dog tired."

"Can we have this chat tomorrow?"

"I mean, look, somebody like you, owns a good business, nice mom, you've gotta have somebody who can help you out. Don't you have some more family?"

"What I told you before is what's happening. Remember what happened in September? Planes crashing into the World Trade Center, the Pentagon, and Pennsylvania? It's just like I said. My business has just dropped by about half. The dot-com bubble burst on us too and caused us to lose our largest corporate account. No one is buying travel. Everybody in the travel industry is suffering."

"So can't you just fire some people and cut way back? You've been doing this a long time so I'm sure that you've been through bad times before."

"There's never been anything like 9/11. Never." John held up his empty glass and the bartender nodded. He wiped the sweat off his empty glass and rubbed it across his forehead.

"How about this: I tell you more about why I'm doing this if you answer something for me? Sound fair?"

She shifted in her seat. "I knew it! Great. OK, go ahead and ask me." He waited until his drink had arrived and the bartender had left.

"So it's cool to ask you anything?"

"Sure. You just gotta be sure to explain what's up on your end."

"Who's Tonya's father?"

"What? You can't, uh, that ain't part of this conversation."

"You agreed that I could ask a question."

"Well, let's just keep my little sweetie and who her daddy is out of this."

"Hey, you didn't say that anything was off limits." He looked back at the clock. "Look, it isn't really my business anyway. Just forget I asked."

"Goddamn, I can't believe you asked that."

"Hey, I know. Out of line."

"Alright, alright. Look, I can tell you about that. It's just that I've never talked about it with anyone."

"Well you don't have to start sharing it with me. We can just skip this and ..."

"Jamel's her daddy."

"Jamel? You mean that guy that you work for?"

"Yep. He's the one."

"But this guy, you told me some bad stuff about him."

"Yeah, I know. He's a shit. But it happened. Never even told him."

"Really? Why not?"

"Look at what he does, man. And you only know a little bit about him. Do you think he would be any kind of father?"

"Guess not."

"That man has no heart, no feelings for anyone but himself. He is one cold-ass dude and that is a fact."

"How do you mean that?"

"What I mean is he gets off on fucking with people's heads."

"Give me an example."

"OK, here's one. Let's say Jamel is having a problem with one of his competitors, or maybe someone who's working with him, so he needs to send them a little message, you know, like straighten your ass out."

"What do you mean by a 'message'?"

"He messes with folks in a couple of ways but his favorite is to jack up their car so they crash it."

"What, like he messes with the brakes or something?"

"Yeah, something like that. Something that makes the car wreck while they're driving it."

"So the guy's good at being a dealer and knows a lot about cars."

"No, not him. He doesn't know shit about cars. He has someone that does it for him. So then, after they crash their car, if they ain't in the hospital, he calls them and says 'Sorry about your car. I noticed the other day that it had this strange knocking sound, so I spent a little time working on it for you.'"

"Interesting. So they get the message and they stop whatever they're not supposed to be doing, right?"

"Oh yeah. One dude he sent a message to got so banged up that he was in the hospital for a couple of weeks. Jamel sent some flowers to his hospital room and the guy knew what had happened."

"That's an interesting method for dealing with business problems."

"Guess you could say that. Another thing the bastard did was threaten to hurt Tonya if I ever tried to fuck with him. If he knew that she was his, it would only make things worse."

He moved back to the center of the booth. "So I guess that you've got to be careful when you get back, huh?"

"Don't worry about that. Jamel won't know a thing."

"So how did he end up being the father?" asked John.

She pulled her drink from her mouth, laughing. "How the hell do you think it happened? Did your mom forget to tell about where babies come from?"

"No, no, I mean were you involved with him? Were you guys dating or something?"

"Dating? Now that's funny. No, it wasn't like that. We both just got wasted really bad one night drinking Jack Daniels. When we woke up he just kind of acted like nothing happened. Hell, he's damn ugly anyway. Just glad that my Tonya got my good looks." She brushed her hair back. "And, now this will freak you out: He's queer."

"No way. Now I think you're pulling my leg."

"Wish I was. Can't stand faggots. Goes against the Bible and everything."

"So how do you know he's gay?"

"I just kinda suspected after I was around him for a while. Just little things. But then, the night we hooked up I found a bunch of fag magazines under his bed. Some magazines called 'Jocks' or some crap like that. Bunch of naked guys kissing each other. Nasty."

"That's really interesting."

"And then, 'bout a month later, I saw some letter open on his desk from the 'Lambda Defense League of Durham,' thanking him for sending them $5000. So I looked them up in the phone book and damn if they ain't some kind of group that provides legal help to fags and lezzies."

"Whoa. So, the father of your daughter, the drug kingpin, is gay?"

"Pretty good, huh? And I ain't never told nobody that either."

"And he donates to the Lambda Defense League. My God. So what in the hell did you …"

"Hold on just a minute." She held up her hand "Now it's your turn to do some talking. I said too much already, anyway."

He smiled, took off his glasses, and cleaned them with a cocktail napkin. "You're right. I got a little carried away with what you told me. You sure did shock me with that one." He put his glasses back on and ran his hand across the top of his head.

"I need the money because Lucy has to have a kidney transplant." He laced his fingers together on the table and gazed down at them. "And I haven't told anyone either, so you have to swear that you won't say a word." He placed a finger under his glasses and rubbed his eye.

"Oh God. Your sweet little girl. What's wrong with her kidneys?"

"Some rare disease. Kids that have it don't live very long without a new kidney."

"Damn. I worry all the time about my little girl being sick. I'm sorry."

He wiped his eye again. "Thanks."

"Don't you have insurance to take care of something like this?"

"I used to. I had insurance for everyone in my company, but we lost damn coverage about a month before Lucy was diagnosed because I couldn't pay it a few months ago. God, I messed up on that one. No one will cover us now."

"Tonya and I had a hard time getting insurance, so Jamel got us set up on some kind of plan. He put us and some of his other people on it."

He looked up and smiled. "So you've got group health insurance through your job. Now that's funny."

She smiled back. "I guess so. How much is this thing that Lucy needs going to cost?"

"The doctors told me that with everything, the operation, recovery, therapy, drugs, it will cost a couple hundred thousand dollars."

"Umm. I see. I'm sorry, John. Real sorry." She put her hand on top of his. "I guess I understand a lot better now."

"Thanks." He leaned back in his seat and pulled his hands down to his lap.

"But hey, you've got family right? Can't they help out? How about a bank? Banks lend money to rich people like you, don't they?"

John shook his head. "Look, Wanda, I might look rich to you, but I'm not. I've made a good living, but running a business like mine, there just isn't a lot left over. I've got nothing to fall back on. Same for my family. My mom got stuck with a huge bunch of bills when my stepfather died in 1985. All he left her with was a broken business, $130,000 in unpaid taxes, and about $90,000 in bank loans. My attorney and I had a lot of the debt reduced for her, she paid what she could, and I helped some. I've been paying her a salary out of my company for the past few years so that she will have something to live off of. She works temp jobs when she can find them, but lately she hasn't been working. Basically, I'm all I got and I don't have anything to fall back on. Believe me, if I saw another way to get the money, I would. I went to my bank before all this came up to try to get some money to help my company, but they turned me down. Think about it, who's going to lend any money to someone in the travel industry right now?"

"Damn. That's terrible."

"That's why I'm here working with you."

"But, what about Lucy? Is she having problems right now?"

"She's doing fine. The doctors at Duke have tested her and they don't think she's at risk for any problems before a donor comes along. She takes medications that help and they make her a little hyper, but that's all. She seems normal to me. Didn't even suspect something was wrong until she started having lower back pains. As far as the operation, it is a damn hellacious procedure, but the doctors say she'll do fine. There is a lot of stuff to do afterwards—therapy, medications, things like that. She'll be in the hospital for several weeks."

"How did you come up with the money to buy the product? Shouldn't you be using that to pay for Lucy's operation?"

"I have to use what money I have left from something I call my 'Russia Fund.'"

"What's that?"

"Something else that was good but stopped after 9/11. A few years back, this Russian professor from Carolina called and bought a business class ticket from me to fly from RDU to Moscow. Business class for that kind of trip is four thousand and change."

"Damn, that's a lot."

"Yeah, you're right. And this guy comes in to get the ticket the next day and starts to leave but comes back and asks me to look up what the cost would be if he just flew economy. So he says that he's changed his mind and that he's going to just buy the cheaper ticket. He hands me the business class ticket back and I tell him that we can just 'void' the ticket since he changed his mind within the reporting week when we have to turn in our ticket sales to the airlines and that it won't be a problem. Then, when I start to tear up his business class ticket, he stops me and asks if he can have the receipt from the business class ticket anyway, since I would just be voiding it. Then he gives me this big smile and says 'University have very good reimbursement policy for professors.'"

"Good job. That even sounded a little like a Russian. But I still don't get it." The bartender returned to their table. He asked for a glass of water. She ordered another drink.

"He gets me to issue a business class ticket, I void it like it never happened and he wants to keep the receipt. Then he buys an economy class ticket for $700."

"So the sneaky ass Russian turns in the receipt for the expensive ticket and makes a couple of grand!"

"Yep. Only I didn't get it at first. But then I started getting calls from other Russian professors who all wanted me to void their tickets after they changed their minds and if I didn't mind, would I include the business class ticket receipt in the envelope when I mailed them their cheaper ticket. After I did a few more and the same thing happened, I put it all together. So I started charging them a $500 service fee every time they did this. And professors kept calling— from Virginia, Maryland, Alabama. Real nice guys, very friendly. Did twenty or so tickets a month for a long time. I mean I didn't do them all personally. As the business grew, I had my manager, Mary, take over. But then 9/11 happened and they all stopped calling. Haven't done one since then. I had to dip into the fund occasionally, like when I helped my mom and for the business. So now, I've got enough to fund this little venture and then it'll just about be depleted." The bartender returned with their drinks.

"Cool story. So the Russians scammed their universities and you skimmed a little off the top?"

"Guess so. I was just providing the service. I wasn't the one that was doing anything wrong."

"Pretty damn smart. The Russia Fund."

"That's what Mary started calling it. Has a nice ring to it. Kind of James Bond sounding."

"What about Lucy's mom? You've never said anything about her."

"She's not around. Not an option. That's a topic I don't want to get into."

"Damn, I just can't stand to think about Lucy being sick. If my little Tonya needed to have some kind of operation, I'd be doing whatever it took to make her better, just like you."

"Speaking of family, is yours around Durham?"

She laughed and shook her head. "Family? I guess you could call what I had a family."

"What do you mean by that? Surely you've got a mom around somewhere. Brothers, sisters, somebody. Who takes care of Tonya while you're working?"

"I've got help for Tonya. Someone who loves her and helps out. It's the aunt that took care of me after my mother skipped town, that sorry whore. Damn sorry bitch. I can still hear her loud-ass voice screaming at me when I was little, out in the neighborhood playing with my friends. 'Wanda, Wanda, get your little ass in here cause I got to go to work right now. Get over here right now.'" She took a sip of her drink, set it down and then took another, longer sip. "Some days I'd be in the house, minding my own business and wham!" She smashed her hand on the table. "She'd smack me upside the head so hard I'd fall down crying. Once I got to be as big as her, you better believe that stopped." She took another long sip.

"I'm sorry. Maybe I shouldn't have asked."

"Nah. It's OK. One thing she did teach me was not to take any shit off anyone. She taught me how to look out for myself, how to fight back, how to take what I needed. I'll at least give her a little credit for that."

"I guess it's better not to have her around now."

She snorted. "Wasn't my choice really, not to have her around. When I was fourteen, she just left town. Dropped me off at my aunt's house and said she had to take care of some things out of town for a few days and never came back." She shifted in her seat. Her gaze moved from him to the blackjack table. "Sorry ass whore. That's what she did you know. She was a whore." She turned back to him. "She'd make me dinner and tell me to go to bed and she'd head out to sell herself to anyone who'd pay. Most mornings, if she came home at all, she'd have some john with her. She drank too much too. One night I heard her out on the porch try to get some guy to give her two bottles of vodka. She ended up doing it for one bottle. She was a cheap whore too."

"You said your aunt raised you then? You started living with her when you were fourteen right?"

"Yeah, that's about right. I was starting to get wild too. With my mother, I started doing what I wanted when I was thirteen. Maybe that's why she left me. I don't know for sure. Anyway, I ran with some girls who were doing just about anything they wanted. We never went to school, stole shit from stores, started drinking beer and dealing a little pot. Smoked a lot of pot that year myself. Some of the girls had boyfriends. Couple of them had babies when they were fifteen or sixteen. None of the boys seemed to care for me much. Guess I was a late bloomer." She smiled.

"Well, my aunt put a stop to all that. She wasn't that much better than my mom in some ways. Tried to beat me a few times for staying out late and drinking, but I told her what I'd done to my mother when she tried to pull that shit on me."

"What kind of work does your aunt do?" asked John.

"She worked in the cafeteria at the Durham VA Hospital and we lived in a better neighborhood. She drank a lot too, just beer. But she made me go to school, made me get a job after school to help pay for things. I finished high school. One of my teachers told me that I could go to college if I just tried a little harder." She finished her drink. "I had it pretty good compared to a lot of people I grew up around. Most people I ran with are in jail or dead. A few of them are living on welfare and got six kids with six different fathers. I've done pretty good for myself. It was tricky at first, but since I connected with Jamel, things have run pretty smooth. The man's heart is black as night, but he's smart."

"How so?"

"He's connected."

"Like how?"

"He's connected to some cop. I got busted one time and he bailed me out. Not like bailed me out by putting cash down and then I get out and a few weeks later I got to go to trial. Nope. He said that he just used his connection to get me out."

"You mean they just let you go?"

"Yep. I don't know how he did it, but he made it happen. Got me out of a few other jams too. The guy knows how to run a business."

"Sounds like you feel that you owe him. Is that why you've stuck with him and this business?"

"Don't know how to do anything else. I couldn't have raised Tonya by myself anyway trying to work some McDonald's job that didn't pay worth a damn. I only have to work a couple of nights a week, so my aunt takes care of her while I'm out and I bring home the money. My aunt loves Tonya too and I help her out with money. I got enough cash to do what I want. I got lots of time to spend with Tonya and I can keep a close eye on her. Can't let her get into trouble like I did."

"What happens if you're arrested?"

"Won't happen. Like I said, with Jamel's connection and my brains, I ain't going to get busted." He nodded and she crunched an ice cube from her drink.

"Besides, I ain't going to be doing this too much longer anyway. You and I make a couple of runs and then I'm out of here."

"You mean you're planning on quitting?"

"Yep. The way I figure, we need two or three good runs and then you will have the cash you need and I'll have the same amount. Then Tonya and me are taking off. I gotta good place in mind. Somewhere safe."

He leaned forward, his arms resting on the table. "What about Jamel? Can you just quit working for him?"

"Yeah. I'll just slip away."

"You told me he needed you to help him move the product. What's he going to do without you?"

"He ain't going to be too happy but I got some ideas on how to cover it with him. Besides, a lot has changed since we can't move stuff by using the airlines anymore. It's time for me and my little girl to move on."

"Would he try to find you?"

"Doubt it. Anyway, I know how to become invisible. If there's any trouble with him, Tonya and me will just disappear." She stirred the remaining ice in her drink with a straw. He took off his glasses and rubbed his eyes.

"Speaking of disappearing, I'm ready to disappear to my cabin. I need to get some sleep and so do you." She nodded. He stood up and placed $20 on top of the tab that the bartender had left. They walked out of the bar and onto the deck of the ship to return to their cabins.

The wind blew her hair and she brushed it away from her face. "You've got to promise me again that you ain't going to tell anyone about all this stuff we just talked about. I just told you some things that I shouldn't have."

He looked out over the ocean. The night was clear and full of stars. "Won't tell a soul. Seems to me that both of us shared a little too much tonight. No one knows Lucy is sick. Not Lucy, not my mom, nobody. I want to keep it that way."

"I forgot already," she said. "I've never seen so many stars."

* * *

John slept off and on and woke up at 5:30 a.m. as the ship was slowing down for its port stop. They had three cabins. Lucy and Tonya were sleeping in his mother's cabin so he and Wanda could leave without disturbing them. He had an hour until he needed to knock on Wanda's cabin to wake her. He sat up on the edge of the bed, rubbing his hand across his face. He put on his glasses and stared at the other bed. On it were the items they would need: a handheld GPS unit, binoculars, seven hollowed out wooden sculptures, an old khaki safari vest with $35,000 in one-hundred dollar bills sewn into the lining, and a large, black Nike gym bag to carry everything.

Luckily for John, he had become acquainted with Paul Jelton through his work. Paul operated a "helitour" company that charged tourists large amounts of money to see all the beauty of the Mayan ruins by air. John and his staff had booked hundreds of customers with Paul's company. In return, Paul would send commission checks and often provided free trips to John's VIP travelers when they were in port. Whenever Paul visited his brother, who happened to live in Richmond, he'd always make a special trip to Durham to take John out to dinner. Paul had given John the address of a man in town that would provide them with a car and cell phone for the day. John told Paul he wanted to do some sightseeing on his own and needed to make sure he could contact someone if he lost his way or the car broke down. He slipped on his clothes, grabbed the day bag, and slipped out the cabin door.

Up on deck, the sun was rising over a calm sea. He paused a moment to watch it clear the edge of the sea. He smiled, thinking of how tourists flocked to the ocean's edge at sunset, wherever they might be in the Caribbean. He always favored the sunrise, but most people on vacation were too determined to enjoy the nighttime activities, which made sunrise gazing difficult. He pushed open a door and walked into the ship's coffee bar. At any other time of the day, it would be overflowing with guests, but this early in the morning, John only saw a group of four occupying a table near a window that overlooked the deck. They were laughing loudly, reviewing events from the previous evening. They had the sloppy look of partygoers who had decided to enjoy the entire evening and a little of the morning all in one gulp.

He filled up a paper cup with coffee, picked up a bagel, and sat down on the far side of the café. His table had a copy of yesterday's USA today and he glanced over the business section. The headlines had been the same for the last three months—corporate layoffs, another dot-com failure, several airlines contemplating bankruptcy filings, and an accounting scandal. It took thirty minutes to finished two cups of coffee, his bagel, and the entire newspaper.

After his fourth knock on her cabin door, John heard Wanda grunt and he whispered through the cabin door that he'd be back in fifteen minutes to get her.

He returned and she opened the door. "I told you that we needed to be moving around, ready to go at 6:30 a.m."

"I'm ready to go. What's wrong, you wake up early again?"

"Yeah." He rubbed his eyes under his glasses. "Do I look tired?"

"Nah, not really."

"I just want to get this thing done, that's all. You sleep OK?"

"Hell yeah. Like a rock. I can't believe how good I feel every morning when I wake up on this big boat. Could've slept until lunchtime. This cruising life is really the way to live. How soon 'til we do this again?"

He turned and started walking down the hall. "Well, it all depends on how well this goes, so get your ass moving."

She fell in behind him. "Man, you worry too much. I told you, these guys are happy to have our money. They know me and they know I can move the product. Just take it easy."

He stopped and turned back to her. "Wanda, look, you're forgetting this is just one piece of the puzzle. I'm glad you feel like you've got this all figured out, but you don't." She kept walking past him. "There's a dozen other things besides today that need to work out for us before either one of us can relax. I'll take it easy after that. I suggest you get more serious about what's happening."

She pushed open the door to the deck. "Whatever, man. Let's go."

* * *

They left the ship at 7:15 a.m. and took a ten-minute taxi ride to a tiny, dirty, cinderblock home a few blocks south of the city center. Just as John reached up to knock on the door, an old man opened it. He pointed them to a Ford Pinto parked beside the house. He started to argue about the condition of the car, but the old man cut him off. "You take, bring back car, I give you half of money back." He handed the man $400. His grin revealed a total of three teeth. He gave John a thumbs-up signal, repeating "give half back, give half back." The phone was on the passenger seat. Wanda threw her bag in the back seat and picked up the phone. She sat down in the passenger seat and dialed the number she had memorized. John walked around and got in behind the wheel.

"Hola, Jose. We're here. How long until you fly in?" She waited. "I don't like the sound of that, Jose." She listened again. "I hear you. But I don't give a shit if you're sick, you've got to show up." She looked over at John and rolled her eyes. "I got your cash on my lap, friend. You show up with my stuff and it's all yours." She listened for a few more seconds. "Alright, alright, but remember, we're here with your cash and you don't want to screw anything up with this. If this works out, we'll be back in a few weeks for more." She brushed her skirt while she listened. "Sure, sure. But don't be late. We'll give you an extra few minutes, but if you don't show by then, the deal's off and we're going to buy our shit from someone else." She paused again. "Yeah, OK, yeah … right. See you then." She punched a button on the phone and smiled at him.

"So, what's up?"

"It's just the normal stuff. Every buy I've ever been on has something come up like this. There's always some last minute shit. Don't sweat it."

"You said this guy was reliable."

"He is." She turned and looked out the window. "There's

always some kind of change before you meet. You start haggling again about the price or they say they can't get the amount of keys you wanted."

"So what does that mean? Are we going to get screwed over by this guy?"

"Nah. They all want the money, especially now since things are so much tighter. I should've started hitting him up for a better price." She waved her hand toward the front of the car. "Let's get on with it."

The car sputtered, spit, and groaned as he drove out of town and onto a dusty, rutted dirt road. John had to search hard for each gear, grinding and cursing until the stick shift settled into place. Only the first three worked, so thirty miles per hour would be their maximum speed. After a few miles, the poor condition of the road made it apparent this was the maximum speed for any vehicle. There were more tiny homes and dirty children playing in dusty yards while chickens drifted across the road. He had seen "behind the curtain" many times at tourist areas across Mexico and the Caribbean. The stark difference in how people lived in these places was not new to him, but he noticed her interest and nodded when she commented on the poverty or pointed out a new example of squalor. After an hour on the road, they came to the first intersection with another road.

"Does this look like the where we turn?" He opened the door and stepped out.

"Hell if I know. He just said that when we got to the crossroad, turn right and go about four miles to the airstrip. I mean, how can anyone get lost in this place? There are only two roads."

"Yeah, I guess you're right. Well, we're a little early. That's good 'cause I want to look around a little when we get there," he said as he got back in the car. "I don't know what we're going to do if this piece of crap Pinto doesn't get us back to the port."

"We'll be fine. Look, I'm sure that if we have a problem with the car, Jose will help us."

They found the airfield as instructed after ten more minutes of driving. The road and the airfield ran parallel for two-hundred yards and then blended together for a quarter mile before end-ing. He drove to the end and stopped. Stepping out of the car, he removed the binoculars from his bag and he scanned the field. He couldn't have imagined a more ideal spot for an exchange. The airstrip appeared to have been groomed recently. It seemed natural, especially in light of their reason for being here, that in this place there would be a greater demand for a remote airstrip to be well-maintained as opposed to the roads.

"How does it look?"

"Looks to me like the perfect place to buy seven keys without anyone watching." "Let's do something with the car right now, just to get it out of the way."

He got back in and drove to a small grove of scrub trees that were at the other end of the airstrip, and parked the car beside the trees, camouflaging it. They waited without talking for twenty minutes. When the appointed hour arrived, both of them got out of the car, walked to the center of the air strip, and looked west.

"Look, there he is. Just like I said. Man, the guy is always on time."

"Is this guy rich enough to have his own plane?" asked John.

"Don't know. All the other meetings were at hotel rooms. He seems like someone who has a lot of money to me. I mean, just looking at his clothes, his jewelry. But I don't really know."

The Cessna flew in low but not low enough to land. It was two-hundred feet above them as it passed and the plane's right wing dipped twice before it began to rise at the end of the landing strip. It circled around while they moved off the runway. The plane landed from the opposite direction in which it had arrived. Once it reached the end of the runway, it circled around and taxied back to where they were standing. He saw a pilot and a passenger. The pilot left the engine running and waved at them, smiling. They watched as a small, black duffle bag was dropped from the passenger side and then a small boy, perhaps ten years old, hopped down from the same side and ran around the back of the plane, carrying the bag.

"Jose didn't show." She shouted over the roar of the engine.

"What should we do? This doesn't feel right."

She held up a finger and walked toward the boy who had stopped ten yards from them.

"Where the fuck is Jose?" The boy shrugged his shoulders and pointed at his stomach. She nodded and the boy handed her the black bag. She walked back toward John and motioned to him to follow her away from the airstrip.

They both knelt down and she unzipped the bag. "Something is weird here. I don't like that Jose didn't show up. Let me take a few minutes to check everything out. Leave our bag here. Look back at the plane, smile, give them a thumbs-up, and keep your eyes on them."

He did as instructed. The boy stayed in place and returned the gesture. She unzipped their bag and pulled out the small plastic testing kit. She picked out one of the seven blocks of product from the black bag and slipped a pen knife through the plastic wrap that protected it. She withdrew the pen knife from the block and dropped a thimble-sized portion into a test tube that was filled with a clear liquid. Then she poured another liquid into the test tube, corked it, and shook it gently. She smiled at him and held up the test tube, displaying the results, which were coffee colored, indicating that the purity was very high. She repeated this procedure on the remaining blocks. They were all of similar quality.

She motioned to him to lean over. "We got the good stuff. Give the kid the vest and let's go back to the ship. I'm hungry!" He slipped off the vest and threw it toward the boy. The boy took the vest and walked back to the plane. He couldn't see what was happening but after a minute, the pilot held up the vest in the window and smiled at John. The pilot busied himself with opening each section of the vest and thumbing through each stack of hundred-dollar bills. They saw him nod to the boy, whose feet disappeared from John and Wanda's view as he climbed back into his seat. He gave the same enthusiastic thumbs-up motion the boy had. The engine revved back up and the plane taxied to the end of the runway. It took off with both pilot and passenger waving to them.

"So is this the way it's supposed to go?"

She was kneeling down by their bag, transferring the blocks of cocaine from the boy's bag to theirs.

"Yeah. I'm just still not sure why Jose didn't show." She finished packing and stood up, holding the bag out for John. "Look, let's just go now. Everything's fine." He looked over her head at the plane.

"Wait just a second." He lifted his binoculars to watch the plane. A minute later he leaned toward her. "Something strange is happening."

"What?"

"They're not turning back to head home; they're flying low."

She took the binoculars and trained them on the small plane. "Could be going somewhere different, who knows?"

"Maybe." She watched and saw the right wing dip twice.

"Oh shit. You're right. They just signaled to someone on the ground."

"You sure?"

"No doubt about it." She handed the binoculars back to him.

"We've got to get out of here."

She started moving past him and he grabbed her arm.

"Hold on, let's think for a second."

"No time, we've gotta move."

"Wait. If someone is coming, we're screwed if we get back in that car and start driving. There are no other roads and who knows whether the piece of junk is going to fall apart."

"We got no choice. Let's get moving and maybe we can get some kind of jump on them."

"We're dead if we get in that car." He pointed to a group of ten palm trees that was behind them, one hundred yards from the runway. "Go over there, we need some cover." They jogged to the trees. "Gimme the phone."

"Yeah … but what're you going to do with it?"

"I'm going to get us another ride out of here." He punched in a phone number and put the receiver up to his ear. "Paul, hey, it's John. Yeah I'm fine, everything worked out with the guy you connected me with for the car and phone but look, the car is crap and broke down on us. We're stuck at some airstrip about twenty miles west of town. OK, so good, you know where it is. Can you send one of your guys to pick us up? Thanks, man, thanks. Great! Right, OK." He was silent for moment. "Sure, sure. I gotcha. OK, got it, fifteen minutes? Thanks, Paul. I owe you big for this one."

"Amazing. We're getting rescued by a helicopter, huh?"

"If we're lucky." He pointed to the sky. "You hear that?"

"Yeah. Sounds like the plane is coming back." They moved behind the palms. He saw the plane clear the trees at the far end of the runway.

"They're coming in too high and fast to land." Using the binoculars, he watched the boy tap the pilot on the shoulder and point back to the area where they had left the Pinto. They couldn't follow it from where they were hidden, but the engine noise faded away and after a few minutes, John came out from under the trees and found the plane with his binoculars, rising and shrinking as it flew west.

"Goddamnit. That fucking asshole set us up."

"OK, now let's just keep our heads."

"I'm betting that our friend arranged a special greeting party to meet us as we drove back to Cozumel."

"No shit."

"But they also could be coming here."

"I can't believe this is happening. What if I call Jose again and ask him a few questions?"

"That's a good idea. Go ahead and call now."

She dialed the number. "No answer. We're screwed if your friend with the helicopter doesn't it make here soon." They both watched the road. After two minutes, he tapped her on the shoulder and pointed up. He could hear the faint sound of a helicopter coming from the east. She watched the sky with a frown. Soon the helicopter was visible and they headed back out to the runway, waving their arms. The pilot landed a hundred yards away. John helped her climb in. He handed the bag to her and then ran around the front of the helicopter and climbed in beside the pilot. He smiled and shook his hand. The pilot handed him a set of headphones and motioned to him to put them on.

"Thanks, man. We are happy to see you!"

"No problem, my friend. This place may look a little barren, but someone would have come along and given you a ride or helped with the car. Paul said you guys were his good friends and that if you wanted to take a free ride around for fifteen minutes or so before we head back, that would be fine."

He stared out across the runway and the pilot accelerated the engine. The helicopter started to rise. "Uh, yeah, that sounds great. We were looking for a special area of Mayan ruins that is about ten miles west from here. Swing out that way and maybe we can still see it," requested John.

"There ain't any ruins in that direction, but if you want to go that way, it's fine with me." The pilot flew west for ten minutes. "See, man, I told you there's nothing out here."

John looked around. "Yeah, you're right. We must have misunderstood. Go ahead and take us back in." The helicopter turned and flew back toward the city. Their return flight path took them back over the airstrip, just as John had hoped. As they got closer, he motioned for her to look down. They both saw the dirty white van that was parked in the middle of the airstrip and the three men walking toward the Pinto. The men stopped and looked up as the helicopter flew over.

"See those guys?" The pilot, pointed down at the men. "They would've helped you with the car. Are you sure that you just want to leave it here?" He nodded. She turned as they flew over the men. The tallest one was carrying a sawed off shotgun. John turned back to her and she flashed a weak smile, wiping her forehead with her hand in mock relief.

* * *

The ship continued its journey back to Norfolk the next day. The seas were rougher and the skies less inviting than when they began the cruise. They had secured the product inside cheap, wooden sculptures of some Mayan God. To better insure their safety, they worked out a simple system that had one of them carrying the bag that held the product at all times. He knew cabin stewards were instructed to watch out for suspicious cargo. They met in his cabin just after dinner.

"I'm going to come to your cabin at midnight. I set it up so the girls will be with my mother."

"What?"

"We've got some work to do before we land in Norfolk tomorrow morning."

"What work? I'm going to be sleeping. Don't be waking me up on my last night at sea."

"We've got to make arrangements so that if the port authorities check us, they won't find anything."

"We did that already. The statues will keep everything safe."

"They're not enough. We're going to take it one more step."

"What?"

"We're going to dump everything overboard tonight."

She laughed. "Yeah, right. Drop our stuff in the ocean after we almost got ourselves killed. Good idea. Then we'll be safe but we got nothing to show for it. What kind of bullshit plan is that?"

"We're going to drop it off so that we can come back and get it."

"What do you mean? Let it float out in the ocean and we'll just scoop it up next time we're on the cruise ship?"

"No. We're going to sink it so that it stays on the bottom. Then we're coming back out on a boat to pick it up. Look at this."

He opened a large duffle bag that contained diving gear—masks, flippers, and snorkels. He dumped the contents onto the bed and unzipped a compartment on the bottom of the bag.

"What in the hell is that shit?"

"This is how we make sure we don't have anything to worry about with the port authorities. We take the statues and waterproof them." He lifted an electronic device the size of cigarette pack and held it out to her. "This is a signal beacon that we attach to each statue. I've got a receiver that can tell us where each signal beacon is." He reached into the bag and handed her an orange balloon that would be the size of a basketball when fully inflated. "These balloons are remotely inflatable so that when we pick up the beacon signal, we can inflate the balloon and then scoop up the package when it comes to the top."

"You're going to drop our shit overboard and then hope we can come back and find it just floating on top of the water?"

"Yes. It's the only way to be sure that nothing happens."

"Sounds a little messed up to me."

"It's safe. I've worked with this equipment before. I've spent a lot of time on boats, diving and fishing, and have used this equipment before to bring things back up to the surface. It works fine."

"You mean nothing is going to get lost?"

"Don't know that for sure. You want to lose a couple of kilos or get busted in Norfolk?"

"I don't want either one. You better tell me some more about this plan."

He sat on the bed. "Tonight, around 2 am, we'll be just off Cape Hatteras. You and I will prep all these items so they're secure. We'll go down to the lowest deck and drop each one in the water. It's good that the seas are choppy, that way no one will hear the splash."

"OK. I get all that. But you say we're just going to come back and get it?"

"Yeah. After we disembark in Norfolk, I'll make up something about you and I needing to go to Wilmington for a work emergency. My mom will take my car and the girls. We'll only be gone for one night. We'll drive down to Hatteras and get on a boat that I've rented and go out to pick up the statues."

"You're going to take me out on the ocean in some little boat you've rented?"

"It's not a little boat. It's a forty-foot, deep sea fishing boat. Like I said, I've spent a lot of time at Hatteras. My stepfather owned a big boat like the one we're using. We pretend we're going fishing, locate the product, and come home. Easy."

"You sure we just shouldn't try to do something else with the stuff? Sounds too risky to just throw it in the ocean and then hope we can find it."

"It has some risk, but less than other options I've considered."

"What about paying someone on the crew to bring it out for us? Don't you have some special connections or something?"

"No. Bad idea. They check the crew more than they do the passengers."

"Shit. Why didn't you tell me about this plan sooner?"

"Didn't matter. I knew you'd agree. Plus you don't know

anything about the port security in Norfolk. This is the only way. I figure that if we lose a couple of packages, we'll still be good."

"What if we lose all of them?"

"Won't happen. I know how these things work. You're going to have to trust me on this. It's the only way to be sure."

"Well if you say so. You've worked a few miracles already, so I guess this shouldn't be any different."

"Don't you guys have risks when you move product around on airplanes or by car? Didn't you say that people who transport the stuff count on a portion of it not getting past all the security, but you make enough money on it so it doesn't matter?"

"Yeah, that's right."

"So it's just part of the business, right?"

"Yeah, I guess you're right." She looked over at the small porthole that allowed the cruise line to charge twice as much as other cabins because it had a fabulous ocean view. "Is this little boat trip going to freak me out? I've never been out on the ocean except on this cruise ship."

"I doubt it. The weather's going to be better tomorrow. Taking out a boat like this is just like driving a car to me. You might even like it. Have you ever been fishing?"

"Sure, at a little lake with a cane pole and worms."

"Well maybe I'll even show you how to catch a tuna."

"You mean one of those big ass tunas? We can catch one of those while we're out?"

"Sure, you can catch a big one if you know what you're doing."

"Let's get it on then." Her face brightened. "My little girl will be so happy if I bring home one of those big fish. You ever been to that aquarium in Monterey California?"

"No, but I've heard of it. It's supposed to be a pretty neat place."

"Well Tonya and I've been there and she's seen some big tunas. Do they taste good, like can tuna?"

John smiled and shook his head. "So much better you won't even believe it. I cook them on the grill all the time. Best fish you can eat. Let's hope we have reason to celebrate and have a little tuna party."

* * *

The next morning, they made it down to Hatteras from Norfolk in two hours. His mother took the girls home from Norfolk and was elated to have them overnight at her home. He drove the rental car while she slept. They arrived at the Blue Marlin Marina in Hatteras at 11 a.m. and their rental boat pickup wasn't until one. John looked over at Wanda sleeping and his eyes began to feel heavy with the weight of the trip. Before long, he was asleep.

"Hey, John. John. John, wake up."

"Huh, what. What is it?" He bolted upright, rubbing his eyes.

"You're having a dream. Mumbling something."

"Hmm, can't remember."

"Is this the place where we get the boat?"

"Yeah. What time is it?"

"One-fifteen."

He put his glasses on and pushed open his door. "Damn. Come on, we've got to get going." He stood up beside the car and then leaned back inside the door. "You got your bag?"

"Sure."

"Stay here with the car. I'm going to take care of the papers for the boat."

He opened the back door and took a baseball cap out of his overnight bag. He needed coffee. Putting on the hat, he walked thirty yards to the marina office and store. Hatteras had only two marinas and he was known at both of them. He would have preferred to be anonymous and rent a boat somewhere else. Hatteras jutted out into the Atlantic, which made it the closest point to their drop site. He didn't have another choice. He pulled open a squeaky screen door and it slammed hard behind him.

A tall, sixty-year-old man with sun-ripened features and thick gray hair smiled at him. "Well, if it isn't the world's best fisherman. How ya' doin' my friend, John Manning?" Franz Koening owned the Blue Marlin Marina. He held out his large, rough hand

and John took it, patting John's shoulder as they shook hands. John had never seen him wear anything else except faded blue overalls and a white t-shirt.

"Hey, Franz, doing great. How 'bout you?"

"Just fine. Just fine. I saw your name on the rental list. You and Travis heading out to pick up a few tuna?"

"Nah, Travis isn't with me today. Taking out someone from my work. She's never been fishing before so I promised I'd take her. We've been working up in Norfolk. Figured I'd pop down and show her the ropes."

His smile broadened and he rubbed his chin. "Hmm, a lady friend from work. Sounds kind of interesting. Aren't you going to introduce me?"

"Can't do it today, Franz. And I can see your dirty mind starting to conjure up something that isn't there. We just work together. That's it."

"Hey, my friend, I'm not thinking anything. Great weather today, you know. Perfect for a romantic boat ride."

"OK, Franz, that's enough."

"Hey, maybe you could turn it into a moonlight cruise? Want to borrow some of my Barry Manilow tapes?" He snorted, slapping the countertop beside the cash register.

"Yeah right, Franz. Screw you." He pointed to a clipboard hanging on the wall. "Just give me the papers. I'm already late. Someday I may need your help with my love life, but not today."

"Just joking with you, my friend. Here's the paperwork. You know where to sign. What's up with Lucy? Travis?"

"Everyone's fine. I'm hoping I can bring Lucy down here next year. Don't think she's quite ready for the deep sea trip yet. Maybe some surf fishing. Travis is doing good too."

"Super. I look forward to meeting your little girl." He tore off the top copy of the form that John had signed and handed it to him. "Papers are all set. You're good to go, my friend."

"Thanks, Franz. Wish I could stay and chat a little more, but we've got to head out."

"No problem. Can I get you a bottle of red wine for the trip? Maybe some candles?"

"Yeah, man. I'm glad you're having fun with this. Remind me next time to just lie to you and say I'm going out by myself."

"I'll remember that. Have fun. The boat's all gassed up and ready."

He waved as he walked out. She was walking on the pier, looking at the boats.

"I said stay with the car."

"Ah! Damn, man. You scared me. Don't sneak up on me!"

"Sorry. I wanted you to stay in the car."

"I had to get me a look at some of these fancy boats. Look at these fish. That's a tuna, right?"

"Yep. Kind of a small one, though."

"You sure we'll catch one?"

He glanced at his watch. "Doubt we'll have enough time. Wind is light so we should make good time getting out, but we've got a lot to do. If we run out of time, we'll just buy one from someone here at the dock."

"Is it fun to catch them?"

"Yeah, but it's hard work."

"See that bright red one? That's us. Go ahead and get on board and I'll get the stuff from the car."

* * *

She peppered him with questions during the first half hour and he did the best he could to answer them over the roar of the engine. From a small drawer in the boat's cabin, she had found an old blue baseball cap with "Skipper" printed on it. She wore it during the last hour of the two-and-a-half hour trip while she drove with John standing close by. After taking a reading from the boat's GPS unit, he signaled to her to step aside and he took back the controls. He throttled down and put the engine into neutral.

"This is it. Keep your fingers crossed."

He took out the binoculars and the remote control unit. It powered up and he extended the antenna.

"Tell me again how you know how to use this thing."

"Well, actually, this is the first time."

"What! You said you knew about this stuff from being

around boats all the time, and fishing and diving."

"Yeah, that's how I found out about it, but I've never used it before."

"We've dropped all our shit in the ocean with some balloons attached to them and now you're telling me that this is the first time?"

"Just because I haven't used it before doesn't mean that it won't be fine. This equipment is the very best. I talked with a dozen different people before I bought it. The Navy uses the same stuff. They drop things from submarines and then a boat on the surface can pick it up later, you just need to know the GPS coordinates."

"OK, whatever. Navy, GPS, I don't know nothing about that stuff."

"One thing you should know by now is that I plan things out very carefully. Besides, do you think I want to lose anything?"

"Yeah, but, damn, I mean what if the water's too deep, or some fish eats the shit or something?"

"The water depth is fine, I know all about that from being here so many times. But there are some things that could muck this up. Things we can't control."

"Like what?"

"Like, I don't even know what. But wouldn't that be the case even if you were moving this stuff around some other way?"

She closed her eyes and took a deep breath. "Sure, I mean, yeah things can go wrong in a lot of places. Shit happens."

"Right. So relax. Let's see what happens." He turned back to the device, removed a well-worn piece of paper from his pants pocket, unfolded it, and placed it beside the device. It was a copy of the directions along with John's own notes scribbled in the margins. Running his finger down the page, he stopped at a line of five numbers and typed them into the keypad.

He held the unit out to her. "Here, you do the honors. Just push that green button labeled 'go.'"

"Sure."

She pressed the button and they walked to the back of the boat. Taking hold of the binoculars around her neck, Wanda put them up to her eyes and scanned the ocean.

"It'll take a couple of minutes to reach the surface."

A soft splash from behind caught their attention. John turned and saw the red balloon bobbing in the water, one-hundred-and-fifty yards from the boat. "Thar she blows. Didn't even need the binoculars."

She punched his arm. "Wow, you are one smart dude. We're right on top of the thing. Let's hurry up and get over there and make sure everything's cool."

It was. After they picked it up, John drove north for fifteen minutes. The second package presented itself less than one-hundred yards from the boat.

"Another bulls-eye," said John, throwing his hands up in the air.

"Can't believe it."

"Man, I didn't expect it to be this easy." She held up her hand and he reached over and tapped it with his fingers.

"Man, I'm going to have to teach you how to give a real high five. That was weak."

"I'm hoping I'll have five more occasions to practice."

The next three pickups were much the same, but they ran into problems with the last two.

"It's not happening on this one either. We did well on the first five, but something just didn't click on number six and seven."

"Hold on, I'm still looking."

"We're not going to have enough daylight. If we can't find this last one in the next ten minutes, we've got to head back in."

She lowered the binoculars. "Please, let's keep trying. If we don't, it's just like we left one-hundred grand out here in the ocean."

"It was bound to happen. We've done well."

"Come on John. Why don't you just turn on one of those big spotlights? That'll help us."

"Can't do that. No bright lights. It would draw attention."

"So we'll just come back in the morning, right? We know where to look now.

"They're lost. Didn't inflate. We did well."

"We gotta try something. Let's just make another circle. Please, we both need that money."

"Nope" He walked from the rear of the boat to the steering console and she followed him. "I tell you what. Let's get back in and go buy some tuna. I'll have you and Tonya come over for a tuna party. We'll cook it on the grill. We'll have a lot to celebrate in a few weeks. You said you've already sold pretty much all of it, so you and Tonya come over with the cash, and we'll celebrate."

"Sure. We'll have a tuna party. My little girl is going to be tickled about that."

"We'll celebrate our success, split up the cash, and then we'll be done. No more boat trips."

Her face tightened. "Done? You said we'd do this run again if everything worked out."

"I'm done. You sell what we have right now, we split the profits, and then we're done."

"Goddamnit, John! I can't believe that you don't see how good this can be for all of us. There's more money for both of us with another run." He turned toward her.

"Do you realize that we almost got killed? Cut this out. You and I will not be doing this again. Never. Besides, if you really wanted to, you could do this without me."

"Yeah sure. I'll just drop the shit off the cruise ship and rent me a big boat and come out here with my remote control balloons."

"A smart woman like you will figure something out." Wanda stared at him, expecting John to say more. "Yeah, there is something else." He pushed the throttle forward and the boat picked up speed. "Doesn't selling drugs bother you? Besides being illegal, it kills lives. I mean people lie, cheat, and steal to get drugs. It starts a bad cycle. I'm not saying I'm some kind of saint or something like that, but I think about stuff like that." He continued to look straight ahead, avoiding her gaze.

"Oh, good. So now, all of a sudden you got some morals or something." She put her hands on her hips and paused. "So, tell me this, you're a businessman right?"

"Yeah."

"So, I sell a product that's against the law. But I don't deal with the scum like crack heads and people that steal shit to buy dope. The folks that buy from me are kinda like you."

"Oh really?"

"Yeah. They want the stuff; they got the money, the fancy cars, so they buy it from me. I even got a few college kids from Duke buying from me. Some of those rich-ass college kids drive BMWs. I'm not putting a gun to nobody's head to make them buy the stuff. I'm just giving the people what they want."

"It's an interesting way to look at it."

"Hell, used to be you'd get busted for drinking a long time ago. Pot's against the law, but now they got people smoking it because the doctor says it helps people with their cancer. And all that shit about crime and people stealing to get drugs. So what?"

"What do you mean?"

"Think about it for a minute. If someone buys a plane ticket from you and they fly somewhere and steal something from someone, is that your fault? All you're doing is selling them the ticket. How they got the money to buy the ticket, that's not your concern, is it?"

"I guess not."

"And what they do while they're flying around, that's not your problem, is it?"

"No."

"So, I'm not responsible for how they get the money. That's their choice. I'm just giving them something they want and I get something I want. That's all it is. A business, just like any other."

"I'll give you credit for your argument. But there's something about your business that's very different from any other."

"What's that?"

"People get killed doing what you do. It almost happened to us in Cozumel."

"Hey, it's just a problem to be solved. Isn't that what you like to say?" He nodded. "So, what if I come up with a way so that it's not so dangerous for you?" He looked at his watch.

"Hey, look, just drop it. You're never going to convince me you can make it safer. You might be used to all this because you're in this business, but I'm not and I don't plan on getting used to it."
"Just, just do this. Think about it. Do that, alright? You owe me that at least."

"I'll think about it. Now let's get back home."

* * *

Two weeks later, Wanda and Tonya came over for dinner. As promised, John was making dinner and grilled tuna was on the menu. Since returning from the trip, Wanda had updated John twice on her sales efforts. Tonight, along with homemade coleslaw and rice, she had brought the black Nike bag back for John. It contained his portion of the money she had made from selling everything.

It was a sunny, mild afternoon and John and Wanda sat on the deck, watching the girls play in the backyard. The previous summer, he had installed a custom playground set that included three swings, a fort, two slides, a six-foot climbing wall, and a sandbox. Lucy and Tonya had settled on the swings; the sweet music of their laughter filled the backyard.

"That sure is one beautiful little girl you've got. I've always thought of Lucy as a little on the shy side, but whenever Tonya is around, my daughter's a different person. You're lucky to have her." He pulled a beer bottle from the cooler beside him and handed it to her.

"You know it," she said, opening the bottle and taking a long drink. "She's my precious girl. Best thing that ever happened to me, becoming a mom. Pretty weird, huh? All the wild shit I did, all the problems I had when I was young. Then along comes my little sweetie and everything seems good. Like the past kind of went away. Know what I mean?"

"I do. Kids have a way of wiping out the bad things. They make you focus on what matters, that's for sure." John took a drink from his beer, wiped his mouth with the back of his hand, and pointed to the Nike bag. "Anyway, let's talk about what happened." She smiled. "Worked out pretty much like I said. Didn't get quite as much as I thought for each, but we still scored big. I had to pay a little more than I thought to some dudes for connecting me up with the buyers, but that's cool."

"Hold on. What do you mean you had to pay a little more to some folks? You never told me about paying people."

Wanda twisted the bottle cap between her fingers. "I did tell you about this and it ain't that much compared to how much you're making."

"The way you're describing it sounds bad to me. You had to pay people for connecting you with people who bought the stuff. What's up with that?"

"That's the way it works. We talked about this while we were driving down to Hatteras. When someone hooks you up, you gotta give them a little piece, especially when you dealing with people you don't know. I had to sell the stuff as far away as possible from Durham so that nothing would get back to Jamel. I did one deal with some guy from Canada."

He leaned forward. "So break it all down for me."

"We had five keys. I sold them for around $45,000 each. So we're at $225,000 total. I had to pay the people who hooked me up with the buyers about $5000 each. That left around $200,000 after some other things I had to pay for. You get back the $35,000 that we used to buy the stuff, and then we split the rest. So you and I get around $80,000 each."

"Eighty-thousand for just a few days of work. I never would've believed it."

"Damn right. Now when are we going again?"

"I won't do this again. I can't go on another trip. That's it."

"We could make more. I know you need it."

"I'll figure out something else. I can't roll the dice again."

"Whatever. You're a fool if you turn your back on this thing. This can be a sweet ride for both of us. I've got to go to the bathroom. Which way?"

"Use the one upstairs. Just go up the steps and it is the first door on the left."

After she went inside, he pulled off his glasses, rubbed his nose, and wiped his eyes with the back of his hand. A creak signaling the opening of the side gate caught his attention, and then he heard a loud voice. "Well, hello, everyone!" Travis walked into the back yard.

"Uncle Travis! Uncle Travis!" Lucy squealed, running the short distance from the swing set to Travis. She jumped into his arms, almost knocking him down. “Will you come and play with us? I want you to push me on the swings. Really high, OK?” Lucy smiled and hugged him.

“You bet I will, my little Lucy.”

Tonya had walked a few feet from the swings. She stood behind a tree, looking at Lucy and Travis. John bounded off the deck and stood between Travis and the house. “Hey man, you should’ve called first. This is a bad time for you to be here.”

Travis stepped back in response to this sudden onslaught. “I-m, I’m sorry man. Hey, I just wanted to say hello to my sweet little Lucy. I won’t stay long.”

“You can’t stay at all.”

Travis nodded toward Tonya. “What’s up with Lucy playing with this girl? I didn’t know that you had these kind of-“

He pointed his finger at him and grabbed his arm. “Don’t you dare say it. Come over here.” He jerked him away from the girls and through the gate.

“I’ll be right back Lucy. Uncle Travis’ll be right back.” John let go of his arm Travis proceeded to rub the bicep.

“Tight grip there buddy.”

“Cut out this crap about blacks. You remind me so much of Hank sometimes. And I will not tolerate any of that crap around Lucy.”

“Chill man. I came to say hi to you and Lucy.”

“Look, this is a bad time for you to be here. Call me before you come over next time.” Wanda had returned to the deck and sat in a chair, watching them.

“Now, I don’t get this. Looks to me like you’re having a little dinner party. The table’s all set and I’m not even invited.”

“You gotta go. I’ll explain later.” He kept walking and pulling him along. They stopped beside his car.

“I’ll send Lucy out to talk with you because if I don’t, she’ll kill me. Don’t keep her long and don’t come back in.” He turned and began walking back to the house. “Look, I’m sorry I got a mad. You just surprised me, that’s all.”

“Whatever man. Just wanted to hang out with you guys.”

“Like I said, I’ll explain later.” Lucy was watching from the gate.

"Daddy, why can't Travis stay? He wants to have a tuna party too."

"It's just not a good time for Uncle Travis to visit right now baby. Why don't you go out and …"

"I'm not going to stay for the party if Uncle Travis can't stay!" she shouted. "If he can't stay, then I'm leaving," she huffed as she pushed the gate open, stomped past him, and then broke into a run when Travis waved to her and opened his arms.

John returned to the deck.

"Now this is a real surprise. Why didn't you ever tell me that you had a brother?"

He picked up his beer and sat down beside her. Tonya was sitting on her lap.

"Tonya, honey, I need to talk with your mommy about something just for a minute. Can you go back and play on the swings for a little while?"

"What about Lucy? Is she leaving with that tall man?"

"No honey. She's just talking to him for a minute or two. She'll be right back."

Wanda set her down and nudged her toward the swing set.

"I was embarrassed for you to know about my brother. That's why I haven't told you about him. His name is Travis."

"OK. Travis."

"It's like this. He's a bigoted … I'm mean he doesn't like Hispanics, blacks, or anyone else that isn't lily white."

She stared at him and leaned back in her chair. "That's it?"

"Yeah. I don't like his attitudes and I don't like Lucy being exposed to them. He picked it up from his childhood and I'm embarrassed he's never realized how wrong he is."

"What does Lucy think about him?"

"Thinks he's God. Loves to be with him. He feels the same way about her. He's a good person, it's just, like I said, I just feel embarrassed by his attitudes.

"How come you aren't the same way?"

"I guess we're just different. I don't know."

She shifted in her chair. "You sure what you're telling me

ain't the other way around?"

"What do you mean?"

"Maybe you're embarrassed to have Tonya and me around here and have him see us."

"That's crazy. I'm offended that you'd even say that. Don't you think that you would've notice by now if I was that way?"

"Probably, but you never can tell about people sometimes."

"I don't care what color someone's skin is and my Lucy is the same way."

She turned to look at Tonya playing. The gate opened and Lucy skipped through, breaking into a run when Tonya held her arms open. Both fell on the ground laughing upon Lucy's impact.

"What does he do?"

"He's an administrator for Durham County. He's the liaison between the county government and the Durham City police department."

"OK."

"He's just a paper pusher. He's the contact person for anyone in county government that has to deal with the police department and if the police department needs help from the county, they contact him.

"Oh."

"He goes to a lot of boring meetings and writes reports on what's happening. It's a crappy job, but he stays with it." He looked back over at the girls. They were out of hearing range. "He likes to jazz it up a bit with Lucy so you may hear her describe him as a policeman, but he's far from that."

"That's easier for Lucy to understand."

"And it sounds a lot more glamorous."

"That's true."

He sat forward in his chair and rested his elbows on his knees. "Except for this thing that I hate about him, he's a decent person. And, like I said, he loves Lucy as much as I do. He's not perfect, but he's my brother."

"Can we eat now? I'm starving."

"Sure. Get the girls and I'll get everything ready. I'm hungry too."

XIII – January 2002

Jamel trusted no one—especially his lieutenant, Roxx, who considered himself a lady's man. His typical response when introduced to new people: "The ladies like to spell my name with three 'Xs' because they say I'm a wild-ass, triple X ride!" which always elicited a round of laughter due to Roxx's appearance. At five-feet four-inches tall, and two-hundred-and-seventy pounds, with a well-shaved scalp, typically beaded with sweat, even in the winter, Roxx's comical physical presence seemed to magnify his lack of intelligence, and added to Jamel's distrust of him.

Jamel first hired Roxx in 1997. They had their ups and downs, as would be the case with most employer-employee relationships. The most difficult period between them occurred two years ago when Jamel discovered Roxx was diluting his product to increase his earnings. Jamel had always stressed to his staff that he wanted to distribute a high quality product. Jamel suspected Roxx wasn't following company procedures, so he had someone buy an ounce from him and tested it. Results showed that Roxx had cut the product by mixing it with 40 percent baby formula. As a result, Jamel calculated Roxx owed him $35,000 plus a penalty of 25 percent for damaging his reputation. Though Roxx proclaimed his innocence, he was persuaded to confess when Jamel produced a pizza cutter and indicated his intention to not-so-surgically remove Roxx's big toe with it. With his hands and bare feet bound to the folding chair he was sitting in, Roxx felt at a severe disadvantage and did his best to assure Jamel he would never violate company policy again. Jamel indicated his happiness with this confession, but rolled the pizza cutter across Roxx's left big toe anyway and, in the process, removed half of the toe next to it. This event sent a strong message to the rest of his staff that he would not tolerate this type of behavior. Jamel knew that any successful business needed to have discipline and strict enforcement of management directives.

A week after this encounter with Roxx, Jamel arranged for two additional salespeople to receive a special pizza delivery. First, he visited a local toy store and purchased a dozen large dolls just to cut the big toes off of each doll's foot. He then visited a pizza restaurant and paid the manager $100 to place the doll's toes on the two pizzas he had ordered for suspected staff members. After receiving the pizzas, Jamel noticed a definite change in all his staff members. His message had had its intended effect.

Since the toe and pizza incidents, Roxx had become very reliable and Jamel often delegated small tasks to him, most of which Roxx dispatched without error. So when Roxx brought the news to Jamel that a competitor had brought in a substantial amount of product, Jamel believed him. Roxx had come by Jamel's house at 10:30 p.m., with a bag of Taco Bell. He was one of a few people that knew where Jamel lived. Jamel took a taco from the bag that Roxx held out for him, and they both sat down on the couch.

"I'm a telling you Jamel, this is some serious shit. I heard it from two dudes now. They got their shit from someone over in Chapel Hill. They done told me that there's been a bunch of shit come into some people in Raleigh. I mean, I know this ain't where we sell most of our stuff, but you know there ain't been jack to speak of since them Arabs blew up New York. You gotta do something about this man."

"Shut the fuck up. I don't have to do nothing. Look who knows what's up, OK? Maybe somebody did manage to get some stuff into the area. Shit happens. It don't mean that someone's moving in on my city. Did you hear about anything happening in Durham?"

Roxx's cheeks bulged with food. He shook his head from side to side and wiped his mouth with his sleeve. "Nah man, but this is fucked up. You got to get some more info on this. If you don't, people'll start bringing that shit over here and then folks'll be saying you let them shit on you. You know what I mean? You can't let these fuckers just walk all over you."

"Shut your fat ass mouth. You ain't got the brains to start talking shit about how I run my business."

"I know man, I know. You the brains, I'm the muscle, right?

"Whatever."

"I mean, shit, man, I lose out too if someone starts moving in on Durham, you know? I'm just pointing out the obvious, bro."

"I told you never to call me 'bro'. Bro' rhymes with toe and you know that you don't want to be reminding me about that."

"C'mon dude. Don't be saying that shit. Just watching your back dude." Roxx's hand shook as he took a long drink of ice tea. He closed his eyes and took several deep breaths.

"Would you like it better if I didn't say anything about what I heard?"

"That's the first smart thing you've said. You need to be telling me shit like this, but don't be giving me your opinion on what should be done about it. Besides, we don't even know it's true. Where are the guys that told you about this new supply?"

Taco sauce dribbled down his shirt. "You know that fat bitch I've been doing the nasty with lately, Kaneesha?"

He nodded. "Well, we was in a bar and she recognized the dudes, said they were dealers. So I figured I'd see if he had anything to sell, you know, check out the competition. They told me they done sold out, and fast. They said they would be getting more from someone over in Raleigh, maybe in a week or so. Said to come back to the bar any Sunday night. If they had something to sell, they'd be in around midnight."

Jamel shook his head slowly. He picked up a napkin and cleaned his fingers. "I hope you asked them some more questions, like where'd they get it, and how much could they score for you."

"Of course, dude. I asked 'em all those questions. But you know how it is; they ain't giving up nothing about where they got the shit from. Nobody talks about that. But they told me the price. Get this: They're asking double the normal price for an ounce. I told 'em to fuck off, but they laughed and told me that was cool with them. They'd sold the last load they had so fast that they might be selling the shit for even more when I see them again."

"Anybody who can bring the shit into town can pretty much charge what they want," said Jamel.

"Uh, umm, I know, dude." He took a long drink of tea.

"You've got to get us some shit to sell Jamel. I mean, you scored a small load back in December, but we ain't had shit to sell since then. I've gotta make some money."

"So does everyone else."

"What's up with that? You got anymore coming?"

"Can't say for sure. The airports are locked down tight, and nobody can move the shit across the borders because they tightened them up so much since 9/11."

"What about scoring some weed? We could make a little on that."

"Fuck weed. I ain't going back to selling that nickel and dime shit. I've come too far to go back to hassling with that low dollar shit. And don't let me hear about you or anyone else selling weed."

"Sure man, sure. I'm just trying to come up with something."

"Don't think. It ain't what you're good at. Leave that to me." He watched him and waited a minute. "Gotcha. Look, I gotta get my ass back to my crib and get some sleep."

"Uh, what man? What did you say?"

"I'm leaving."

He waved his hand at the door. "Yeah, man. Here, take this trash with you when you go. Every time you bring that shit over, my damn house smells like Taco Bell for three damn days."

He huffed and gathered the remains of the meal and then stuffed the remaining half of a burrito in his mouth before leaving.

Jamel slumped down onto the sofa and put his feet up on the coffee table. One thing about Roxx: He was too stupid to be a talented liar. He heard a similar story from another employee. He needed to find out who was bringing in the product and then deal with them if they tried to sell in Durham. He had fended off competitors before, so he wasn't concerned about that; he was more interested in who their supplier was and how he could hook up with him. Maybe he could strike some sort of bargain and get connected to their supplier. But that could be dangerous. He'd look desperate, which he was, but it wouldn't help his business for others to know. Since 9/11, he'd only brought in one small shipment. His frequent email inquiries to suppliers since October had continued to bring the same response: nothing available, too dangerous, forget it, etc. Lately, several of them quit responding. He had plenty of money saved in a Bahamian bank and planned for the day when he would leave Durham completely. He never imagined his supply would dry up. Even if he'd saved enough already, he wasn't ready to retire. The last two years had been especially lucrative. He swung his legs around onto the couch and stretched out, lacing his hands behind his head and staring at the ceiling.

* * *

Two days later, Wanda waited in McDonald's for Roxx. She despised him but she found it useful to pretend otherwise. He was a reliable source of information and because he was the closest person to Jamel, he could often tell her what was on Jamel's mind. She knew Jamel would find out someone was bringing product into the area. Because of this, she had taken great care to sell to sources outside of North Carolina. Still, she knew that some of it would find its way back here. If Jamel was on the hunt for the source of the new supply, Roxx would know. She watched him walk in. He waved at her, pointed to the short line of customers waiting to place orders, and rubbed his stomach. Wanda smiled. After a few minutes, he arrived at the table with a loaded tray.

"Wanda! Hey there, baby. Ain't you gonna have something to eat?"

"No thanks." She smiled as he set his tray on the table. On it were three Big Macs, two large fries, a large shake, and a large Coke. He couldn't fit into a booth, so they sat at a table near the children's play area.

"Damn, honey, you're looking skinny. You lost some weight?"

"Yeah, I guess I have dropped a couple of pounds. I haven't been eating here as much as I use to. I see you got the usual."

He looked down at his tray and then back at her. "Nah, I've been cutting back myself. See usually I get three fries, but today I only got two. Maybe you can tell that I dropped a couple of pounds too?" He laughed and slapped the table next to them so hard the salt and pepper shaker fell off. "That's some funny shit, now ain't it? Me dropping a few pounds. Ain't that some funny shit to think about!"

"Yep, that's some funny shit." She watched him pick up the first Big Mac and take a bite.

"Why do you stuff those things in your mouth like that? If you don't quit eating like that, some day you're gonna choke to death on a damn Big Mac."

He rubbed his shirt sleeve across his mouth. "Guess if I die that way, I'll die a happy man!" Bits of lettuce and bread slipped out of the corner of his mouth as he smiled at his own joke. "So what's up with you? How's business?"

"Don't ask me dumb shit like that. You know there ain't no business to be done."

"Just asking, that's all."

"You got any idea when Jamel's gonna have some shit to sell?"

"Maybe soon, not sure. Went by his crib last night."

"How's he doing? Was he in a good mood?"

"Ha, now that's some more funny shit. He ain't never in a good mood. You heard about what's been happening?"

"Yeah, I heard some shit's been getting in. Haven't heard anything about Durham. You heard anything?" He chewed and shook his head. She looked away again.

"Nah. Durham's still dried up. Some shit landed in Chapel Hill, maybe Raleigh." You can bet it's heading this way." He stuffed a dozen french fries in his mouth. "Jamel'll shit his drawers when it does. You know he don't like folks bringing stuff into his town."

"I heard the shit's been coming in from Richmond."

"Richmond, huh? Now I ain't heard that. You gotta name?"

"No name. You know how people are. They don't say shit when they don't have to." She looked down at her watch.

"You in a hurry, baby?"

"No. I'm mean I've got leave in little while."

"Ain't you gonna get something to eat? You want some fries?"

"Sure, I'll take a few."

"So someone's been moving shit down here from Richmond." Roxx smiled and wiped chocolate milkshake from his chin with his sleeve.

"That's just what I heard. You know how the shit goes, you hear it from one person, no big thing, but then someone else says it, then maybe you start believing it."

"Maybe you and I should try to score some shit from Richmond. You know how desperate everyone is. We could rake in some fuckin' cash, huh?"

"You lookin' to lose another toe?"

"Hell no. I ain't gonna lose shit. If Jamel tries some shit like that on me again, I'll put a cap in his ass so fast he won't know what hit him."

"Now I'd like to see that, Roxx. I didn't know you could do anything fast."

"You just watch me." He belched and rubbed his stomach. She flapped her hand in front of her face.

"Thanks, dude. You just fucked up my appetite."

He snickered. "Now let's get back to you and me getting some dope on our own."

"No thanks. I wouldn't do that to Jamel. He's an asshole, but he's been there for me a couple of times. Anyway, don't you think he'll get us some stuff soon?"

He shrugged his shoulders. "Everything's been fucked up by all this 9/11 bullshit. Someone needs to waste those Arabs that did this shit. Then we can go back to business."

"Why don't you do it Roxx? You can put a cap in someone's ass so fast they won't know what hit them."

"Damn right! Let's you and me both go. We could both kick ass and then we'd be fucking heroes. Clinton could give us a medal."

"Clinton's gone dude. Look, don't be saying anything to Jamel about what I told you."

"What do you mean?"

"The thing about Richmond. Keep it between you and me." She pushed the table back and stood up.

"Oh you know I ain't gonna say nothing. Everyone knows Roxx keeps his lips sealed." He looked down at the empty wrappers on the table. "Unless he's gotta couple of Big Macs in front of him!" His enormous stomach shook the table. "Damn, that's some funny shit. Chris Rock ain't got shit on me, huh? Ain't I the funniest dude you've ever met?"

"Yeah, man, whatever. You keep me laughing"

He grabbed her hand as she started to leave.

"Hold on now, baby. Why don't you and me get together later tonight? Maybe have a little Jack and Coke, smoke some weed. You know I get even funnier when I get a little wasted."

She pulled her hand away. "Nope. You be good now."

"Damn, baby, you're always just teasing. You know you're so fine."

She turned and walked toward the door, flapping her hand over her shoulder to dismiss him.

XIV - February 2002

Every first Tuesday of the month, John took Mary to lunch to discuss the business, review a few reports, and make some decisions about the future. Mostly they talked about the staff. He depended on her to keep him updated on how everyone was doing. She would fill him in on how each person was performing, who might be having personal problems, and how everyone was getting along in the office. He thought of her as his secret agent, but double agent might have been a better description. She kept him posted on important staff matters, but she did so carefully and never revealed her sources. She kept the confidence of all the staff members. As a result, he always concurred with her suggestions about hiring and firing. She had never been wrong.

"How about those sales, huh?" she smiled. "I've got someone in mind who wants to come back to work."

"Hey! Mary, John, how you guys doing, huh? Having that power lunch meeting, eh?" asked Papa, a short and stocky fifty-five year old Greek man with a dark complexion and heavy eyebrows, who owned the restaurant. John was amazed at how Papa managed the place. The restaurant was always packed, but he only ever noticed Papa, his wife, daughter, and son-in-law working.

"Yeah, Papa. Gotta run the business, right?"

"You know it, John. How's that little Lucy doing?"

"Oh, she's the same. Way too smart for me."

"Smart is good, my friend. I'll take smart any day."

"Listen to what she said to me a few days ago. She was bringing up her current favorite subject, which is that she wants a sister right away. So I try to change the subject, but she looks me straight in the eye and says, 'Now Daddy, I don't think that talking about my school right now is relevant.'" They both laughed. "I mean, where in the hell do they pick up these words? Relevant? I didn't know the meaning of that word until high school."

"Hah, that Lucy is a hoot!"

"We all know that Lucy is brilliant, but she just heard that on some TV show," said Mary.

"Maybe. She just slings these words and phrases out all the time and they are almost always, well, you know, relevant."

"Good one, John. So guys, what can I get you for lunch today?"

"Just give me my usual Papa," said Mary.

"I'm gonna pass on my usual Papa. Just bring me the Greek salad."

He leaned in. "What, no Gyros platter with fries?"

"Can't do it anymore. Got my mom and Lucy telling me I'm fat." He patted his stomach. "Dropped six pounds so far."

Papa stood back up and smiled. "I thought so." He rubbed his hands on his apron and looked over his shoulder at a couple standing by the cash register. The loud crash of plates breaking on the floor made everyone look toward the kitchen. Silverware chimed as it bounced on the tile floor.

"Damn that son-in-law. I'm spending more on broken dishes now than I ever have."

"Aren't you Greeks known for smashing dishes?" asked Mary.

"Gotta go, guys. You want sweet tea, right?"

"You bet," said John. "A guy can only cut back so much."

He left without responding. She picked up a report and turned it for him to read.

"Sales are coming back."

"I know. What's making it happen?"

"Not sure. I guess everyone's catching up on those missed vacations." Papa's wife placed two glasses of tea in front of them.

"How's the morale been lately?"

"Couldn't be better, really. You've been helping."

"I'm not sure I've been doing anything different."

"You're more relaxed. Everyone can tell."

"I always feel better when sales start to pick up."

"I know that, but you've been less stressed ever since you got back from your trip last month."

"You're right. I had to tap into the Russia fund two months ago but I replaced most of what I took out last week."

"Now I see. I knew things were bad, but I didn't know you had to do that."

"It's always like this. The fourth quarter is terrible, even more so this year. Then I worry and fret, and then we get busy."

Looks to me like we're even running ahead of last year." She paused to let him look over the figures in her report. "Things are better. So should we bring Susan back?"

"I thought you'd wanted Eve to come back."

"No. Eve's great but she's more tied up with taking care of her kids now. Susan's called me once a week since you laid her off in November."

"I like to hear that. She's ready to get busy, huh?"

"No doubt about it. She needs money."

"Yeah, go ahead and get her started right away. She can keep the same salary."

"You need to sit down with her and explain the monthly bonus calculation."

"Did she ever make a bonus last year?"

"I think so. She had a couple of good months last spring."

"I'll make sure she understands how to figure things out. We need people that want to make money." Papa returned with their food.

"Looks like you haven't eaten since last week."

"Feels that way to me."

"You said you lost six pounds. How long has it been?"

He raised a finger in front of his mouth as he chewed lettuce and feta cheese.

"Two weeks."

"It gets easier as you go on. Hang in there."

"Hope so. Gotta tell you something else important."

"What's up?"

"I'm going on another cruise this month. Not sure when."

"That's a bad idea. Things are going to get busier."

"Maybe."

"What could be so urgent about going on a cruise?"

"I didn't say it was urgent. Just important."

"So it is the same stuff as last trip. You scouting out spots for groups?"

"Yeah. I'm going to grow our group business this year."

"What's the big deal about groups?"

"Since 9/11 and all this terrorism crap. People want to feel safe. Groups are safe."

"Why not just fly down to the Caribbean? You won't be gone as long."

"Could do that, but we're also going to be doing cruise groups. I need to market the fact that I've checked out these ships."

"OK. You know what you're doing."

"Thanks. This is important. We're all going to make more money by heading in this direction. Groups have always been the way to make good money, but now the demand will be greater. Besides, people can book their own trips without us now, but no one would dare try to book a group trip without help from an agent. We've got to position ourselves in places where we still bring value to the customer. Group travel is a great place for us."

"Are you going to take Lucy and your mom this time?"

"Doubt it. I can do more by myself."

"When do you think we'll start selling these trips?"

"Not sure. Doesn't matter too much right now because we're so busy anyway, right?"

"Can you wait to leave until Susan starts back?"

"Probably. But you said she's ready to go, right?"

"Yeah, but you know how things are. It might be a few weeks before she can start and then I've got to get her back up to speed."

"It won't take that long."

"Just give me a little advance notice this time, huh?"

"You bet. Let's get going. I've got tons going on today."

She frowned. "You scarfed down your food in five minutes and now you won't even wait for me to finish?"

"They'll put that in a box for you. I'm sorry, dear, but I do need to go."

"We didn't even talk much about the business."

"I know you'll let me know what's going on. Besides, we can't do anything major right now with so much business coming in. Next month we'll talk more." He dropped his napkin on the table and stood up.

* * *

After work that same evening, he met Wanda in the McDonald's parking lot to inform her that another trip was necessary. He would not, however, take on the same amount of risk. He knew her enthusiasm to make another run was still high and that would be his leverage. A light snow was falling as he reached over to open the passenger door to let her in.

"Damn, I hate this cold weather. I need the Caribbean sun."

"I guess your car's not the best for cold weather either, huh?"

"You're right. But it's worth it because I love to put that damn top down when it gets warm." She took her off her coat and placed it on her lap, brushing off a few remaining snowflakes.

"Did you get a new haircut or something?"

"Sure did. What do you think?" She lifted her chin, and brushed her hair back with both hands.

"I'm not much on judging hair styles, but it looks pretty good." She pulled down the visor and looked in the mirror.

"I've decided to start dressing better and making sure I look good. Never know when you're going to run into the right person, huh?"

"I guess so. I don't have much time. I'm just here because you're such a pest about this second trip."

"I know, but you got to think about this. You need some more cash. I need more cash. Together we can score on this thing again."

"I've been checking out some other places to get the money. I don't know if they are going to work out or not, but I can't take the risk of going on another trip with you." He glanced sideways and watched her take a deep breath and tighten her grip on her coat.

"OK, then. Here's my plan." She paused. "I'll do everything."

"What do you mean by that?"

"Just what I said. I'll do everything. I just need you to drop the stuff in the water and then drive the boat from Hatteras to pick it up."

"That's a nice offer, but I'm still going to pass."

She shook her head. "I don't think you're hearing me. You don't have to do anything. I'll bring the cash we need. I'll set up the meeting. You stay on the boat. I'll make the buy. We ride back on the boat, you pack it all up and drop it in the water, like before. We go to Hatteras, jump on the boat and go back out to get the stuff. I'll drive it back here and sell it. I'm gonna buy more than last time. It'll be a bigger score for both of us."

He shook his head and looked at his hands. "Can't do it. But still, tell me why you would go through what happened to us in Cozumel again? You got a death wish?"

"That won't happen again. I've got things covered."

"How do you have it covered?"

"If you're not going, then why does it matter to you?" She leaned back against the seat, easing the grip on her coat.

"Just curious, that's all. Honestly, I've never been that close to having my face blown off by a sawed off shotgun, so I'm wondering why you would take that chance again."

She rolled her eyes and shook her head. "Don't be such a damn drama queen. I've been doing this a long time and what we saw when we were flying over those guys does not mean they were going to blow us away. I'm going to make the swap in a restaurant or a hotel, you know, a place with people around. The guy who's selling me the stuff wants it that way too."

"So, you just get your face blown off in front of a lot of people?" She shifted in her seat and turned toward him.

"You aren't thinking about things in the right way. Sellers are nervous too. They're walking around with this stuff that's worth a lot of cash. They want to meet in a safe place too. And you aren't thinking like a good businessman. What do you think these sellers have on their mind besides not wanting to get ripped off?"

"Making money?"

"Yeah, but not just one time. They want repeat business, same as you. So if you convince them you know what you're doing and you pay them a fair price, then they want you to think of them when you're ready to buy some more, see?"

"OK, thanks for the Business 101 lesson. I get it." His stomach growled and he tightened his coat around his waist.

"Wow! That was loud. You want to go in and get some food?"

"No thanks."

"I thought that you loved McDonald's."

"Oh, I love McDonald's. I've just been cutting down."

"I noticed you've dropped a few pounds. Your face looks thinner."

"Thanks for noticing." He rubbed his chin and neck.

"Anyway, what I was saying is that I'll just convince them I'm going to be a good customer and I'll meet them in a public place. That way they'll be safe and I'll be safe." She smiled and brushed a strand of hair from her eye. He was warm, so he opened up his coat and pulled out his left arm. When he shifted to take out his right arm, she held the sleeve for him. He gave her a quick smile and a nod, then tossed the coat into the back seat. "So that's it. All you've got to do is what I told you. I'll take all the chances. You'll get a fair share, and we'll both have the cash we need."

"It's not a bad idea. But I don't want you to think for a minute that I'm willing to do it."

"I hear you. It's cool. That's why I told my seller about how we did things last time. He offered to hook me up with someone who knows how to do all the stuff that you did. I'd just have to pay him for the help after we scoop up all the stuff off Hatteras. He says his guy can even take care of getting the boat. All these dudes have connections with people in the Bahamas, so my seller says his guy can just drive his boat up from there and pick me up in Hatteras. The way I got it figured, I'll come out better by paying him than if I gave you a fair split anyway."

He chuckled. "You know, Wanda, you're a terrible liar."

She smiled and turned back to him. "No, man, I'm a great liar. I'm the Bill Clinton of liars but this isn't a lie. If you don't want to partner up with me on this, then I've got to find someone who will. Hope you don't mind that I'm using your idea about the cruise ship and all that. I'll throw you a little bone when I get back from the trip for teaching me what to do."

He picked up a napkin from the cup holder and began clearing the foggy windshield.

"I was thinking about going the last week of February. My Tonya's off school that week for Spring Break. Seems like a good time for both of us to go, don't you think?"

"Please don't tell me you're thinking about taking her again. How in the world are you going to manage with her tagging along?"

"I'm not worried. They got those Kiddie Camp things going on while you're cruising. I'm just gonna set her up with one of those for the few hours while I make the buy."

"And when you get back and drive down to Hatteras to take the boat ride with one of your new friends. What happens then?"

"I thank you for being so worried about me and her. My baby will be safe and sound back here in Durham while I go get the stuff from Hatteras. I was thinking that maybe you wouldn't mind picking her up at Norfolk when we get back and she could stay with you and Lucy for a night or two." She smiled, reached down for the last napkin in the cup holder and cleared the windshield on her side. A full moon shone through the thinning clouds, making the snow on the hood of the car sparkle.

"I'll need to get the same split as last time if I go with you."

Her eyes widened in mock surprise. "Now that don't seem fair. I'm the one who's putting up the cash and taking all the chances. Your split should be more like 35 percent."

"Don't be silly about this. Hell, you'll end up with nothing when they leave you at the dock or worse yet, throw you overboard and run off with your product."

"I'm glad for you to be involved, but you've got to contribute a little more if you're expecting to get the same split as before."

"I'll get my mom to take care of both the girls. Lucy's on break that week too. It's stupid to take them. That oughta be more than enough for me to get the same split."

She nodded. "Hmmm. So your mom won't mind taking care of both of them?"

"She'll love it."

"I'd feel OK about not taking her if she was with your mom." She rubbed the back of her head. "Well, then, I think we got ourselves a deal!" She laughed and reached to pat John's hand, which was resting on the steering wheel. John jerked his hand away just before she touched it.

"Whoa, you startled me." He used the same hand to straighten his glasses and smooth over his hair. "I guess we do have a deal." He looked at his watch. "I've got to pick up Lucy from my mom's. I'm already a little late."

She returned her hand to her lap. "OK."

"Here, let me help you with your coat."

"No, thanks, I got it. It's OK," she said, leaning toward the door.

"I'll make the reservations for us, OK? We can use the same schedule as last time. Maybe leave on the Saturday or Sunday after the girls start their Spring Break. How's that sound?"

"Yeah, that's perfect. You sure your mom will be OK with this?

"She'll be fine, I know it. She can handle it."

"OK. Just let me know when you get everything set up."

"Hey, look, I got a bunch of cruise brochures in the back seat here. I had to drop some off at the Woodhaven Retirement Community yesterday. We get a few groups from that place." John turned and grabbed five brochures from the back seat. He thumbed through them and handed a Golden Line brochure to Wanda.

"Take one. You'll need the itinerary to coordinate your meeting. If I were you, I'd try to get it set up for St. Thomas. There's a Holiday Inn there with a patio restaurant overlooking the ocean. Good spot for your meeting."

"I saw one of these on the last trip. I can't make sense out of this thing."

He took the brochure, turned through a few pages, and held it out to her. "Here's the ship we're taking and here are the port stops on this side of the page. We'll leave on Saturday, the twenty-third, and then we'll be in St. Thomas on the morning of the fourth day, which is the twenty-sixth. Tell your guy to meet you at the Holiday Inn around lunch time on that day. The ship will be in port the whole day." He took out a pen and circled the appropriate day. He also added 'Holiday Inn – 12:00 noon.' "Here you go."

"OK. Let me know when you get everything arranged. I'm going to wait to tell Tonya about it. You know how those six year olds are. You can't tell them about anything fun in advance or they just bug you thirty times a day asking if it's time yet."

"Good idea. I'll do the same with Lucy."

"Alright, then. I'll see you later." She opened the door and got out. He watched her until she was inside her car, then he pulled out of his parking space. She stopped and waved from just inside the door and he waved back.

* * *

A week later, Roxx knocked on Jamel's door. The window curtain near the door moved, but the door remained closed. "Roxx, I told you not to come over here unless you call me first. Get the fuck outta here."

"I'm sorry, man. There's something kinda messed up goin' on and I can't figure this shit out." He held up a box of doughnuts. "Hey, I brought you some Krispy Kremes." He removed a doughnut from the box and jammed it into his mouth. "This is some shit you're going to want to hear."

"You alone?"

"Yeah. I wouldn't bring no one else over here." Roxx heard the lock click open. Jamel slowly opened the door, peering over Roxx's shoulder in the process.

"Get your ass in here. Don't ever just show up like this again."

"Sure, sure man. You know I wouldn't be coming over here unless it was something important." Roxx stepped inside, holding out the open doughnut box.

"Get that shit away from me. I can't eat one now 'cause I've got to look at you with all that sugar smeared all over your face. Damn, man, you are one disgusting pig. How many times do I have to tell you, someday all that fat ass food you eat is gonna kill you."

"Oink, fucking oink, my friend," replied Roxx with a smile, stepping into the living room.

"Don't sit down. Whatever you've got to tell me make it quick."

"Dude, your house is always clean as hell." Jamel flapped his hand in the air, motioning for him to get on with the news.

"Well, here's the deal. I went over to Wanda's house a few days ago. Just wanted to check in on her, you know, see how she's doing and shit. I don't see her that much anymore, you know, being that we don't have nothing to sell we ain't got much to talk about. But anyway, I was over there and she was all happy and smiling like maybe she'd won the lottery or something. So I go in and she even offers me a sandwich." He looked at the couch and bent over to rub his right knee.

"I gotta sit down. You know my knee's been bothering me something awful." Jamel rolled his eyes and nodded toward the sofa. Roxx eased into the sofa and continued to rub his knee.

"Well I'm sitting there eating and she's talking on about how happy she is 'cause she decided to take a vacation and she ain't had a vacation in a while. Says she's going to Mexico 'cause it's cheap. Says she scored a free ticket from some guy she knows that works for American Airlines out at RDU. When I ask her if Tonya is going, she says she don't know yet, but probably not. Wanda says she just wants to go by herself, just chill and shit. So I'm going along, you know, listening to her. I even ask her a couple of questions about where she's going to go in Mexico. She says she ain't decided yet. She's got tickets to Mexico City so she figures that she can fly there 'cause it's in the middle and then she can go to maybe, Ocopooco, or someplace like that or maybe Cancun."

"It's A-ca-pul-co, not Ocopooco, you dumb shit."

"Whatever dude, you know what I mean. Anyway she's all excited and I start asking her how she's got the money to be going on a vacation when we ain't had shit to sell for so long. She just smiled and said it wasn't going to cost her much 'cause she had a free ticket, and she was just going to stay in some cheap hotels while she's there." Jamel reached over for the doughnut box. Roxx handed it to him after taking out two more for himself.

"So? Wish I could go somewhere warm. I'm sick of this fucking cold ass weather."

"I know, man, I know. I didn't think much about it either. But then, all of a sudden, I had to take a wicked dump. You know that feeling like when you ate way too much pizza or chicken or something the night before and your stomach just tightens up and you know you gotta make a run for it?"

"Goddamn, Roxx. Look, it's hard enough watching your fat ass eat. I don't want to know anything about how the back half of you works."

"Sorry, man. Anyway, I go back to Wanda's bathroom and get all settled in, you know? So I'm sitting there, just getting things done and I'm wanting something to read. So I'm looking around the toilet trying to see if she's got any magazines or anything and then I find this cruise book lying underneath some newspapers beside the john. So now I'm thinking about a vacation, 'cause you know, I've always wanted to go on one of those big-ass cruise ships. You know they let you eat all the food you want and I heard that …"

"Get to the point."

"OK, OK, so I start looking through this cruise book, I think it was called the Golden Cruise ship, or something, and then I get to this page where they have the places that the boat stops at. And one of the stops is circled and there's writing beside it. There's this circle around some place call Street Thomas which is like below Jamaica …"

"Not Street Thomas, you dumbass. It's Saint Thomas. The S-T-period stands for Saint, not street."

"Yeah, yeah, OK, Saint Thomas. I've heard of that place. Well this writing ain't Wanda's. You know how she writes, it's real neat and pretty, like the way most girls write. Only this writing is sloppy, kinda hard to read. But it says 'Holiday Inn, twelve noon.' So I'm looking at this, and then realize this trip is at the same time as Wanda's trip to Mexico. I mean the date that's circled is February 26, which is next week. So she's been just running on and on about some fucking vacation to Mexico, and here she is planning on going on a cruise."

Jamel shook his head slowly. "But you just said it wasn't her handwriting. How do you know this has anything to do with her? She could have just picked up this cruise book anywhere."

"I thought about that. But beside this writing there's this big long arrow pointing to another spot on the page that says 'J.Z. confirmed' and this is Wanda's handwriting. So I'm sitting there, finishing up my dump and then I'm thinking, damn, what's all this shit about? Is she going to Mexico or is she going to Saint Thomas? So I'm fucking cool about it when I go back out. She makes me another sandwich and she's saying all this shit in Spanish like 'Ola' and 'Grayshous,' saying that she's got to practice for her trip and everything."

"Big fucking deal. Maybe she don't want you or anyone else to know that she's going somewhere different."

"Maybe. But then why does it matter so much? Why not just say that you're going out of town or something, not be talking about one vacation when you're going on another. It's kinda fucked up to me, man."

"Did she say anything else?"

"Yeah, she did. She asked me for the third fucking time if I was sure that I didn't say anything to you about how she heard that the shit that's been coming into town was coming from Richmond. You remember how I told you about that?"

"Yeah." He walked into the kitchen, opened the refrigerator and reached in for a Diet Coke. He rolled the cool can back and forth across his forehead, then opened and drank half of it.

"Roxx, you shouldn't try to think so much, man. This ain't nothing. Who the fuck knows why Wanda is saying all this shit?"

He shrugged his shoulders. "I don't know, man, I don't know. Maybe she could score some free tickets to Mexico, but these cruise ships take some big time cash. If she's going on a cruise, where the hell is she coming up with the cash? I asked somebody who knows, man and they said a week on a cruise ship would set you back three or four large, maybe more if you get some nice room on the boat."

Jamel sat down in a chair across from Roxx, and stared out the window behind him. "Maybe you're right. I ain't had anything for her to sell in a long ass time. It does seem a little fucked up that she'd be spending a bunch of cash on a cruise."

"That's what I've been thinking too. You know Wanda, she's a smart lady and all, but there ain't no way she's saved enough cash to get through this dry spell we've been having. And then she's going on some cruise ship? No way." Roxx pointed at the Diet Coke can and then to himself. Jamel nodded and flicked his hand in the direction of the kitchen. Roxx walked to the kitchen and returned with his drink.

"Whoa. Don't sit back down again. You can head on out now, I've got some shit to do."

Roxx frowned and shook his head. He reached into the doughnut box and removed the last two. "No problem dude. Ain't you gonna thank me for fillin' you in on this shit with Wanda?" He shook his head and pointed toward the door. "Don't seem like nothing special to me. You should just forget about it."

Jamel watched from behind the curtain as Roxx got in his car and drove away. Then he picked up the empty donut box, dropped it into the trash, and grabbed another Diet Coke before sitting down at his computer. He had become adept at using the computer because it helped manage his enterprise and offshore bank accounts.

The Internet also helped him track several of his employees. None of them had any computer proficiency, so Jamel showed seven key employees how to communicate via email. From Durham's main library, Jamel demonstrated how they could get on the Internet and secure a free email address from Hotmail or Yahoo that could never be traced back to them. He tested these employees by sending them a message, which they had to retrieve and reply to in order to receive a small bonus payment. This training period went on for three months. Since he was involved in the initial set up of their email account, he also knew their password, which allowed him to log into their email account and check their "received" and "sent" mail whenever he deemed necessary. As he had anticipated, none of them had taken the time to change their initial passwords.

He had begun this instruction two years ago and to date, only three of the seven employees had continued to use their email accounts with any regularity. One of those three was Wanda.

Wanda quickly adapted to using email to communicate with her customers. Following Jamel's instructions, she used special codes to discuss items of importance. Most importantly, she never reference meeting dates and times in writing.

He logged into her email account and opened her "sent mail" folder, which he sorted to show the most recent messages at the top. Over the past two days she had sent five messages to "JZ-transport@yahoo.com." The most recent one was short and sweet: "Got your message JZ. Will see you at the Holiday Inn at 12 on the day we talked about. Looking forward to some warm weather and a profitable business relationship. Thanks, W." He threw the Coke can, spraying its contents against the wall. Then stood up and paced in front of the computer, before settling down to do some more research.

Through the Internet, Jamel found the itinerary for the cruise that Roxx had described. Shortly thereafter, he had reserved a First Class seat on American Airlines to arrive in St. Thomas one day prior to the arrival of the cruise ship and return home two days after that. He might as well combine a little business with pleasure and enjoy the Caribbean sunshine. There would not be anything of an illegal nature occurring on this trip, which meant he felt free to book the travel in his own name and to pay for last minute airline tickets with cash. He never used credit cards, which made on-line purchases tricky, but he was well-versed in the business of purchasing air travel and knew that he could visit his local travel agency, pay for his trip with cash, and walk out with the tickets. Hotel reservations were less complicated and he secured a reservation for three nights at a hotel that would hold his reservation without a credit card. Wanda had always taken care of purchasing the airline tickets for the past few years, but he knew the local agency she used and the office was close by. He was looking forward to the trip. As for Wanda, he felt calm. There could be many reasons for what was going on. He'd go and observe and make the appropriate decisions after that. There was no need to spend time contemplating what might be happening. He knew it was not unusual for employees to decide to strike out on their own to gain more financial reward. He knew how to deal with the situation if this was indeed what was transpiring.

* * *

Jamel arrived at the agency the next morning and watched as Mary walked to the door from her car and struggled to get the key in the lock. He waited until he saw the fluorescent lights flicker before walking to the front door. She was settling into her desk when he stepped inside the travel agency.

She stood up at her desk, "Umm, excuse me, sir, but we don't open until nine o'clock. I'm afraid you'll have to come back then."

He nodded and pointed his thumb back over his shoulder. "Yeah, I saw that on your sign, but I have an urgent situation. I'm afraid I'm going to have to pay a lot for a ticket because I had a last minute business trip come up. I've already made my First Class reservation with American, so I just need to pay for my ticket and pick it up from you guys."

"Well, umm, OK. Why don't you have a seat at the front desk and I'll be right there to help you." Mary preferred not to be alone in the office with unfamiliar customers. She watched Jamel sit down in front of the desk, and then glanced out the front window. A coworker was walking toward the door. Relieved, she walked over to the desk where he had sat and tapped the keyboard to log in. She smiled and nodded as her coworker walked in and passed the desk.

"OK, so you've got a business trip coming up, right?"

"Yeah. I've got to go to St. Thomas for a few days. Here's my reservation number with American. They said that you could take care of everything with that number." He handed her a small slip of paper.

"You bet. I'll get that all taken care of for you Mr. …?"

"Scott, Jamel Scott."

"Yes sir, Mr. Scott." She typed six keystrokes. "Here we go. Looks like you're headed to St. Thomas on the twenty-fifth at 8 am, and coming back on the twenty-eighth at 4 pm. Does that sound right?"

"Yep. I guess if I've got to go somewhere on business, St. Thomas is not too bad, huh?" He gave her a wide smile.

"That's for sure. And you're flying First Class, right?"

He nodded. "Yeah. Not sure how much longer my company's going to pay for that, but it's OK for this trip."

"American does a nice job with their First Class service to the Caribbean."

"Great. This is my first time flying with them down there."

"Bear with me just a second, Mr. Scott." She continued typing for a minute and then looked back up. "OK, Mr. Scott, looks like everything's good to go. What type of credit card did you want to use for this?"

He reached into his pocket and pulled out twenty one-hundred dollar bills. "Lost my company card last week so they said to just pay for it in cash. Can you be sure and include a receipt so I can send that in for reimbursement?"

"No problem. She typed a dozen more keystrokes and Jamel heard a printer start running in the back. "Be back in just a second with your tickets, Mr. Scott."

Mary stood up and walked to the back of the office. Jamel reached over to the rack of cruise brochures next to him and took out one from Golden Cruise Line. She returned with an invoice and several tickets. As she assembled everything into a ticket envelope, he put the money down on the desk. Then, she picked it up and counted it.

"I owe you $30 change. I'll get that for you." He waved his hand.

"Don't worry about it. Consider it a tip."

"Thank you. Thank you very much."

"Thinking about a cruise, Mr. Scott?"

"I don't know, maybe. I hear they're expensive. Is this the cruise line that sails from Norfolk?"

"Yes, they have a ship that makes a run from Norfolk to the Caribbean. It's a seven-day trip. A cruise is a great way to see the Caribbean. Many of our customers prefer to drive to Norfolk rather than fly to Florida. Even though flying is safer than ever, people are still a little skittish about getting on planes." She placed the assembled tickets on the desk.

"Oh, yeah. That stuff with 9/11 still has people pretty spooked, I guess."

"Well, it did at first. But it seems that 9/11 has affected just about everyone. Has it touched your business?"

"Yeah. We've been hurt real bad. Hoping it will turn around soon."

"I'm sure it will. We've seen a big pick up in business lately. Especially in cruises. They've been popular this year. When were you thinking about going on a cruise?"

"Well, I was thinking sometime in May or June. But like I said, I heard that taking a cruise is pretty steep." He opened the brochure and leafed through the first few pages. "How much would it cost if I wanted to go on one of these trips, renting the cheapest cabin possible?"

"How many people would be in your cabin?"

"Just me."

"May and June are busy months, so it would be a little pricier for travel then. Also, traveling by yourself is expensive. But the Golden Line is really a First Class experience. I'd have to call them to get an exact fare for the dates you'd prefer but I'm guessing the cost would be around $5,000."

He winced. "Ouch! That really is beyond what I was thinking of."

"Well, when you start adding up the costs of a week-long vacation at a resort, you know, lodging, food, and entertainment, a cruise ends up being the best value." She held up her finger. "Hey, I just thought of something neat. Do you have a little flexibility in when you can go?"

"I do, yeah. I can set my own vacation schedule, even on short notice."

"Golden has this cool feature where they will sell some of their cabins at half price if that the ship is not full and you don't mind not knowing which dates you'll be traveling until thirty days in advance. This type of deal works well for some of my customers."

"Hmm, now that sounds like it might be reasonable."

"Oh my God! I forgot to ask you something important. Have you ever cruised before?"

"Never have. This would be my first time."

"This is great. I haven't cruise with Golden myself, but the owner of our agency is sailing out with them from Norfolk this weekend! This will be his second trip with them in the last sixty days. He loves Golden. Why don't you give me your phone number and I'll have him call you. Since he's sailed with them before, he can tell you all about it."

"This guy's going on the same cruise this weekend?"

"Yep. Like I said, he likes the Golden Line."

"Well, he does sound like a good person to talk to. What did you say his name was?"

"John Manning. He's a great guy to talk with. I'll get him to call you. I see your phone number on your reservation record. Can he call you on that one?"

"He can. That's my pager number. I prefer to use that number when I'm traveling. I tell you what; don't have him call me just yet. I'll just give him a call in a couple of weeks. That'll work better for me."

"You bet Mr. Scott. But don't wait too long. We're heading into peak season and like I said, cruising is booming right now. Even if you're thinking about taking advantage of the half-price deal, we should sit down soon and start the planning process."

"Gotcha. I'll think about that."

"I'll staple our phone number on this brochure for you so you can take it with you. Call me anytime. I'm glad to help."

He smiled and took the brochure. Stepping out the door, he was hit with a cold blast of air and the sight of a gray sky.

* * *

John's mother was giddy with excitement at having both Lucy and Tonya for an entire week. The day before John and Wanda were to drive to Norfolk, his mother had called three times with questions. She was less enthused about lying to Travis if he were to ask about John's traveling companion. Even though nothing had come up about the first trip, John made her promise she would not divulge to Travis that John and Wanda were traveling together. John knew Travis would be inquisitive about why his brother was taking a cruise with a woman and his mother understood.

In anticipation of her upcoming surgery, Lucy's doctor had taken her off medication, which meant John didn't need to worry about his mother asking questions regarding Lucy's health and why she would need to give her a pill daily. Lucy understood the pills were her big girl vitamins, so John had covered the possibility that Lucy might disclose this secret to his mother. He would have to tell his mother soon, there was no avoiding it. He would need her help caring for Lucy. But he could wait. His mother was a worrier and she couldn't relax and enjoy the girls if she knew about the surgery. John fought his own worries about Lucy and the surgery. He would break down crying every few days wondering if she would survive and improve. Would this be the last February that she would see? Could he risk leaving her for a week when she may be with him for another month? Could he go on with his life if Lucy were no longer a part of it? It was best not to ponder these questions, but they still invaded his thoughts relentlessly. Keeping busy helped, so he did just that.

The next morning, John and Lucy waited at his mother's home for Wanda and Tonya to arrive. Lucy jumped up and down on the couch while her grandmother held her hands. John smiled as he watched her black curls bounce up and down. John's mother had already informed Lucy of the special things they would be doing while John was gone and that she had stocked her freezer with six different types of Popsicles and four kinds of ice cream.

"Mom, if you aren't careful about the ice cream and sweets, Lucy and Tonya are going to be bouncing on your furniture the entire time they're here," said John, smiling.

"John, you hush up now. A grandmother's got a right to spoil her granddaughter, you know that."

"Yes, I do, Mom. I understand that very well. You've set a new standard for all grandmothers in that department."

Lucy saw Wanda and Tonya standing outside and dashed

toward the door. She opened it and pulled Tonya inside. They both giggled and hugged each other. She whispered into Tonya's ear and they both looked at John's mother and waved. Lucy pulled Tonya down the hall and into the bedroom they would be sharing.

"Hello, Wanda. It sure is nice to see you again!"

"Hi again, Connie. Thanks so much for helping us out."

"No problem, dear. You two want a drink or something to eat before you head out?"

"I guess I'll take some coffee, Mom."

"A Coke would be great for me."

"No problem, coming right up."

He watched her leave and motioned for Wanda to sit down in the seat next to the couch.

"Meeting all set?"

"Oh yeah. We got us one real happy seller. We're not the only ones that are desperate."

Connie returned with the drinks and placed them on the coffee table in front of the couch, then sat down in the chair opposite Wanda.

"So you guys are off again, huh, Wanda?"

"Yeah we are. Gotta take a look around again. Trying to find some good places for those groups that John is working on."

"That's the way the business is heading, Mom. More people are looking to travel in groups now. I wish I'd moved on this kind of idea sooner."

"You'll make it work honey, you always do. You know this guy is one hell of a businessman, don't you, Wanda?"

"I've seen him in action."

"OK, you two. I appreciate your comments but I'm not so sure that I've been worthy of your compliments lately."

"Oh, dear, you can't blame yourself for the downturn in your industry. Who could've known terrorists would crash planes into those buildings? The fact that you're still in business is pretty amazing. Didn't you tell me that two agencies in Durham went out of business in the last few months?"

"Yeah, a few did. It should help us since things are improving."

"Good for you. So it's going to be a good year then, huh?"

"Don't know for sure, Mom. We're only two months in. Things seem to be moving in the right direction. Now all this war stuff is cranking back up. I think the President's doing the right thing and all, but a war is about the worst thing for the travel industry."

"It won't last long honey. Mr. Bush will teach those terrorists a lesson. What those terrorist don't get is that they woke up the sleeping bear. I mean if you think about it, they're like little annoying bees, just buzzing around us. They blow up a few bombs around the world and the bear doesn't move. But when they smash planes into the Twin Towers, well then they've stung the bear pretty hard. So the bear opens one eye, reaches out with his big paw, and swats the pesky bees dead. They shouldn't have disturbed the sleeping bear."

"Good one Mom."

The girls ran back into the living room where they were sitting. Tonya jumped into Wanda's lap and pulled her head down so she could whisper in her ear. Wanda smiled while she listened to her.

"Yes, baby. All you want."

"Lucy! She said I could have all the ice cream I want!" She jumped off her mother's lap and they joined hands, swirling in a circle. The adults smiled and Lucy tripped and Tonya fell on top of her. They screeched with delight.

"Well, Wanda, now I know I can give Tonya all the ice cream that she wants, but is there anything else you want to tell me about?"

"She's a good girl, Connie. I'm glad she's going to be with you while we're gone. You've already been around her a little. I trust you to do whatever you think is best."

"Does she take any medication or anything like that?" asked Connie.

"Nope. My little honey never gets sick. She's a healthy, happy girl."

"I left some phone numbers on the counter, Mom. If anything comes up, just try the first two numbers. You can contact us by phone if you need to. I know that both of us will call a couple of times anyway." He stood up and stretched.

"Daddy, are you guys leaving now?"

"Yes, honey, we're going. Looks to me like you're going to have a pretty good time while I'm gone. Can I have a hug before I go?"

Lucy took three steps toward John and lunged for him, wrapping her arms and legs around his mid-section. He fell back down on the couch laughing.

"Daddy, now you've got to promise me that you're going to be good on this trip, OK? I want you to listen to Wanda and do what she says and you got to be really nice to everyone on the big cruise ship. OK?" She climbed into his lap.

"Shouldn't I be saying something like that to you, my little sweetie?"

"Oh Daddy, I'm going to be very good while you're gone, I double cross promise and pinky swear." She held up her pinky and he hooked his pinky finger with hers. His eyes welled up with tears and he swallowed hard.

"I love you, Daddy. You're the best Daddy ever." She wrapped her arms around his neck and pressed her lips against his cheek. She held the position for five seconds and then, glancing at her grandmother, she blew hard making a loud raspberry sound. She jumped down off his lap and he took a tissue out of the box on the table to wipe his eyes.

"Oh my goodness, Lucy! That was the wettest raspberry you've ever given me you little rascal!"

Wanda knelt down and hugged Tonya. She motioned to Wanda that she wanted to whisper something into her ear. She brought her mouth up to Wanda's ear.

"That's good honey. I'm glad you told me. Do you remember all the things we talked about?"

"Yes, Mama. I remember. I promise I'll be real good for Miss Connie." She turned and smiled at Connie and then buried her face into Wanda's shoulder.

"I know you will, Tonya. Remember that Miss Connie knows how to get in touch with me if you really need me, OK?"

"OK, Mama. Can I go back to Lucy's room now?"

Lucy grabbed Tonya and pulled her down the hall again.

"Bye, bye, Daddy. See ya' later." He wiped his eyes again.

"John, she loves you so much. Have you ever met a better Dad in your whole life?"

"He is the best Dad I've ever met." John's mother beamed with pride.

"Thanks. Can you tell us what that secret whisper was all about?"

"She just wanted me to know that she wasn't scared anymore to stay here with Lucy and Connie. Yesterday and earlier today she was saying something different."

"Well that's good news," said John.

"Let's go. I'm ready to get to some warm weather." She turned toward the door.

"Now you two just relax and have some fun, OK? I'm going to take good care of those two precious girls. You just do your work and don't worry about them for a second."

"We know they're in good hands, Mom. Thanks again for watching them for us." Connie walked over to John and they hugged.

"You still want to leave your car at the shop while we're gone, right?" John asked Wanda.

"Yeah … umm … I almost forgot about that. You're going to follow me over there?"

"I'll be right behind you. Thanks again, Mom. I'll call you tonight."

They walked to Wanda's car, which was parked behind John's in the driveway. Connie went back inside and closed the door.

"Sorry I caught you off guard."

"Yeah, what's up?"

"It's better if you don't leave your car here. You know, just safer for everyone. Follow me. There's a well-lit shopping center parking lot a few blocks away. You can just leave it there. It'll be safe."

* * *

Later that day, they stood in line to board the ship. They hadn't spoken much during the three-hour drive from Raleigh to Norfolk. He drove and thought about Lucy's surgery. She asked a few questions about their plans for moving the product and he indicated they would use the same process as before. He had purchased some newer equipment and felt they stood a better chance of recovering all of the product. When they stopped for a bathroom break, she bought a copy of People magazine and read the rest of the way. As they stood in line to board the ship, he felt someone touch his arm and call out his name.

"Well John Manning, what in the world are you doing on this cruise?"

He turned around to see Lucy's teacher, Cindy Alston-Capps, smiling at him.

"Wow, Cindy, this is a surprise."

"The feeling's mutual. I didn't expect to find you on this cruise."

"It's strictly business. I am researching group packages for my travel agency. It's an untapped market. And you, why are you here?"

"A few months ago I decided that I needed a change, so I booked a cruise. Now, this is the second singles cruise I've been on in the last two months. I took another one over Christmas break and had a blast." She glanced at Wanda. "I see you've got some company on this trip. Hi, I'm Cindy Alston. I'm his daughter's teacher."

"Nice to meet you, Cindy. Wanda, Wanda Johnson."

"This is a working trip for us, you know. With being in the travel biz and all, she and I sometimes take trips together. Separate cabins and everything."

"Well that's very interesting. So you're not on this cruise because it's a singles cruise I guess?"

"No, I didn't even know it was a singles cruise. I guess this works out well for you since it's Spring Break."

"Perfect really. I don't have to take any vacation time. But even if I did, I'd still be here. Like I said, these singles cruises are a blast for me. Now it looks to me like you've lost a little weight."

"Thanks, I have lost a little. So I take it that things haven't worked out with your husband?"

"You could say that. It's a long story. Maybe when we get a chance to chat on board, I'll give you some details." Wanda tapped him on the shoulder and he turned to receive documents from the gate agent, who had been waiting while he chatted.

"Can we go ahead and get this check-in stuff done? I'm hungry and I want to take a nap."

"Sure, Wanda. Look, here's your cabin number, key, and check-in documents. I'll just get my separate cabin key and paperwork and then we'll be done. Well, Cindy, we're boarding now. I'm sure we'll be running into each other. You know it's not a very big ship."

"Now that's what I heard. So you've been on this boat before?"

"Yeah, a couple of times."

"Well then you would be the perfect person to show me around the ship. Maybe then we can talk about how much the class has missed your reading to them. I don't know if you know this or not Wanda, but John has a magical way with children. He used to read to Lucy's class quite frequently."

"Actually, Cindy, I do know how good he is with kids. I've got a six-year-old myself and she thinks that John is great." She turned and walked toward the ship. He smiled at Cindy and as he turned, collided with another woman who was boarding. His boarding documents spilled out in front of him on the ground. He mumbled an apology. Cindy bent down and picked up a few documents that had landed near her.

"Damn, that was embarrassing."

"Understand. Hey, I do want to talk with you later. I owe you an apology for how I reacted when you asked me out that day. I'm hoping that's not the reason why you haven't been back to visit the class."

"Oh no, I understand. I just haven't been back to visit your class because I've been under a lot more pressure lately. The business got socked by 9/11 and the bad economy. I've just been too busy trying to hold things together."

"Well, that's fine, but I still want to talk with you about coming back and visiting the class. It was nice to have you around." They both stood back up and she handed John the papers she had collected.

"Thanks again, Cindy. See you on board."

"Sounds good, John, I'll be looking forward to that."

* * *

The second day after their departure, John and Wanda were eating lunch in the small restaurant on the top deck of the ship. She was ecstatic to be back on board and was overflowing with details on how well she was sleeping and enjoying the food. He was sleeping better also, but he was having less success sticking to his diet due to the abundance of food.

"I'm not kidding you. I fell asleep at 9:30 last night and I didn't wake up until 9:30 this morning! Can you believe that? Twelve hours. That hasn't happened to me since I was a teenager."

"You do seem more relaxed."

"You just looked at my plate for the third time since the waitress brought our food. Take some."

"Thanks, but I've gotta pass. I need to keep losing weight. Going on a damn cruise right in the middle of a diet is nuts."

"Maybe so, but you've gotta enjoy it too. Why don't you just save up and have a nice dinner like we did last night?"

"I'm planning on it. Remember that woman that I was talking to when we were boarding the ship?" asked John.

"Yeah, I think so. Her name was Cindy, right?"

"Yeah."

"So what's up with Miss Cindy?"

"She asked me out for dinner tonight. How about that?"

"Wow. Now that's funny."

"Doesn't seem funny to me. She's a dynamite lady and a great teacher."

"No, I don't mean like funny, like you shouldn't go out with her. I just mean that she doesn't seem your type."

He stabbed his forked into his salad and put a piece of chicken into his mouth. "Well then, since you seem to know me so well, what is my type?"

"Don't get all pissy on me. If you don't want me to say anything, then just tell me to shut up."

"Well it's already out there now, so go ahead and tell me why she's not my type."

"I'll do it if you promise to calm down and not get all pissed off with me."

"Fair enough."

"Well for one thing, isn't she the one you were talking about when we had that tuna party at your house?"

"OK. So she did lie to me about her pending divorce."

"That's right. So now you just want to forget that she lied to you?"

"Things have changed now."

"How?"

"She explained to me why she lied."

"What did she say?"

"She was pleased that I asked her out, but she felt uncomfortable because she was Lucy's teacher, and she wasn't in a good place to start thinking about dating yet. She said that she lied about her divorce because it was the first thing that popped into her head. She apologized and thought she might have hurt my feelings since I haven't been back to help out with the class." He took the last bite of his salad.

"And now she's all smiles and asking you out?"

"Damn right. And I can't wait."

"Wait for what? Don't you see what's happening here?"

"What the hell are you getting at?"

"All I'm saying is that I know this type of woman. She's on this singles cruise, looking hard at all the men on board and sees you. Since she knows you kinda like her, she's thinking she's got herself some nice company for a few days. She doesn't have to be lonely, right? Then she keeps looking around, seeing who else she can meet that might be better and then she just leaves you high and dry."

"So, now I see. You don't think she's not my type. You're saying I'm not good enough for her. That when she meets someone else, she'll just dump me. Is that what you're saying, because if it is, then I'm canceling my promise not to get mad at your observations and I'm going to tell you to fuck off and we can just end this little chat." He stood up and she reached out to grab his arm, but he stepped back.

"Hey, don't be getting so mad. I'm just trying to look out for you." He walked to the ship's railing; she followed.

"Hey, just forget about what I said. All I'm trying to do is help you out, that's all."

He stared down at the water, brought his hands together on the rail and placed his chin on top of them.

"Hey, John, you there?"

"I heard you. Just leave me alone for a while, will you?"

"Sure. But look, you kinda scared me just then. I thought for a second that you were going to jump off the ship."

He rubbed both eyes with his left hand, put his glasses back on, and turned to look at Wanda. "Thought about that before. Would've done it on the last trip if it wasn't for Lucy. My life would be over without her."

"Please don't say things like that. You're fixing things. Lucy's going to be OK. You're getting the money she needs. She's going to be fine, you just wait and see. I just know that she's going to be OK."

"I'm not going to get sunk down in all this shit right now. You pissed me off, I yelled at you, I got sad, now I'm moving on. I'll see you around tomorrow."

"OK. Have a good time. Hey, aren't we supposed to be in St. Thomas tomorrow?"

"No, we're at sea all day tomorrow. We'll wake up the next day in St. Thomas and get our work done." He walked away and disappeared back into the ship.

"Good, I'll see you tomorrow."

* * *

Jamel woke up in St. Thomas at 7 a.m., the morning John and Wanda were scheduled to arrive. He sat up in bed and switched on the Today show.

"Dude, you wake up too early."

"Yeah, sorry, my man. You're gonna have to hit the road 'cause I've got to take care of some business today."

"You could've let me know about that. Maybe I wouldn't have let you keep me up all night."

"How late you stay up is my decision," said Jamel. "I'm paying the bill."

"Guess so. You got some cash for me?"

"Yeah, over there on the desk is an envelope." He got out of bed, walked to the desk, and counted the contents of the envelope.

"Thanks for the tip. Sure you don't want me to stay for a little more fun this morning?"

"Can't do it. But you might hear from me after I take care of my work today. Never know."

"Hope so, lover. You gonna give your Big Bobby a kiss goodbye?"

"Nah, get out of here."

"Ok, you ain't got to be rude about it." He collected his clothes, dressed by the door to the hotel room, and left.

Jamel wasn't concerned about what he would discover when Wanda arrived for her meeting. After all, the pieces of the puzzle were already starting to fit together. He and others knew that someone was bringing in a sizeable amount of product into the area. She went out on her own and starting running her own show. It happens all the time in the business world. Truth be told, he had a little more respect for her. As was the case with so many other problems he had resolved in the past, Jamel would come up with a solution to this one. If it ended up being true, then there were appropriate ways to remedy the situation. After all, that was the game. Problems arise, problems get resolved. Unlike other enterprises, he couldn't pursue legal means to put an end to Wanda's efforts. He knew companies required employees to sign non-compete agreements to protect certain company assets. Because of her involvement in the transportation of his product, it was understandable that Wanda could steal contact information about his suppliers. He wouldn't expect his suppliers, if indeed Wanda was buying from ones he had used in the past, to alert him to Wanda's new enterprise. They'd be just as happy to take her money as his. Besides, he hadn't been a very good customer lately anyway. With transportation being so difficult, Wanda was in a position to get product at a greatly reduced rate. She could get much more for it, too. Jamel realized that she could possibly be making twice as much as he had been before everything went crazy after 9/11.

How did she solve the transportation issue? That question kept bugging him. Could it have something to do with the cruise ship? Maybe she had discovered some method by which she could move the product that way. He couldn't imagine there was another reason to take a cruise ship all the way to St. Thomas for a meeting. But a cruise ship might allow for multiple ways to transport the product. Pay a crew member to be the mule maybe. Perhaps the security was less strict than what one faced at the airports. If she had discovered a way to use a cruise ship to move her product, he would be sure and pass along extra special congratulations to Wanda for her ingenuity.

After a leisurely breakfast and an hour of reading the previous day's USA Today, Jamel looked up from his outdoor café seat to see the ship being guided into St. Thomas Bay. A conversation with a shore crew member the day before revealed that the ship was scheduled to arrive at 9 am. He was also advised that it took about an hour and a half for the ship to be secured, and that the passengers would begin walking off the ship thirty minutes after that. To mesh with the tourist crowd, Jamel had purchased a cheap pair of sunglasses and a straw golf hat. To enhance the disguise, he had covered his nose and cheeks with zinc oxide.

Right on schedule, he observed the first passengers walk down a short gangway and onto the white concrete of the dock area. There was no security and the passengers walked another three-hundred yards to a small fence door where a cruise line employee smiled and pointed them to a variety of waiting buses, taxis, and minivans. He spotted Wanda as she stepped onto the white concrete. She had on a loose white blouse and khaki shorts.

A short, stocky man with blonde hair and glasses walked off the ship with her, carrying a black Nike sport bag. After the two passed through the gate, the man gave Wanda the Nike bag, spoke for a few more moments, and then left, walking toward the main shopping area. She watched him for a couple of minutes before lifting the bag onto her shoulder and stepping into a waiting taxi.

He smiled as he watched through his binoculars. Nice, predictable Wanda with her black Nike bags. She said they brought her good luck. She had brought one on every trip they had made together. Even had a kid-sized one for her daughter. It was puzzling to see someone with her, and hard to imagine she would have a stranger carrying her bag. He packed his binoculars in his back pack and left the café.

Jamel found a taxi and advised the driver that his girlfriend was in a green cab down by the dock. He told the driver that he had devised a plan to surprise her with a wedding ring and he needed to follow her for a while before he could reveal his surprise. The driver smiled and nodded. He drove down to the dock area and fell in behind Wanda's taxi. The driver was careful to follow Jamel's instructions and stay several cars behind her so he wouldn't be spotted.

After driving around the city for thirty minutes, they arrived back at the cruise ship. Her cab stopped, she stepped out, and walked over to another one and got in. His driver looked back at him with a frown. He advised him that she just got mad at the driver. He explained to the driver that his girlfriend was very attractive and quite often men would make annoying proposals. The driver looked back at him and they both smiled and nodded at Jamel's good fortune.

They followed her again the short distance to the Holiday Inn Resort. He instructed the driver to pass the hotel while he turned to watch her get out of her cab and entered the resort. He suspected the veranda restaurant overlooking the bay would be the spot that Wanda would pick for her meeting. He had dined there the night before and it was an ideal place to meet someone. Just enough privacy to discuss important business matters, but not too much privacy to be concerned about one's safety should the meeting not go well.

He ordered the driver to continue up the steep cliff road another mile to a small hotel bar that offered a clear view of the Holiday Inn's restaurant, then paid the driver and walked into the bar. Tourists occupied four of the eight tables. When he brought the veranda restaurant into view with his binoculars, he saw Wanda directing two bus boys to position three Japanese screens around a table near the edge of the restaurant, closest to Jamel, which created more privacy for her meeting. Jamel watched her hand the busboys some money before she sat down and put the black bag between her feet.

His waitress brought him a pina colada. At the same time, a tall, well-dressed man in an olive drab suit and light blue dress shirt stepped through the screens and shook hands with Wanda. He sat down across from her and placed his dark brown briefcase between his feet. The man leaned in close and began speaking to Wanda, who was sitting back with her arms crossed. Their waiter interrupted and she waved him away.

He watched the man finish speaking and lean back in his chair. She leaned forward and thrust her finger at him. She grew more animated and the man slid his chair back. Her head jerked with her words and the man held up his hand. She continued and the man held up his other hand. She leaned back in her chair. They were both silent. The waiter returned with two glasses of water and she waved him off again.

He set the binoculars down and laughed. She played the game well. He drank half his pina colada and resumed watching. Every meeting with a new supplier brought surprises. Prices changed. Amount of product changed. Nothing would be as agreed upon. You yelled at the supplier, argued about the price, threatened to walk away from the deal, and then you got down to deciding whether or not you wanted to buy what they had to sell. He'd been through it dozens of times. He was fortunate in that he had a reliable group of regular suppliers, but that would not be the case for her.

He watched her stand up and start walking away from the table. The man reached over and touched Wanda's elbow before she moved through the screen. He pointed to her seat. She frowned and returned to her seat. The man held up a menu so that she could see it and he pointed to an item on it.

Thirty minutes later, Jamel had finished his breakfast as had Wanda and her guest. She was smiling, leaning across the table and the man was laughing. He clapped his hands together and her head flung back as she laughed. The waiter came and took away their dishes. They both paused and he watched as the man slid his briefcase toward Wanda's feet. She pulled it up to her lap and opened it. After examining the contents, she closed the briefcase and used her foot to slide the black Nike bag toward him. He brought the bag up to his lap and looked through the contents. The transaction was complete.

They shook hands and the man walked away. No doubt he would be eager to secure the contents of his bag from possible theft, as would she. As she bent down to pick up the briefcase, the wait staff removed the screens that had created additional privacy for their meeting. Panning the rest of the restaurant, Jamel noticed the same man that had carried her bag off the cruise ship, sitting four tables away. His face was obscured by sunglasses. Jamel watched her turn to the man and he saw the man smile and give a thumbs-up. Jamel watched as the waiter brought the man a salad. It took him about ten minutes to eat it, then he threw some money on the table and left the veranda.

So, she had a partner. An interesting turn of events. He raised his hand to catch the waiter's attention. He ordered a beer. There was much to do and he needed to get back to Durham.

* * *

"You were right. The guy did want to jerk you around on the price," said John. The ship was moving out of the St. Thomas harbor and he had met Wanda in the casual dining area.

"It was about what I expected. Things are always changing. The person, the price, the schedule, whatever. One time I was with Jamel and I watched some guy try to double the price. You just have to be ready to walk away. Today, the guy decides he wants to jack up the price, so I get up and start to leave. He calls me back, we yell at each other, then we end up back to the original price. If you think about it, the same shit could've happened to him. I could've showed up and started talking about how I couldn't get my hands on enough cash. Hell, the only reason he might have started in on this higher price thing was to keep me from haggling for a discount."

"And you've got everything stashed away, safe and sound?"

"You bet. Now all we gotta do is relax and cruise back," said Wanda. She took a sip from her rum and coke and looked out the window at St. Thomas Bay.

"Hey, what type of boat is that?"

"Cigarette boat. Very fast. People in your line of work like them," said John.

The long thin boat was moving out from the port slowly. It was thirty feet long. One man was driving and two women were lounging on the rear seat. They were dressed formally, perhaps in preparation for a dinner on a nearby island.

"There's a company down near little Washington that makes them. Can't remember the name. You know where little Washington is?"

"Yeah, around Greenville, on a big river, right?"

"Yeah, the Pamlico. Why did you ask about that boat?"

"Just reminded me about this awful trip I had on one of those boats."

"I thought you told me in Hatteras that you'd never been out on a boat before."

"Yeah, I guess I forgot about it until I saw that boat."

"So what happened?" He leaned back in his seat.

"Well, it was maybe about four or five years ago. Jamel called me up and told me I had to take care of something. Says some guy he owes a favor to has got some kind of legal problem, big trial, or some crap. He says that I got to take this guy who's a witness in the trial on a trip so that no one can find him. So next thing I know, I'm dropping Tonya off at my aunt's house and I'm flying to Fort Lauderdale with some old guy. Jamel's given him some downers and the guy's just out of it.

"So I've got to drag him through the airport. We meet some other guy who drives us to some boat place and we get into a, what's it called again?"

"Cigarette boat."

"Yeah, we get into this cigarette boat and start hauling ass to some deserted island over in the Bahamas. The boat's so damn loud, my head is pounding. The old guy is just sleeping. Then we get to this place that Jamel told me was going to be some kind of beautiful resort, but it's just a couple of nasty old shacks. The guy drops us off with a couple of boxes of food, a lot of rum, and he says he'll be back in three days."

He smiled. "So you were stranded on a deserted island. Some people would love that."

"No one would've loved this deserted island. It had a well, but the water tasted like someone had pissed in it. Jamel gave me instructions to keep the old guy filled up with booze and to slip him more downers whenever I could. So here I am on this deserted island with some old guy who's either drunk as shit or sleeping and I've got nothing to do and no idea whether I'm going to get picked up in three days or not."

"How big was the island?"

"Very small. I could walk across it in about an hour. Nothing but palm trees, birds, and ocean."

"Who was the old guy? Did you find out anything about him?"

"Nothing. Jamel says don't talk to him, don't ask any questions, so I don't. Never did find out anything about why this guy was so important. He paid me three grand, so I was OK with it. Needed the money."

He looked out the window and watched the boat pick up speed. The driver turned back to the women and said something that made them sit up straighter. The boat accelerated and the sound was overwhelming, even though they were a quarter mile from the boat.

"Bet those bitches have a headache by the time they get where they're going."

"After you've been on a boat, you get use to the sound."

"Not me. Only cruise ships for me." She raised her hand to signal the waiter and he arrived with two menus. He held one out for John, but he waved it away.

"I'm going out with Cindy tonight."

She continued to review the menu.

"Fine. Guess you guys are hitting it off."

"You could say that. She's a pretty lady. A little short on intelligent conversation, but nice."

She turned and stared out the window. The sun was setting and the clouds had a strange orange tint.

"Aren't you going to say something else about how she's not my type?"

"Nope."

"Good. Thanks for not getting into that again."

"So, I guess we'll just meet at your place in the morning to start packing up everything, right?"

"Well, yeah, that's what we talked about. But umm … why don't you just wait and let me call you before you come over? I may …"

"Have company?"

"I was going to say something else."

"That's cool. You should enjoy yourself, you know? I mean, I saw a pair of earrings in your room yesterday when we were packing for the meeting."

"Well, yeah, she did leave those there by accident. Anyway, we don't have to pack tomorrow. We've got a full day at sea tomorrow and then we'll be in Nassau for a day, so we've got plenty of time to pack up. What do you have planned for tonight?"

"Not sure. Maybe play a little Black Jack. I saw a good movie last night. Might just stay in and watch another one."

"You might want to go to one of the dance clubs or something. This is a singles cruise so you never know, maybe you'll run into someone interesting."

"Maybe. Thanks for thinking about me. I'll be fine."

"Sure, sure. Well, I'll see you in the morning. I'll give you a call, OK?"

"You bet."

* * *

The next day, at lunch, Wanda found Cindy near the bar in a lounge where most passengers enjoyed playing bridge or board games. Cindy's cabin steward had been nice enough to tell Wanda where Cindy was when he came upon Wanda knocking on her cabin door. She was reading and had a cup of coffee on the end table beside her. A couple sat at the bar with their backs to them. They were laughing and talking to the bartender. She sat in the chair beside Cindy and smiled.

"Hey, aren't you the woman who works with John?"

"Yep. Name's Wanda. You're Cindy, right?"

Before Cindy could answer, she leaned across the small end table that separated their chairs. She clutched her blouse in her hand and pulled her closer.

"I'm not here for a bunch of chit chat, girl. I'm going to do a little talking with you, you hear? And you're going to smile all pretty at anyone that might be watching. Got it?"

"Get the hell off me. Are you crazy?" She tried to pull away, but Wanda held fast.

"You could say I'm a little crazy. So listen up and nothing bad is going to happen to you. You put that smile back on your face right now. Do it."

She complied.

"Now I'm going to tell you a few things and you're going to listen. Nod your head when I ask you a question and just keep smiling. Don't do nothing else."

She tried to pull away. Wanda tightened her grip and the blouse ripped.

"If you keep pulling away, I'll rip this motherfucking blouse right off you."

A drop of her saliva had landed on Cindy's cheek. They both noticed.

"Guess you could say I can get a little worked up. So don't fucking push me girl. See, this man you've taking a liking to, he's with me. We got some important work to do together. I need him thinking about that work and nothing else. See, he don't need no distractions like some bitch trying to get him in the bed and have a little fun while she's on vacation. So, this is what's going to happen. When you see him again, you ain't going be flirting with him and carrying on like you've been doing. You're going to smile and talk real sweet to him about how much you like him. You're going to tell him he's one of the nicest men you've met in a long time and that he's good looking. Yeah, don't forget to say that." She paused and glanced over Cindy's shoulder to observe the couple at the bar still in conversation with the bartender. "Then you're going to say that you've been doing some hard thinking and you're going to be getting back together with your husband. Tell him that you called your husband today and talked with him. So you just tell him that. Real nice, now. I don't want his feelings hurt. After you do this, you just walk away. If you say something about our little chat, then I'll fuck you up bad. Just do what I'm telling you and you'll have a great trip and I'll be able to get my work done."

Wanda released Cindy's blouse and stood up. Cindy immediately pulled back, almost tipping over her chair. Then she stood up and brushed her hands across her blouse.

"Don't forget something now, my girlfriend. I'm a crazy woman. If you don't do what I just told you, I'm going to get a little crazier. Might turn out to be the worst vacation you ever had if you don't."

Cindy turned and knocked over the end table that held her cup. It crashed to the floor, and the bartender's head popped up above the couple at the bar. Satisfied that it did not need his immediate attention, he returned to his conversation. She rushed out the door as Wanda smiled and waved goodbye.

* * *

When Wanda arrived at John's cabin at 1p.m., she could see he had already been working on their project. He had emptied the floats, spare rope, GPS monitor, and extra plastic baggies. She dropped the old briefcase beside the GPS monitor.

"You're going to get the biggest kick out of something." He pointed to a chair next to the bathroom. She sat down.

"So, what's up?"

"You were right about Cindy,"

"What do you mean?"

"I mean, when you said she wasn't my type, you were right. See I've been lying here thinking about it and we've had some fun together these last few nights, but you know, there's just no spark between us. I don't know if we just don't have much in common, or what, but it's not happening for me."

"Really?"

"Yeah. So, I was thinking I need to go ahead and let her know my feelings. I mean, the last thing I want to do is lead her on and have her think that we might go out more when we get back to Raleigh. As I'm trying to figure out how to do it, guess what?"

"What?"

"She calls me. Right at that moment, the phone rings, and it's her. She starts into this long story about how much fun she's been having with me and that I made it a great vacation for her, but that she's just spent the last two hours talking with her husband on the phone and they decided to try and work things out."

"Hmm. That's all she said?"

"No that wasn't all she said. I mean, she said a lot of nice things about me, complimentary things, things I haven't heard about myself in a long time. Felt pretty good. I mean, we talked for a while so we both said a lot of stuff, but basically, that's what happened."

"Told you."

"I know, that's why I wanted to tell you about it. It made me laugh for a few minutes after I hung up, thinking about how you said she wasn't my type. I mean, we both had a good time and all, but she and I just don't fit. Have you ever chased something in your life, or tried to get something that you think is going to make you feel happy and when you get it, you realize it wasn't important?"

"What do you mean by that?"

"I mean that, damn, I can't believe that I'm telling you this." He looked down at his hands. "I've been very lonely for the past year. I thought if I found someone I would feel better, you know, the loneliness would be gone. Hell, maybe I'd even get married again if it worked out. But, now, after this little thing with Cindy, I'm seeing that I don't need to be so consumed by that thought. Part of my loneliness was that I just haven't felt like anyone could want me anyway. I've been overweight, stressed, balding, you know, just not the kind of guy that women are on the hunt for. Now, after finding out what Cindy thinks about me, I realize I was just being down on myself for nothing. Women do like me, and I'm getting myself back into shape, slimming down, and everything. Why are you smiling like that?"

"No reason."

"I gotta tell you, this has been the best damn vacation I've had in a long time."

"Me, too." He pointed at the supplies on the bed.

"So, now, what do you say we make this a profitable vacation too!"

"I'm ready."

XV - March 2002

John knew he couldn't keep Lucy and Travis apart for long. He had to do everything he could to keep some distance between the three of them while this project was going on with Wanda. But Lucy was too attached to Travis and John knew how much Travis loved her.

So a week after he and Wanda returned from their trip, he called Travis and told him that Lucy wanted to see him and asked if he could pick her up from school the following Friday and take her to Chuck E. Cheese. He hadn't wanted her to spend the night at first but Travis was insistent.

"Uncle Travis, Uncle Travis!" shouted Lucy as she ran out the side door of her school, frantically waving at him. When he saw her, he crouched low, raised his hands up like claws and ran toward her. She squealed with delight as he approached her. She leapt toward him, he caught her, and in one smooth motion twirled her around in a circle before lifting her high above his head.

"Oh, my gosh, you little beauty. I cannot believe how big you are now. This might be the last time I'll be able to lift you up like this." He set her down and knelt down to her level.

"I am getting bigger because I've been eating all my food and running and playing. My Daddy said that if I do those things, I'll grow up big. And look at this." She put her finger on the tip of her front tooth and moved it back and forth.

"Uh-oh. Looks like someone is ready to lose their first tooth. Wow, you are a big girl."

"And when it comes out, the tooth fairy is gonna come and bring me some money and I'm going to save my money so I can get a new doll called Beach Girl Brittney because she loves to wear her bathing suit and go to the beach, just like me."

"Hmm, a Beach Girl Brittney doll. And tell me, what color hair does this beach girl doll have?"

"Black hair, just like me. But her hair is straight and not curly like mine."

"And does this doll have a big, beautiful smile, just like you?

"Yes, just like me."

"Well that is very interesting because something funny happened to me when I was driving here to pick you up."

"What happened?"

"Well, I was just thinking that it has been so long since I've seen you, that … how long has it been since I've seen you anyway?"

"A long time."

"That's right, it's been a very long time. So anyway, I was driving over here to pick you up and I was driving right past this store called The Toy Depot. Do you know that store?"

"Yes! I love to go to that store. It's my favorite."

"I thought it was. So, I decided to go inside, just to see what kind of stuff they had. I was kinda hoping they had something for me."

"They only have kids' stuff," Lucy explained. "They don't have any stuff for grownups like you."

"You're right. So I was getting ready to leave when I saw this big stack of boxes. And inside the boxes were these pretty dolls called …umm, what was that name again?"

Her eyes grew wide. "Beach Girl Brittney!"

"That's it, that's the one." Travis had tucked a section of the box into the waistband in the back of his pants and covered the gift with his shirt. He stood up, reached behind his back, and held it out for Lucy. She grabbed it with both hands and looked at the package closely, screaming and hugging the box tightly when she recognized its contents. Then she leapt toward Travis, who caught her and brought her up while she hugged his neck.

"Whoa there, my darling, you almost choked me to death." She released her grip and he set her back down.

"I can't believe it Uncle Travis. A Beach Girl Brittney doll just like I wanted. It is my most favoritest doll ever."

"I'm glad my darling because you are my most favoritest little girl ever and my most favoritest little girl should have her most favoritest doll." He smiled and winked.

"I can't believe it. You're the greatest uncle ever in the whole world."

"Thanks darling. Now how about you and I go somewhere fun? Maybe Chuck E. Cheese?

"Can I play some video games?"

"You can play video games for as long as you want, my darling."

* * *

Sixty tokens and three hours later, they pulled into the driveway of Travis' home, which was between Durham and Raleigh. Even though the house was small, he relished his privacy: and his two acres of land surrounding it provided him this. To Lucy, Travis' house was a playground. There were no rules about picking up toys, or what you could eat, and she could stay up late. His refrigerator was empty except for ice cream, beer, and milk. Travis always had six or seven boxes of her favorite cereal.

"Here's the movie, darling. You remember how to put it into the DVD player?"

"I know."

"I'm going to make you a big ice cream sundae and then we can watch the movie, OK?"

"Will you put extra chocolate stuff on it?"

"You bet, my darling. And I'll give you extra whipped cream too." She walked into the living room, inserted the DVD, and stacked her two favorite pillows on top of each other. His living room had a large screen TV, a DVD player, stereo, and a dozen large pillows. A minute later, he walked in with a three-scoop sundae, loaded with chocolate syrup, whipped cream, and three cherries on top.

"Yum, yum."

"Here you go, darling. Just the way you like it."

"Thank you. Do you want a bite?"

"No thank you. Uncle Travis is full from eating too much pizza." He grabbed a worn bean bag chair and placed it beside Lucy as the movie started. Just then Travis' cell phone rang. He smiled at her, looked down at the phone but no caller ID appeared.

"Excuse me for a second, darling," he said, standing up.

"Hello, Hanson." He listened. "Hold on, just hold on for a second." He covered the phone with his hand. "Lucy, darling, I've gotta talk to this person for just a minute. You keep watching the movie, OK?"

"OK."

He walked back into the kitchen and out onto his back deck.

"Are you a goddamn idiot? I told you not to call me again. Fuck you. That's it. Don't call." He slammed the phone shut and leaned against the deck railing, looking out into the backyard. The phone rang again.

"What?"

"Yeah. Great. Take care of it yourself." His face tightened and he laid the phone down in his lap. He listened again. "You finished? Well listen to this. I don't give a shit about your threats. Get out of my life and leave me the fuck alone." He held the phone a few inches from his ear and continued to listen. "No, can't do it. Did you lose your fucking hearing?" He listened and sat down on the only piece of furniture on the deck, a white plastic beach chair. He bent forward and ran his fingers through his hair, shaking his head as he listened. "Why should I believe that?" His voice calmer. "Yeah, how much? Not enough." He rolled his head in a circle as he listened, rubbing the back of his neck. "How the fuck do I know this will be the last time?" "OK. Leave half in the usual place along with the pictures. I'll let you know when it's done. It'll happen in the next two weeks." He stood up and looked at the full moon as he listened. "Can't do it sooner. Take it or leave it. If you leave the cash, then I'll know you want it done. I'll expect the other half after it's done, that's it." He folded his phone back together and clipped it back onto his belt. He rolled his head again, rubbing his neck, then opened the door and walked back into the house. Lucy was sitting on the floor, arms wrapped around her knees, and head down.

"Hey, my darling Lucy. What's wrong?" She kept her head

down, her back was shaking.

"I heard you yelling at that man on the phone." She sobbed. "I got scared and I couldn't eat my ice cream anymore."

"Oh God, my darling. I'm so sorry." He walked back to the window that looked onto the deck and closed it."

"Lucy, Lucy, look at me darling," he said, reaching down and lifting her chin. "I'm sorry you had to hear all that. It's just that sometimes I have to yell at people because of my job. I know it sounded scary to you, but sometimes I just have to yell." She listened and nodded, rubbing the sleeve of her sweater against her nose. He brushed a tear off her cheek with his finger. She relaxed and leaned against his body, as he put his arm around her.

"Are you enjoying the movie?"

"I was."

"Can I watch it with you now?"

"Yes. Do you want a bite of my ice cream?"

"Well, that is very nice. I will take a bite, my darling. I'm sorry I scared you darling, but you do know that sometimes people need privacy when they are talking on the phone, right?"

"Yes, Daddy tells me that he needs to talk on the phone in privacy."

"Yes, darling, that's right. So when grownups need privacy, you know that it's important not to listen, right?"

"Yes. But I didn't try to listen to your privacy. I just heard because the window was open."

"I know, darling, but if you happen to hear someone talking and they want privacy, then you have to remember that what they are talking about is a secret, OK?"

"I know, Uncle Travis. I know about secrets and stuff like that."

"I'm sure you do, darling. So you know that it's important not to say anything to anyone about what you heard me say on the phone, right?"

"Yes, sir. I won't say anything, I promise."

"I know you won't, darling." He returned the spoon to her and she took a large bite of ice cream. He licked his thumb and wiped a bit of chocolate from her cheek. She took another bite of ice cream. He leaned back into his bean bag chair and they continued watching the movie together in silence.

* * *

John picked up Lucy the next morning. Her usual protests to stay with Travis longer were met with smiles. He let her finish her third bowl of cereal and they left. Travis followed them out and drove to work.

"Travis, hey man, what's up with you?" asked Jim Keefer. They were both filling their coffee cups in the staff lounge.

"Hey, dude. Not much. How 'bout you?"

"Same old stuff, man. Check this out." Jim turned his head to reveal a bandage covering the top part of his ear. "Some guy put a Tyson on me, man."

"What! What the hell are you talking about?"

"Didn't you hear, man? Everyone's calling me Evander Holyfield."

"You mean some perp just bit your ear, like Mike Tyson did?"

"Damn straight. I know he wasn't trying to pierce it for me. He even spat a little piece of it back in my face."

"Wow, man. When did this happen?"

"Two nights ago. Got called in as back up to help with a big bar fight. I was helping our guys load a few of the bad ones into a squad car and another cop let one of his guys get loose. Perp was handcuffed and everything. Didn't see him coming."

"Guess it could've been worse man. Could've lost something more than just the tip of your ear."

"Damn straight, like I haven't been thinking about that."

"What's it look like under there?"

"Nothing really. Lost a piece about the size of a dime. Doc says it's easy to patch it up so that no one can tell."

"Maybe you should just leave it. Kinda like a war wound."

"Might just do that. Hey, man, umm, Joe's looking for you. Says that he needs to talk to you when you come in."

"Fuck, man, what did I do this time?" He took a long drink

of his coffee.

"Might be good news. The boss man was smiling."

"Hmm. Well, I guess I better get on in there, right?"

"Yeah, see ya' round."

"Yeah, take it easy Holyfield." He walked out of the lounge and down the hall. When he reached the lieutenant's office, he knocked and was waved in by a large, balding man, who was just finishing up a phone conversation. Joe Smalls had been on the Durham police force for thirty years. He told the new recruits that if they made it as long as he did, they'd be just as fat as he was due to all the late night donuts and sodas. Joe was well liked by everyone, including Travis. He had a reputation for being hot-headed, but he looked out for his men and always went the extra mile to help them. He liked to brag he was the only boss that could kick you in the groin and pat you on the back at the same time.

He hung up the phone. "Well, well, Mr. Hanson. I need to have a little chat with you my friend. Why don't you take a seat?" Travis eased himself into the worn wooden chair across the desk from Joe.

"Hey, Joe. Can't we just start off with a little, 'How's it going Travis?' or, "Hey Joe, how's your kid doing at NC State?""

"Forget that. You know me. Not too good on the small talk shit. Listen, my friend, you're being watched. Couple of folks higher up have been singing your praises."

"Really? Tell me more."

"You know those two drug busts you made last month?"

"Sure. One guy from New York, the other guy from New Orleans."

"Got calls from higher ups from both places. They've been trying to bust both of these douche bags for a long time."

"Always aiming to please." He leaned back in the chair and laced his fingers together behind his head. "So what are the head honchos around here saying about me?"

"They're telling me that I need to get you moved up. Back to where you were before all that trial shit you went through."

"Well, Joe, it's about time."

"Maybe so. That trial was a goddamn nightmare for all

of us. I'm just glad it worked out for you. Anyway, you can't go through something like that and not have it stick on you for a while."

Travis leaned forward in his chair, and placed his fist on the desk. "But, Joe, it's been five fucking years. Five long years busting my ass to show them and everyone else that the trial was some bogus, trumped up shit."

"I know, man, I know. Look, you got shafted. We all know that. But it's politics. You played it right, just right. Now the time has come to put that stuff in the past."

"Goddamn right. I put it in the past a long time ago." He slumped back into the chair and took a drink of coffee. "Anyway, looks to me like it's time to start putting things in motion. Don't know how soon. I've gotta work out a few other kinks and everything, but I wanted to give you a heads up. Don't be saying anything around here until I give the go ahead. You know that Fischer's been pressing hard to move up and he ain't going to be smiling about you moving up ahead of him."

"Screw Fischer. I've been doing this twice as long as that little pussy. He seems to know what he's doing and everything, but you gotta put in the time too, right?"

"Well, you know, man, they want results. You and Fischer have been bringing in the good collars over the last two years. He'll be moving up soon enough."

"So, how long do you think?"

"Month or two. Maybe a little longer. You'll be getting a nice little pay raise too."

"I know. Still not enough for all the shit I've had to eat these past few years."

"You've been doing good my man. Like I said, that trial is all in the past now."

"Thanks, Joe. Couldn't have done it without your help."

"Sure you could have, it just might've taken you another five years if you didn't have me looking out for ya'!" Joe stood up and walked out from behind his desk, and walked Travis to the door. He held the door open for him and patted him on the back.

"Sure is nice to have you patting me on the back instead of

kicking me in the nuts."

"Just keep that in mind pal. Don't mess around with this. If I have to, you know I'll kick your ass if you screw it up."

"Sure, Joe, sure. Thanks again," said Travis. He walked out the door and back to the main hallway.

* * *

Just as Jamel hung up the phone, Roxx banged on his front door.

"What do you want? I don't have time to fuck around with you."

"Just came by to hang out, bro. What's up with you?"

"Nothing. Go away."

"Now, come on, Jamel. Let's go get some food or something. Whad'ya say? Wanna get high? I picked up some killer homegrown shit from this guy last week. This stuff will flip you out." Jamel turned around and walked into the living room. Roxx took that as an invitation to follow.

"Too tired. I've gotta relax."

"Tired? From what?"

"Who the fuck knows, man. Just tired."

"Well then you need to try some of this weed. It'll chill you like you've never chilled before." He pulled a plastic bag and a pipe from his coat.

"Put it away. I don't want you getting high here and just passing out on the couch."

"Come on. Just try a little."

"Fuck no. Got it?"

Roxx jammed the bag and pipe back into his coat pocket. He looked into the kitchen and then back at Jamel. Jamel nodded his permission, and Roxx walked to the refrigerator and opened the door.

"You ain't got shit to eat, man. Couple of apples and two slices of pizza."

"Then get the fuck outta here and go get your own food."

Roxx walked back toward the living room, and picked up a

photo of a red convertible mustang laying beside Jamel's telephone. Another picture underneath was a rear shot of the car, enlarged so that the license tag number was visible. He squinted at the pictures. "Hey, this is Wanda's car. What the hell you doing with pictures of her car on your desk?"

Jamel leapt to his feet and snatched the photo from Roxx's hand in one swift motion. He set it on top of the other photo and slid two other scraps of paper under the photos. "Don't you know better than to be looking at people's shit? Keep your fucking eyes and hands away from my shit."

"But, what the ..."

"It ain't nothing. It's just some stupid ass idea, that's all. I just got an idea that this dude I know who knows someone that collects old mustangs might be interested in Wanda's car. So, I just asked her if I could take a picture of it and see what the dude might pay. You know, Wanda loves that car so she'd never sell it, but she said go ahead. She seemed like she wanted to know what she could get for it anyway."

"Wow, dude, that's pretty damn fucking cool of you to do that for her."

"I'm always looking out for my crew. She liked that I was doing it for her. But look, don't say anything about it. She told me not to make a big deal out of it. I don't think she'd go through with it anyway, you know. She loves that damn car like a kid."

"Sure, dude. I ain't going to say shit to any one, especially Wanda. I'm cool man. I'm cool." Roxx started walking toward the door. "I'm gonna get outta here like you said. I gotta get me some food."

"Yeah man. Don't be getting hungry. I'm going to just hang out here and relax."

Roxx left and Jamel walked into the small bedroom that he used for an office and peered from behind the curtain. He watched him get into his car. Roxx looked back at the front door and then reached for his cell phone. Jamel stepped back from the window and hurried out the front door. He jogged to the car and tapped on the driver side window.

"Hey, man. Hey wait up, Roxx." Startled, he let the phone

slip from his hand, and rolled down the window.

"Changed my mind, man. Let me in quick, it's fucking cold out here." Roxx gave an awkward smile and nodded. He reached over and unlocked the passenger door just before Jamel opened it. Roxx grabbed the phone from between his legs and slipped it into his inside coat pocket.

"McDonald's, my man. Let's roll. Gotta get me a Big Mac."

"I thought you was just gonna chill?" Even in the cold, a line of sweat had formed on Roxx's brow. He wiped it off. "I was just thinking about hittin' the drive through and just taking it home."

"That's cool. Let's roll."

"What happened to you wanting to just chill out?"

"Don't know. Just felt hungry all of a sudden. And get that weed out. Let's stoke up the appetite a little."

Roxx pulled the bag and pipe out of his pocket and handed them to Jamel.

"Goddamn, it's cold. Man I ran out of the house to catch you without even getting my coat. You got anything like a sweat-shirt or something I can wear?"

"Yeah, look in the back seat."

He turned and picked up a white Duke sweatshirt. There were three large ketchup stains on the front. "This must have been the shirt you were wearing the last time you hit McDonald's, dude. God I hate fucking Duke."

"Yeah. I was fucking wasted last Saturday. Spilled shit all over me."

"Got another one?"

"Yeah. Look around for the Carolina one."

"Got it." He turned back around and slipped the oversized sweatshirt on, pulling the sleeves up over his forearms. He opened the baggie that Roxx had handed him, filled the pipe, took a lighter out of the ash tray, and lit the pipe, breathing deeply. He held the pipe up to Roxx's lips and Roxx did the same. Roxx exhaled and Jamel put the pipe back up to Roxx's lips and relit it. Jamel leaned his head back. "You're right. I can feel this shit already."

"Told you. It's good as hell. We'll be flying high by the time we get to Mickey D's."

"Oh fuck, man, don't let me forget after we get the food, I gotta make a call and pick up some cash from this fuckhead who owes me about five large. Help me out and I'll cut you in for 10 percent."

"Sure, man, sure. I'm here for you Jamel. Do I need to break out any of my 'special equipment'?"

"Naw, man. Nothing like that. Just gotta get the cash."

Ten minutes later, they pulled up in front of an abandoned tobacco warehouse near downtown.

"Turn down that alley over there, then go about a hundred yards and you'll see a place where you can drive into the warehouse."

Roxx followed the instructions. He drove the car into the warehouse and turned off the engine. A group of cinderblocks with two-by-six's on top for seats were set up twenty-five yards away. Fast food cups, plastic soda bottles, and used syringes littered the area around the ramshackle seating.

"Let's get out and eat over there."

"Too cold. This is the place where you want to meet some dude to pick up a wad of cash?"

"Yeah, man. I've used it a bunch of times. It ain't that cold in here, you'll see." Jamel got out and slammed the car door. A group of pigeons fluttered away to the far side of the warehouse. He walked over to the seating area. Roxx stayed in the car shaking his head. He ate his fries slowly, staring at Roxx. After two minutes, Roxx got out and sat down next to him, starting in on his second Big Mac.

"Give me your phone, man. I gotta go ahead and call that dude and get him over here."

He sat up, removed the phone from his pocket, and handed it to him. Jamel hit the 'redial' button and glanced at the phone as it displayed Wanda's home number. He winced and looked over at Roxx as he jammed the remaining third of his Big Mac into his mouth. Jamel closed the phone and drew back his hand. He brought the phone forward rapidly, smashing it into the back of his skull. Bits of lettuce and bread spewed out of his mouth as he fell forward onto the gravel and dirt. Roxx placed his right hand in front of him to break his fall, then rolled over to his left and looked up at Jamel.

Jamel fell on top of him and jammed his right fist downward and forward under Roxx's nose, forcing his mouth open. His left hand came smashing down, cramming a Big Mac deep into his mouth. He stood up and delivered a kick to his chest. Roxx was coughing and pulling himself forward on his elbows. He stepped sideways and raised his foot again, slamming it hard between Roxx's shoulder blades. His head fell back down into the dirt. Jamel whipped off his sweatshirt twirled it over one time, and wrapped it around Roxx's face. He drove his right foot down hard into Roxx's back and pulled back on the sweatshirt.

Roxx's hands grabbed at the cloth covering his face. His body convulsed with panic as Jamel pulled tighter. After three minutes, Roxx's hands dropped down into the dirt. He held tight for another two minutes and then released his grip. His limp head hit the ground with a sharp thud. Jamel pulled the sweatshirt away from Roxx's head.

"Damn, Roxx," he shouted. "I done told you about watching what you eat. I told you over and over this McDonald's shit was gonna kill you some day. Now looks like you've gone and choked yourself on a Big-ass Mac, homey. Fucking helluva way to go, now ain't it?" He wiped the sweat off his forehead with the sleeve of the sweatshirt, and sat back down on the makeshift seats. He flipped the top off of his Coke cup and gulped it down.

"Fucking hell, ain't it, Roxx," he shouted again. "Now if you would've been a smart guy and not picked up the phone and tried to call Wanda, well then I wouldn't have had to smack you upside the head with it, now would I?"

Jamel looked down at the broken phone. Getting down on one knee, he picked up three large pieces of the phone, then gathered ten smaller pieces, and put everything into an empty McDonald's bag. Then he grabbed Roxx's Coke and drank the rest of it. Glancing around the area, he collected the items he had touched and put them into the McDonald's bag. Slipping off his shoes, he began sweeping the dirt and gravel clear of his shoe prints before walking back over to Roxx's car and picking up the pipe, baggie, and lighter from the passenger's seat. He proceeded to dust off the seat, dash, and door handles with the sweatshirt and walked out of the warehouse.

* * *

It took Wanda three weeks to sell all of the product. When she finished, she called John the next day to tell him the good news and suggested they get together so he could collect his share.

The next day, John sat in his office, staring at the clock. Thoughts of Lucy's upcoming surgery weighed on his mind, making it difficult for him to focus on work. Despite his frequent meetings with her doctor and the reassurances he received, he could not shake the thought that something could go wrong. Even though the exact date of the operation was dependent on the arrival of a proper donor match, her doctor was certain that based on where Lucy was on the list, the procedure would happen before the end of April. Meeting with Wanda would be a welcome distraction. The money was less of a concern now. His company was busier than he had expected. He looked down at the phone on his desk and every line was busy. This was always a good sign. As he walked out of his office, John stopped by Mary's desk.

"I'm going out for the rest of the day. Got to meet someone about a work thing"

"Sure. Did you see the invoice for that group cruise I booked?"

"I did. Good job."

"It was the same group of people that were planning on going last year but cancelled after 9/11."

"So, they're going out in October?"

"Yeah. Got more deposits than last time. When all is said and done, the group may be twice as large as what they planned for last year."

"Fantastic. Gotta go."

She nodded and looked down at her desk calendar. "Hey, hold on a second. Today's the twenty-fourth. Remember I set up a presentation for you with that church group who wants to go on a mission trip to Barbados? They're expecting you at the church at 5:30 today."

"Damn, forgot. There is no way I can do it today. I've got to pick Lucy up from school. I promised that I'd take her out for pizza. I can't break that promise to her. You go. You'll be managing the group anyway."

"I get nervous doing those types of things. If you talk to them, I know we'll get the business."

"Just do the best you can. They'll like you; that's what matters. Be sure to tell them about your experience in the industry and how many groups you've handled before." Her phone rang. It was difficult to understand her lack of confidence. Her ability to manage customers and people in general was the best he had ever seen. She took down a phone number, promising to return the call in just a moment.

"Alright. But don't do this to me again. If we don't get the group, then it'll be your fault, right?"

"I'll take the blame. But don't think about it like that. You'll do fine."

"Does Lucy know you're getting a new car?"

"No, but I made sure I got one in her favorite color and that it has a built-in DVD player."

"So is that the car?" She motioned toward the new minivan in the parking lot.

"No. I'm picking it up tomorrow. The salesman gave me this one to drive just for today. These vans have a smooth ride and when you're driving, you're riding up high. Of course, anything's better than the old car I'm getting rid of."

"If we stay this busy, we'll all get new cars." Her phone rang again and he motioned for her to pick it up.

He saw Wanda's car as he pulled into the McDonald's parking lot. She waved at him from inside, the Nike bag at her side.

"You look happy."

"I'm always happy at this kind of meeting."

"Why's that?" He took a seat across from her.

"Why do you think?"

"Enough said. You eating?"

"Can't eat here. Had a friend who used to eat here too much. They just found him dead. Choked to death on a Big Mac."

"I hope you're kidding or you're just saying that to keep me from eating here."

"No. Cops found him in an old warehouse with wrappers all around him and food stuffed in his mouth. Weird shit, too because he was fat as hell and I used to tell him that all the McDonald's food he ate was gonna kill him some day."

"Damn. Was it a good friend?"

"Work friend. I liked the guy and everything. Life is messed up. One minute you're boppin' around, having fun, the next, you're choking on a Big Mac."

"How 'bout we change the subject?"

"Fine with me. This thing's just got me thinking, that's all. Something shitty can happen to you and then it's all over." She shifted the bag on her lap.

"So, you got something in that bag for me?"

"Yep. One-hundred-and-fifty grand. We scored on this one."

"Wow. That's better than you thought."

"What can I say? I'm good at what I do."

"That you are." He held out his hand and she gave him the bag.

"Lucy's been bugging me to get together with Tonya. Can we meet you guys here next week for dinner?"

"Guess that'll be our farewell dinner, huh?" She looked down at her hands and picked at a nail.

"Nah. We can't have our farewell dinner here. We'll let the girls eat and play and have fun. Then I'll take you out for a real celebration dinner."

"Hmm, a celebration dinner? Well, I might go but it depends on where you take me."

"Well, I'd say that after your incredible sales success, you deserve to go to the very best place I can think of. I'll let you know tomorrow. I've got to pick up Lucy."

"I'll walk out with you." They left the restaurant and stopped beside his minivan.

"Looks like you got yourself a new car?"

"Needed one. Haven't told Lucy yet."

"Did you get the minivan with the DVD player?"

"Yes I did."

"I've been thinking about getting one of these myself."

"So you like it, huh?"

"Love it. Just what I've been thinking about getting. Nice color too."

"Why don't you drive this one today and I'll take your car? This is just a loaner until my car comes in tomorrow. I want to surprise Lucy and I'd rather have her see the real car."

"Really? I'd love that."

"I'd kinda like to drive your car too. She'll get a kick out of riding in it."

"OK then." She handed him her keys. "Meet you here tomorrow to trade back."

"You bet."

"And don't forget about taking me out. I want to go to the most expensive restaurant there is."

"OK. You deserve it. Saturday night, it's a date," said John, smiling. He hoisted the Nike bag over his shoulder.

"Damn, this bag is heavy!"

"Won't be so heavy after our date on Saturday."

"You're funny."

"I wouldn't pack that bag in a car, too valuable."

"Way ahead of you. Gonna put it in the safe at my office."

" Okay, see you tomorrow."

XVI - March 28, 2002

When John woke up in the hospital, memories of the incident rushed back into his consciousness. *Daddy, Daddy, please wake up. Please help me. I'm bleeding, Daddy, really bad. Daddy, you've got to wake up and help me. I'm coming sweetie. I'm coming to get you out. I'll help you my sweet Lucy. I'll help you.*

He turned his head and noticed his mother's bloodshot eyes, filling with tears, as she held his hand. Wanda dabbed her eyes with a tissue.

I'm cold, Daddy. I'm bleeding all over and I'm cold. Wake up, Daddy. Please wake up, Daddy, please.

Ok, sweetie. Daddy's coming to save you. I'm coming right now, sweetie.

He couldn't speak because his jaw was wired shut. As the room came more into focus, his eyes opened wide, asking the question they knew he would ask. Wanda shook her head.

"She's, she's not here, John. She didn't make it."

When he woke the next day, Wanda was still there. He turned his head away from her and she took his hand. It had not been a dream.

"I'm so sorry, John. I'm so sorry."

Tears streamed down his face as he tried to cry out. His Lucy was gone. She took a tissue from the box beside his bed and dabbed his tears. He pushed her hand away. She took out another tissue and put it in his hand. He wiped his eyes and nose.

"The doctor said it would be best if you just keep sleeping."

He nodded.

"My sweet, sweet John. I'm sorry. I'm just so, so sorry."

He held his hand up and wrote in the air. The nurse had left a pad and pencil, knowing he would have questions. She handed him the pencil, and held the small notepad up in front of him while he wrote.

"You and Lucy had an accident while you were driving home." He shook his head and wrote more.

"Oh, to Lucy." She sniffled and took a tissue from the box. "Oh God, John. I'm so sorry. She got cut bad by a piece of glass and just lost too much blood." He winced and grunted. He twisted his body and slammed his hand down on the bed. The pencil bounced onto the floor while his body trembled.

"I'm so sorry. They said that your leg is going to take a while to get better but you're going to be fine." He held his hand up again for the pencil. She retrieved it and handed it back to him.

"Where is she? Lucy?" He nodded. "Oh God. No one knew how long you might be asleep. We buried her two days ago." She dabbed his eyes with her tissue. "Your mother is going to be here later today. One of us will be here every day until you get out. The doctor said that you'll need to stay another three or four days before you can go home." Wanda heard no response; he had drifted back to sleep.

* * *

After his release from the hospital, John was haunted by thoughts of Lucy. He tried to distract himself by reading and watching TV. The accident, her voice calling him, her damaged body—the images and sounds pervaded his mind. In a recurring dream, he was lying in bed with her, his face an inch from hers, trying to breathe in her breath but she wasn't breathing. Suddenly, she would open her eyes, smile, and say, 'Daddy, I'm so cold, could you get me a blanket?' A trickle of blood ran from her scalp and across her face onto the pillow. He'd bring in a blanket, only to find her lying in her bed, now soaked with blood. Her dull, blank eyes were like those of the great white sharks he'd seen at Hatteras. He'd reach down to pick her up from the bed, but she was gone. Then she reappeared at the doorway, waving at him, motioning him to follow. He'd walk from the bed to the doorway, but she had already begun walking down the hall. In the hallway, he'd find her holding hands with Travis, both of them waving goodbye. He'd run as fast as he could, but the hallway grew longer with each stride. She'd look back, smile, and wave as she and Travis jumped off an edge into a black chasm. When he made it to the edge, they were gone. He'd wake from the dream, sweating and silently screaming her name, breaking down into tears as he lay in bed, realizing again that she was gone.

His leg was healing, but movement still brought pain. There was a nurse that came by for an hour in the morning to check on him. She made breakfast and encouraged him to get cleaned up and ready for the day. Her perkiness only aggravated him and after three days, he fired her. Pain medication did not provide enough relief, so he started drinking.

One evening, after imbibing half a fifth of bourbon, he fumbled for the TV remote and accidently started the VCR, which contained a home movie of his trip to Disneyworld with Lucy eighteen months ago. He sat frozen, staring at the screen, tears running down his cheeks. He watched Lucy laughing and running to hug her favorite, Cinderella. The next scene showed her smiling and dancing to the sounds of a parade with all of the Disney characters. Later, she had informed him that every princess in the parade had blown her a kiss. His shoulders shook and the sobs grew deeper. Attempts to turn off the VCR failed. He grunted out her name and threw the remote at the VCR. The torture of the home movie continued.

He grimaced, limping to the VCR, and switched off the tape. He would not go on living. He wanted to be with her, to hold her, to talk to her—that was what mattered. He walked with great care to the garage, opened the door to his new van, and wrestled his broken body into the seat. He started the engine; the garage door remained closed. He was leaving to see his sweet, sweet girl.

Wanda arrived to check on him, as promised. She pulled into the driveway just as the fumes began seeping out from underneath the garage door. She struggled to lift the door, but couldn't. She ran to the front door. Locked. In desperation, she removed her sweater and wrapped it around her right hand to break the glass and unlock the door. She ran through house and threw open the door that led to the garage. "John!" she yelled, as she punched the garage door opener. She headed into the fumes, fanning with one hand and coughing into the other. Slinging open the car door, she grabbed his wrists and jerked him out of the seat. She crashed onto the floor, knocking over a box of old newspapers. He fell out of the seat but his legs remained in the car. The pain woke him and he grunted in agony.

"John! John! Wake up! I'm goin' to get you out of here!"

He rolled over on top of her. Pushing him off, she stood and grabbed him under the arms. She dragged him out and fell down in the driveway, vomiting from the fumes. He lay on the concrete beside her, coughing, writhing in pain.

"Why, why?" He mumbled. She wiped her eyes and mouth.

"If my little girl died, I'd think about killing myself, I know I would. But is that what she would want you to do? Think about her, about what she would want."

"All I think about. Don't want to live!"

"I know. I know." She stood up and brushed the dirt from her arms. "Let's go back inside and talk. I'll get you cleaned up." She held out her hand and he slapped it away. She went into the garage, turned off the car, and came back.

"You know how stubborn I am, so you can just lay there until you let me help you back into your house." He wiped his hands across his face and pushed himself up, only to fall back down. She held out her hand again and he took it.

* * *

The next day his mother moved in. At dinner that night, she did her best to distract him and make small talk. Lucy's absence hung in the air like a thick, cold fog. It clouded everything.

"I haven't heard from Travis in a while. Has he been by?"

"No."

"I've called and left four messages. When I call, his voicemail says that it is full. I wish I knew what was going on with him."

"Don't care about Travis," he grunted. She turned her attention to her salad. "See him at the funeral?" he added.

"No. I haven't talked to him at all."

"Call his boss?"

"No, but I did call his friend Jim at work. He said that he hadn't seen him in about a week and that if he heard anything he'd call me. You'd think he'd at least tell me he was going out of town."

"Last summer? Girlfriend?"

"Yeah. He did disappear last summer for a while with some girl. I need him to fix my car. That rattling sound is back and it's driving me crazy."

"Hmm."

* * *

The next day Wanda arrived at noon to relieve Connie. She sat on a chair beside John, who was resting on the couch.

"You on suicide watch?"

"Guess you can call it that. I just came for a free lunch." He stared at the ceiling. She leaned back in her chair and watched TV. Connie had turned the sound off.

"How's Tonya?"

"She's fine."

"She ask about Lucy?"

"No. I told her what happened." He felt the tears began. He turned away from her and wiped his eyes.

"This morning she asked a lot about you. I told her how you were doing." She reached down for her pocketbook and pulled out a sheet of paper.

"She made you this 'Get Well' card." She held out the paper but he did not reach for it.

"Not now. Save for later."

"No problem. How's the leg?"

"Hurts like shit."

"Sorry."

"Percocet?"

"Sure." She walked to kitchen and returned with a glass of water and the pill. He sat up on the couch.

"Break it up. Can't chew." She did. "Thanks."

"No problem. What do you want for lunch today?".

"Not hungry. Help yourself."

"I'll get something in a second." She leaned back in her seat and watched the TV.

"I decided that Tonya and I are going to move."

"Move? Where?"

"Remember me talking about Monterey?"

"Yeah. 'Quarium, right?"

"Yep. Well I've been thinking a lot more about it and I want to get the hell out of here for good. I put down a deposit on a small house that we can rent for a year. It's south of Monterey, near Big Sur."

"Wow. When?"

"Two or three weeks. Not sure yet." She studied her nails. "I've got an idea that may help you."

"What's that?"

"Come with us. We're going to drive, take our time, and see the sights. You could use some time away from here."

"Cross country adventure, huh?"

"Guess so. I've never done anything like this. Tonya's excited."

"I bet she is. She can go to the aquarium whenever she wants, and eat a lot of tuna, right?"

"Yeah."

"I've thought about running away. Everything here reminds me of her."

"I thought so. If you came with us you'd get a chance to clear your head."

"It is a good idea. Mary can pretty much take care of the business."

"That's good."

"I'll think about it." She studied her nails again. "It's a nice thing to offer. I don't think I've said thanks for all you've done since the accident."

"You don't have to."

"Yeah, I do. You've been a good friend through all this."

Tears formed in his eyes and he turned his head to the back of the couch. She reached over and put her hand on his shoulder. He reached up and put his hand on top of hers. She looked down at the floor and cried with him. After a few minutes, she took a tissue from the small table beside the couch and blew her nose.

"I'm going to make a sandwich now. You sure you don't want something?"

"Yeah, I am a little hungry. Wish I could have a sandwich. Tomato soup is fine."

"No problem."

XVII - April

Wanda and Tonya had begun packing. They were to leave at the end of the month, which was two weeks away, but Tonya insisted they start right away.

"I've been thinking about it Mommy and I decided that I'm going to take all my toys."

"You can't take them all, baby. We've already talked about this. We don't have enough room to take everything."

"But that's not fair."

"I know, honey, I know. But I'm going to get you some new toys when we get there, I promise."

She sat down on the floor, jutting her lower lip out and crossing her arms.

"Don't be mad, honey. We've got the new minivan now and we can take a lot of your things, just not all of them. We might even have an extra person going with us."

"Who? Who's coming with us?" The pout disappeared.

"Well, I'm not sure yet. John may come with us. He's still thinking about it."

"Really?"

"Yes, honey."

She watched her smile grow and then fade. Tonya's gaze fell downward.

"I wish Lucy could go."

"I do too, honey, I do too. She's in heaven now, honey, you know that."

"I know, Mommy. I just wish she could go with us. Then we could play dolls while we ride in the car. I wish she wasn't in heaven."

"Me too, honey."

"Mommy, does everybody go to heaven when they die?"

"Almost, honey. Bad people who are mean and hurt other people don't go to heaven."

"Mommy, are you going to die?"

"No, honey, not for a long time." She sat beside her and wrapped Tonya in her arms. "Are you scared that I'm going to die?"

"Sometimes."

"You don't need to be worried about that. Everybody dies, but that hardly ever happens until a person gets real old." She pulled her closer and stroked the back of her neck. "You know I love you more than anything. You don't need to worry about me dying. That's not going to happen for a long time."

Wanda heard a car door slam. She stood up and walked over to the bedroom window. It was Jamel's car. Someone banged on the front door. She panicked. They had not spoken since she and John had made their second trip. She was surprised he had not tried to contact her. If he came in, he would see that they were leaving. There would be questions.

"Mama, someone is knocking on the door. Aren't you going to let them in?"

"Yes, honey. Umm, but, I need you to play a pretend game of hide and seek. Follow me. She opened the closet door and bent down pushing aside two boxes of old clothes that blocked a small opening in the closet wall.

"Honey, do you remember when I showed you this little hiding place?"

"Yes, Mommy."

"OK, honey, now you get in there." Wanda reached over and took a blanket from a shelf. "Here, honey, here's a blanket for you. Get inside right now. I'm going to close the door and cover you up with these boxes, you know, just like hide and seek." Wanda grabbed her wrist and pulled her down toward the opening.

"I need you to promise me something?"

"But Mama, it's dark in there. I don't want to go in there. It's too scary."

"Tonya, sweetie, I don't have time to talk about this. Just

do what I say right now. Listen now. You cannot come out of here until I say so. No matter what happens, you and I are playing hide and seek, and you have got to stay inside this hiding place. Do you understand? Do not come out, no matter what." Tonya nodded and eased herself into the opening.

"Ok, Mama. I'll hide."

"You'll be fine in here, sugar. Remember, this is hide and seek so don't come out until Mommy says so, OK? Now I'm going to close this door, but don't be scared, just think about being on the cruise ship and playing in the pool, OK? Remember how much you liked that?"

"Sure, Mommy, I'm hiding now. You better go see who is there. It sounds like they're mad now since no one has come to the door."

She moved the boxes back in front of the opening, closing Tonya in, and then locked the closet door from the inside. Rushing out to the kitchen, she knelt down beside the refrigerator, and felt around for her handgun. As her fingers touched the barrel, Jamel kicked the front door; the sound of splintering wood permeated the air as the door frame gave way.

Only one hinge held, which did not slow him. He was through the door and she watched helplessly as he raised his silencer-equipped HK 9mm and fired a round into her leg. She cried out and pulled her hand from behind the refrigerator, grabbing the injured leg. She swung her body out of the way just in time to miss Jamel's foot as he attempted to kick her in the chest. He shoved the refrigerator away from the wall and picked up her gun. It was small and he slid it into the pocket of his jacket.

"Oh, Wanda, were you not looking forward to seeing me? That's a pity, because we have so much to talk about." He grabbed the back of her shirt collar and dragged her to the bedroom.

"You shot me in the fucking leg, you asshole. What are you doin'?"

"Looks like I did the right thing now don't it my dear?"

"Hold on, Jamel. Look, I can explain some stuff."

"We're just going to chat, my love. Now, where is your sweet daughter? Wouldn't want her interrupting our discussions, would we? Please tell me right away so she won't get dragged into this." He dropped her in front of a small wooden rocker and motioned for her to sit. She pulled herself up, wincing as she eased into the chair. Rocking back and forth, she pressed her hands against the wound.

"Now, lemme just show you what's in store if you don't tell me everything I need to know." He put his foot on her hip and her hands moved to push it off. He jammed his finger into the open wound and twisted it.

"Stop. Goddamn it, stop!" She tried to push his hand away and he drove the finger in deeper. "OK. OK, just stop. God that fucking hurts."

He stood back up and pulled a towel from a half-filled box. "Here, tie it up with this." He threw the towel toward her and she caught it.

"Looks like you're moving. You should've told me. You should've told me a lot of things."

"Found another place, that's all. Closer to Tonya's school. We're not moving far." He walked backwards toward the door, still watching her and then glanced down hallway.

"Where is she?"

"Look, Jamel, wait a fucking minute! Look at my leg! You just fucking shot me."

"And I will shoot you in the other leg unless you tell me right now where she is."

Her face tightened as she wrapped the towel around her leg.

"She's playing with a friend. I'm supposed to call and say when I'm coming to pick her up."

"Perfect." He removed his cell phone from its clip and tossed it onto her lap. "Start dialing."

She picked up the phone and flipped it open.

"Do it." He took off his jacket.

"I'm trying to remember the number. Just give me a fucking minute."

She dialed John's cell phone.

* * *

Ten minutes before he received the phone call, John limped up the long concrete pathway that led to Lucy's grave, placing the cane down slowly with each step. The honeysuckle vines in his yard had just bloomed and he had brought a small handful of the flowers for her. They were her favorite. He had shown her how to pull the flower off the vine and then extract a small drop of sugary tasting water from the flower. She always called them "honeysnuckles."

When he reached her grave, he opened the small folding chair he had brought and sat down. As he bent forward to lay the flowers on her grave, he found that a small handful of honeysuckles had already been placed there along with a small box.
He used his cane to drag the box toward him. A distant streetlight provided enough light for him to see it was a new box of clothes for a Beach Girl Brittney doll. He set the box on his lap and looked around the graveyard. It had rained for an hour earlier in the day; however, the box was dry. Both Travis and his mother knew this was her favorite doll but his mother had yet to visit the gravesite.

His cell phone vibrated in his pocket. "Hello?"

"Hey, it's Wanda."

"Hey there. This is a bad time. I'll call you back."

"Look, I need a favor. Do you mind if Tonya just stays over there tonight? I've got something urgent that just came up."

"What are you talking about Wanda?"

"Good thanks. I know she'll be fine, she just loves to play with your little boy. I'll come over and get her around 8, OK? Yeah, thanks."

"Wait, Wanda ..." The line went dead. The caller ID did not match her number. He placed the box and his honeysuckles on top of Lucy's grave and moved as quickly as he could back to his car.

* * *

Twenty minutes later, he reached her house. Gazing through the broken door, he saw blood stains on the refrigerator and a thin red smear that lead to her bedroom. He pushed the door aside and limped into the room.

"Hey, Wanda? What's going on with all this blood?" he shouted. "I called the cops and they'll be here any minute." He waited. She appeared on the hallway floor, dragging herself. He hobbled toward her. Her left eye was swollen shut and the right side of her face was covered with blood.

"Oh God, Wanda.Wanda! What happened? Who did this? God, oh my God, you're bleeding all over." He eased himself down to the floor and she rolled over on her back. He could tell by her blood soaked clothing that she had been shot in the chest.

"He was here."

"Who?"

"Jamel. He knows. Shot me in the leg and beat the shit out of me." Blood dripped from her mouth and nose. "Got mad because I wouldn't talk and shot me in chest. Thought I was dead."

"Where did he go?"

"Not sure. Passed out. I hope that you didn't really call the cops."

"No, I didn't but I'll call 9-1-1 right now. Where's Tonya?"

"Hid her in the closet and the door's still locked. She's OK. Don't call anyone. They'll just take her away when they see all this shit."

"I'll get her now."

"Wait, don't. Just hope she fell asleep in the closet and didn't hear anything. Take me into the living room. I don't want her to see me like this." He wrapped his arms around her and tried to pull her down the hallway. She cried out. "Goddamn that hurts like shit. Hold on a second. I gotta tell you some things." He took off his jacket, rolled it up, and placed it under her head. He wiped the blood from her eyes and face with a tissue. "Look at me. I've been bleeding too much. You've got to take Tonya out of here. No cops, no ambulance. If they come, they'll just take her away and she'll just go into the foster system. You've got to promise me you'll take care of her. I ain't got nobody else to depend on."

"Wanda, you're going to be OK. I gotta call 9-1-1." She pushed his hand down as he raised the phone up to dial.

"No. No one can know about this."

"Just hold on. I … I don't want you to die. I'm going to go

with you. You know, just like you said. You, me, Tonya. We can start over. We can all be together. You can't die on me!"

"Oh, my sweet John. I knew you'd want to come with us." She moaned and her head rolled to the right. She coughed and blood sprayed onto John's pants. He wiped her mouth. "We would've had a good life together in California, huh?"

"Of course, but just hold on. I'll get some help for you somehow."

"I already thought about it. You've got to take Tonya away from here fast, so no one knows what happened to her. If the cops came you'd have to answer a bunch of questions and they might connect you somehow and then there wouldn't be anyone for Tonya. No, the only way is for you to take her and go. Go now."

He leaned closer to her face, tears streaming down. She looked up and took his face in her bloodied hands.

"Now, you heard what I just said. Are you going to do this for me, my sweet John? You're all that Tonya and I have. Promise me."

"I will, Wanda. I'll take good care of her."

"And you won't wait around here, right? Just get out fast. OK?"

"OK. OK. But hold on, Wanda. I need you. We both need you. Let's figure out something else. Let's get you some help. Please hold on."

"It's too late my dear. It's my time to go. I'm going to see that little girl of yours. I'm going to hold her and tell her how much you love her. Lucy and I will watch over you and Tonya. I'll take care of Lucy; you take care of my sweet little girl." Her face tightened and she coughed again. "Don't let her see me like this. You got to cover me up. Shit, it is so cold in here. I gotta.." Her eyes closed and her head rolled to the right. Her hands slid down his chin and fell onto the carpet. He picked up them up, but they were limp.

* * *

Durham Herald-Sun - April 24th, 2002

Policeman and Suspect Both Found Dead

Authorities report that Durham Police Detective Travis Hanson was discovered dead yesterday morning at the residence of suspected drug dealer, Jamel Scott. Scott was also found dead. Both were killed by gunshots at close range. Police are ruling both deaths as homicides and confirm that Detective Hanson was killed in the line of duty while trying to apprehend Scott. Exact details of the event are not clear at this point. At 7 a.m. yesterday morning, Detective Hanson's car was spotted by a patrol car at Scott's residence. After calling for backup, several officers entered the residence. The Durham police chief issued a statement at 1 p.m. announcing Detective Hanson's death and some of the circumstances surrounding the homicides. In the police chief's statement, he noted that Scott was well known to the Durham police as a major player in the drug business in Durham. The statement indicated that Hanson had Scott under surveillance and may have attempted to apprehend him. The police also reported that there may be a connection between Scott and a woman, who was an associate of Scott's: Wanda Johnson, who was discovered dead at her home yesterday morning. Johnson had been brutally beaten and shot in the chest and leg. She was discovered in her home by a neighbor who noticed her front door was ajar and that it appeared to have been broken open. The neighbor saw blood smeared on the kitchen floor and called police. It is estimated that Johnson had been killed sometime around 9 p.m. the previous evening. The police chief indicated that a full investigation had begun into all of these homicides. More details about the incidents would be released as soon as they became available.

Detective Hanson was a ten year veteran of the Durham police force. He gained some notoriety five years ago when he was indicted on corruption charges, but was later acquitted at trial. He is survived by his brother and mother who live in the area. The funeral will take place on Friday at 3 p.m. at the Rosemont Funeral home, 407 E. Buchanan St. A full police procession will escort Detective Hanson's body from the funeral home to Wellstone Cemetery.

XVI - June 2002

"Mr. John, what's the place called that we're going to?"

"Tonya, remember I told you to just call me John."

"OK, I'm sorry."

"We're going to the Bahamas in that big boat over there."

"It's really big. Does it have a TV?"

"Yes, sweetie. A big screen TV."

"Sure is a beautiful boat you got there, Mr. John Manning." Franz Koening, the marina owner, slapped him on the back.

"Hey, Franz. I was wondering where you were hiding today." They shook hands. "I thought you'd like it."

"Looks to me like you ain't packing up for a fishing trip though."

"Nah. Going to take a little trip down to the Bahamas. I guess you'd call it an extended vacation."

"Can I go and look at that big red boat over there?" asked Tonya.

"Sure, sweetie. Just be careful. Don't go anywhere else, OK?"

"OK, I won't." She skipped toward the boat.

"So is that your first mate there?"

"Yeah, I guess you could call her that. Friend of the family."

"Where's your little girl and Travis? How are they doing?"

"Oh, they're fine, just fine." He looked down at the sand and gravel that covered the parking lot and kicked at a small rock. "They're going to meet us in Nassau."

"Nice. Long family vacation on your new yacht!"

"Yep. That's it."

"Guess your business is going pretty good, huh?"

"Yeah. Things are going well."

"I guess so if you're springing for a big beauty like that one. You got a name for her yet?"

"Nah. I haven't thought about it."

"Bad luck to go on your maiden voyage without naming the boat."

"I'll come up with something." His cell phone rang in his pocket. He pulled it out and looked at the number. "Gotta take this. Excuse me for a second." Franz nodded and walked back toward the marina office.

"Hey, Mary. How are you?"

"I'm nervous as hell, that's how I am."

"Really? You've been running the place since my accident. You'll do fine."

"Maybe. I'm just nervous about how to reach you if anything important comes up."

"I'll check in periodically. You can make the decisions without me. Don't worry."

"Have you figured out where you're going yet?"

"Well, I told you about Nassau, right?"

"Yes."

"After that, I'm thinking about Costa Rica. I hear the fishing is great down there."

"And you still have no idea when you're coming back?"

"Not sure. I just have to take some time off. So much has changed."

"I know. I'm so sorry about Lucy and Travis."

"Thanks, dear." He watched Tonya chatting with the teenage boy filling his boat with diesel fuel.

"Hey, I've gotta go. I'll call you when we get to Nassau, OK?"

"OK. Be safe. We're all going to miss you, especially me."

"I'll miss you too, thanks for all you've done. Bye." He replaced the phone and walked toward the shed where the fisherman brought their catch to be cleaned. Removing a folded sheet of paper from his pocket, he spread it out on the table. It was worn from being folded and unfolded many times. It all seemed so impossible, so crazy. Two days after Travis death, he was at the office after hours, checking his email and there it was. It left him frozen. Then his body went limp and he fell on the floor, weeping for an hour. He sat back up and pulled up the purchase records on his computer. It was all there. That was one thing about selling travel, you could always tell who was traveling and where they were going. You just didn't know why. Now he did.

One of the first ticket purchases Wanda had made was five years ago, just before the end of Travis' trial. John recognized the name of the star witness that had vanished. They had both flown First Class to Fort Lauderdale. The trip she'd complained about. The cigarette boat, the deserted island where the witness couldn't be found, Wanda had been the one. She had escorted the witness, on Jamel's orders.

Then he searched for flight records in Jamel's name. There were only three as he typically flew under a different name. He studied the screen. The last flight Jamel had purchased was to St. Thomas. The dates matched and it all made sense. Everything had been there, right under his nose. Had he seen that flight record before Wanda's death, he could have warned her. She would still be alive. Had he found that flight record, he would have looked further, dug deeper, and found the record of Wanda's trip four years ago. He would have been able to make the connection, to talk to Travis, to find out more. Travis would have told him. Travis wanted to help. John unfolded the message and read it for the last time.

From: TH27705@yahoo.com

To: John@executive-travel123.com

Subject: to my Dearest Brother

My beloved brother,

I'm sure by now you know about my death at the hands of one of Durham's most famous drug dealers. I would love to know what the papers were saying, what the talk was around the station, and what kind of memorial service, if any, I might receive. I'm laughing and crying at the same time as I'm writing this message to you. See, the thing is, I'm the bad guy in all this. I've lived the worst hell that anyone can live for these past few weeks. My only salvation is my death and the small chance that you will understand.

You see, I'm the bad cop. I got involved with drug dealers. I passed along information for money. You name it, I did it for them, for the money. Whenever they needed an insider to tip them off about an upcoming arrest, I told them. If they needed one of their competitors arrested, I arranged it. If someone, an employee or customer, needed a little "warning," I did it. I had my own special way of doing these warnings. All these things had a reward for me. Just like a commission sales job. I'd close one of the deals and get my couple of thousand in commission. I figured it

was all OK. Why shouldn't I make some money helping the drug guys rip each other off? Who would be the wiser? They're all just scum anyway, right?
It got easy, real easy. I saved a lot of the money and now it's all yours. I'll tell you more about that later. There was a price to pay. God was watching and boy did he fuck me over.

I killed her. I killed Lucy. It was me. A thousand times I wanted to fall down in front of you and confess. To tell you everything that I did, how sorry I was and how I deserved any punishment you chose for me. My precious sunshine, Lucy, light of my life. She's gone and I did it. See this guy I'm here with now, he would pay me to do special 'car repairs.' You know how good I am with cars. If he wanted to scare someone, he'd give me their license plate number, I'd find the car and rig it so the driver would have an accident. He'd then contact the person whose car I rigged after the driver crashed just to let them know their recent car mishap was no accident. Nobody was hurt too badly. Heck, even if they were hurt, they were just a bunch of low-life drug dealers.

He ordered a car repair on an old mustang convertible. Gave me a picture of the car and the license tag and I found it. I adjusted the brakes, the steering, just like always. Somehow you and Lucy got in that car. I killed the most beautiful thing in my life and ruined yours forever.

I was the first person at the hospital. But they wouldn't let me see you or her. I started talking to the ambulance crew that brought you in. They told me all the details about the accident. It was bad, real bad. They told me about the car too.

My precious Lucy. Dead. I did it.

For a few days I was floating, numb and dazed. My head didn't clear until I came up with a plan. A smart plan that would end my pain. But there was nothing I could ever do to end yours. That's why I couldn't be around you. Anyway, I wasn't sleeping much and the only thing that kept me going was the plan. Did I mention the life insurance? I took out a $1 million policy on myself after I began to put the plan into action. You're the beneficiary. The documents are at my house. You know where I keep the important papers. Go get the money. Do something decent with it. Have more children. You deserve to be happy.

So, as I'm writing this, I'm in this guy's house. I got him to tell me the whole story. At least pieces of it. He didn't know we were brothers. He described a guy that he saw with this Wanda Johnson woman in St. Thomas. It sounded like you. I don't give a shit how you were involved in all this. You don't have to worry about anything else connecting you to him. Best I could tell, he was only recently looking for you. He won't be passing along any information to anyone now. He's not a pretty sight at the moment. Not sure that you would mind too much, or that anyone would for that matter. I also got him to do a little on-line banking for me. He wired $400,000 into an account that I have in the Bahamas. This is yours. All my account information is in the same place as the insurance papers. There's also $75,000 or so in there. That is most of what I collected for doing some of their dirty work. This guy showed me how to set up a bank account there and move the money around.

Gotta dig that irony now.

Funny thing about being a cop. You learn all about how these drug guys do their business. You investigate how the money is laundered, transferred, covered up. You work a few drug homicides and you learn how to read a murder scene, how to determine the sequence of events. That stuff is coming in handy now. How do you apologize for committing the sin of murdering your brother's child? Simple fact is, you can't. Even if you did come to understand or even to forgive me, I can't go on living with it. The description of this event that you will read about is just the way I've planned it, I hope. Maybe something will go wrong. Jamel's not quite dead yet, but he will soon be. After he is, I'll put his gun back in his hand. I will put his finger over the trigger, my finger over his. All wrapped up. Easy for the homicide boys to figure out. But if not,

I don't care. It's all over for me. I deserve to die.

Make sure that you delete this message.

Don't save a copy of it or print it out. I'm covering the tracks on this end. They'll take this PC apart from head to toe, but there won't be a trace of this correspondence. I'm sure you know the consequences if someone found it. I hope you know how much I love you and how sorry I am. If I were going to heaven right now to see Lucy, I would be so happy. To be with her, to hold her, to talk to her. But I know that I won't be with her. I miss her so much. Please forgive me.

Travis

His head slumped down on the table, on top of his hands. What if he had known? Travis had money and would have given every dime he had to help Lucy. John could have found more money somewhere, anywhere. Why didn't he just ask for help? He'd always been the problem solver, the fix-it guy. Never needed help from anyone.

He stood up from the picnic table and walked over to an empty boat slip. He tore up the note and tossed it into the air. The pieces fluttered down and landed in the water.

"Why did you throw those pieces of paper in the water, Mr. John?"

"Oh, hey, Tonya. You scared me."

"I'm sorry. Have you been crying, Mr. John?"

"Yeah, I have. Were you trying to ask me something?"

"Yes, sir. My mommy told me that I'm not supposed to put trash in the water. In school, they told us it's pollution."

"Your mom's right, but this wasn't trash. We call it a memorial and I'm doing this for my brother. So for his memorial, I'm scattering something important in a place that he liked. My brother and I used to come here to go fishing, so I threw these pieces of paper in the water for him. It is a way for me to remember him." She stared at the scraps.

"My Mommy told me that she liked going out on the big boat with you."

"Yep. She loved the big boats."

"Can I do a 'morial' for my Mommy?"

"Absolutely, sweetie."

"What should I do?"

"Here, I've got a piece of paper and a pen. Why don't you write something on this piece of paper and then you can throw it in the water like I did."

"I can't write too well."

"So why don't you just tell me what you want to write and I can help you."

He led her over to the picnic table, lifted her onto the bench, and then sat down beside her feet.

"OK, now you just tell me what you want to write." Her brow wrinkled as she brought a finger to her mouth.

"Dear Mommy, I hope that you like being in heaven. Me and Mr. John are going to have some fun on his big boat. We wish that you were here with us 'cuz you love big boats. I miss you Mommy and I love you."

"That's a beautiful thing to say." He wrote the words down on the page and handed it to her as they walked back to the empty boat slip. She tore the paper into four pieces and dropped them in the water."

"Mr. John?"

"Yes, sweetie?"

"You said that my mommy and Lucy are both in heaven, right?"

"That's right."

"Do you think they're having fun?"

"Yes, I think they are having fun. Heaven is a good place, a happy place."

"I wish my mommy was still here and not in heaven."

"I do too, sweetie. I wish Lucy was still here, too."

She reached over and took his hand. She leaned against his leg. He caressed her hair and the side of her face.

"This place where we're going, you said it is called Baha-Men?"

"Not Baha-Men, sweetie, B-a-h-a-m-a-s."

"Oh. I guess I got a little mixed up. Do you know those guys called the Baha-Men?"

"No, honey, I don't."

"They sing a funny song that my mommy and I use to dance to. It's called 'Who Let the Dogs out – Ruff, Ruff, Ruff.' She flashed a smile.

"I think that I do know that song. And I like it, too."

"Can we listen to that song?"

"Well, I don't have a copy of it right now, but I tell you what. We'll be making a few stops on the way to the Bahamas. How about I buy you a CD with that song on it?"

"Really?"

"You bet, sweetie. And then you and I can dance and sing the song. How about that?"

"Yeah! So can we get on the boat and go now?"

"You bet. Let's get going."

The End

About the Author

Author Andy Holloman grew up in Greenville, N.C., and graduated from the University of North Carolina at Chapel Hill with a degree in Economics. After college, he started a career in the travel industry and successfully expanded a travel business into an Inc. 500 company. The agency grew through the use of the Internet and the acquisition of three other agencies. In the late 1990s, one of his agency's clients—a suspected drug smuggler—was murdered in Durham, N.C. This incident and the subsequent downfall of the travel agency industry after 9/11, was the impetus for his first published novel, Shades of Gray.

Holloman started writing Shades of Gray in 2003, and then shelved the completed novel in 2006, before resurrecting it in 2011 with encouragement from a friend in a Cary, N.C.-based writers group.

Today, Andy Holloman lives in the Raleigh, N.C. area with his wife of twenty years and their three children. In his leisure time, he attends his children's sporting and school events, supports the local real estate industry, and watches fine films with his wonderful wife. This avid reader and social media goofball also enjoys the beauty of North Carolina's mountains, running, and long walks on the beaches of the Outer Banks. Most evenings he can be found tapping out his next novel, due for release in late 2013.

Visit www.AndyHolloman.com for more information.

Made in the USA
Lexington, KY
17 June 2012